PRAISE FOR *ENGINEERED FOR MURDER*

"... fabulously exciting and emotionally charged debut novel. Highly recommended!"—*Dorothy L*

"... spunky characters and a suspenseful plot."—*Engineering Times*

"This one's a winner!"—Les Standiford, *Deal to Die For*

"... an impressive debut that calls for a sequel ..."—Elroy Bode, *Commonplace Mysteries*

"... ideal for readers who want to probe beyond the superficial."—Marilyn Haddrill, *Night of Shadows*

"... intricately plotted, fast-moving, fun to read ... I can't wait for the next Tory Travers mystery!"—Rangeley Wallace, *No Defense*

"I sincerely recommend this book to all mystery lovers ..."—*Small Press Magazine*

"... fiery, passionate, and sexually explosive ... keeps the adrenline pumping, the pulse racind and the heart thumping ..."—*Gothic Journal*

ENGINEERED FOR MURDER

A Mystery
by

AILEEN SCHUMACHER

Aileen Schumacher (signature)

A Write Way Publishing Book

This is a work of fiction. The events described here are imaginary. The settings and characters are fictitious, even when a real name may be used. They are not intended to represent specific places or persons, or, even when a real name is used, to suggest that the events described actually occurred.

This one is for Richard, forever and for always.

Acknowledgments

I would like to thank the following people: E.T. Henry (those wonderful lunches have kept me going); Ana Reyes; Velicia Chavez; Susan Park; Rollie Steele; Pat Steele (without you it wouldn't even be a possibility); Dick Blum; Catherine Berg; Glenn Calabrese (I'll bet you never had this in mind when you went to medical school!); Greg Smith; Melba Schumacher; Wilfred Schumacher (did you really read *all* of it?); Karen S. Duncan; Sandra Lee Stuart; Nicky Blum-Schumacher (you taught me about persevering in the face of rejection); Kevin Blum-Schumacher (I hope you continue to consult on all my mysteries); Dorrie O'Brien (this page of acknowledgements wouldn't exist without you); and finally, my college boyfriend's roommate, who told me I could never pass Electrical Engineering 201. If it weren't for you, I might never have had to prove someone wrong by becoming an engineer.

PROLOGUE

It was a cool, dry, clear night, characteristic of summer in El Paso. The night brought only temporary relief from the summer heat, when not even the barest hint of clouds sheltered the parched earth from the sun, shining relentlessly down on this far western part of Texas. The most recent memory of rain might be two, or even three weeks past.

People died on nights like this.

Modern desert dwellers tried to escape the heat inside buildings where the whisper of cool air was continuous and seductive with its empty promise of soothing frustrations exacerbated by rising temperatures. But the heat continued to take its toll, and the effect was cumulative, exceeding some secret threshold when least expected.

People killed on nights like this.

Every ambulance driver and police officer in the city knew only too well that summer tempers flared and split-second decisions were made that could alter lives forever. Years of emotion could boil over in one mercurial flash of anger. Feelings normally suppressed could erupt hot and intense, and all the winters to follow would never eradicate the results.

People hid their actions from the light of day on nights like this.

A person acting under the influence of the summer heat might spend years subsequently wondering how he had come to such a juncture. While he wondered, incarcerated by the results of his actions and the unchangeability of the past, the Texas summer would come again, uncaring, seducing still others to actions that were uncharacteristic, even unthinkable, at any other time.

People made irrevocable decisions on nights like this.

Sitting in the late night air-conditioned solitude of a deserted city library, the lone individual left in the Periodical Reference Section compared the image on the computer screen in front of him to a letter sitting on the table next to him. He was a person who measured his frustration not in the hours he spent in the sun, but in years spent pursuing activities he had come to hate. Looking again from screen to letter and back again, he reassured himself that there was no mistake in his conclusions.

He let out a low whistle. This in itself was uncharacteristic for someone so accustomed to fading inconspicuously into any setting in which he was placed, but tonight called for a new expressiveness on his part. Tonight, he had stumbled across a discovery that might provide a way out. Like those heat- crazed individuals committing violent acts in a moment of passion, he did not stop to consider how his discovery might affect anyone else. He craved the belief that he could change his life in the same way early pioneers had craved clear, cool water, crossing through the arid mountain pass that had given El Paso its name.

"Victoria Wheatley and Tory Travers are the same person," he repeated to himself like a mantra. Somehow saying it out loud made it more real, more totally his discovery and no one else's. Still, as satisfying as it was to voice his discovery, he couldn't prevent a knee-jerk reaction, immediately glancing around to make sure there was no authority figure nearby to censure the forbidden act of speaking out loud.

Reassured, he stared off into space for a while, allowing himself to ignore the copious notes and documents that surrounded him. "This could be my big break," he told himself. "If ever anyone had a story drop right into his lap, this is it." For a few minutes he allowed himself to indulge in his fantasy of what life would be like as a "real writer," i.e., one who didn't have to pursue another line of work to keep the bills paid.

If only he hadn't gotten married right out of college. If only his disabled mother-in-law wasn't such a drain on his financial resources. Going back even further, if only he had better withstood the pressure exerted by his blue-collar family on the first child to be sent to college. "Don't major in journalism or English, major in something reliable, something where you can get a good job," he had been told again and again. But fulfilling his family's expectations, and then his wife's, had done nothing to quench the desire that burned like a summer sun in his soul, through all the seasons of the year.

He snapped back to the present, aware of the late hour and that he was expected at work, as usual, in the morning.

He would have to figure out how to use this new-found knowledge to the maximum advantage. The story he could milk out of this connection certainly wouldn't be a panacea to his quest for journalistic renown, but it could provide a start. "My days as an engineering technician are numbered," he assured himself, as he started to gather his papers together.

He left the library, striding out into the inky night. He forced himself to whistle as he walked to his car. It still felt really strange, but he decided that making more noise was a habit he was going to get used to.

In other parts of the city, the summer sun continued to work its ancient spell of madness, unimpeded by the brief promise of relief held in the fleeting night. Acts covered by darkness would soon be visible for all to see. Discoveries made in the night would be illuminated by the relentless light of day, and there would be no turning back.

CHAPTER ONE: PRELIMINARY DESIGNS

Tory Travers critically regarded all five feet ten inches of her reflection in the steamy dressing room mirror of the Las Cruces Women's Fitness Club. This was one of the few places with some humidity in the air during the relentlessly arid New Mexican summer. Sometimes, after working up a sweat and stepping outside into the blinding southwestern sun,

Tory thought she could feel the moisture being sucked right off her skin. Water was at a premium out here, and Mother Nature had a way of scavenging whatever was in short supply. Moisture would be atmospherically stockpiled until the August rainstorms would drench the parched land, and what appeared to the neophyte desert dweller to be a wasteland would overnight be painted green to the horizon.

But it was appearances, rather than humidity or the lack thereof, that held Tory's attention now. The body was okay. Somewhere around thirty, she had actually become comfortable with her height. The fact that she could eat like a horse and not pay for it on the scales hadn't hurt her coming to terms with the fact that petite would never be an adjective that she would experience.

And the face was okay. Without a doubt, her best feature was her startling blue eyes. They contrasted with her pale skin, which was dusted with freckles across the bridge of her nose and cheekbones. Her heritage was from the Black Irish, not the ruddy kind. Her hair, a sleek dark brown verging on black, was blunt cut in bangs across her forehead and curved under a few inches below her chin, hanging a little longer in the back.

No curls, no frills, no concessions to current styles. It sometimes seemed that she had looked this way forever, but at thirty-five she realized the advantage of the fact that she would likely look the same in fifteen more years.

So the problem that currently held Tory's attention was wardrobe-related. The moss green silk blouse would have passed muster anywhere as part of a dress-for-success outfit. It coordinated beautifully with her black and green skirt, which, unfortunately, was at home hanging in her closet. It didn't coordinate so well with her beige slip, which currently comprised the rest of her outfit.

"Damn damn damn damn," Tory admonished her reflection, which didn't come up with any snappy answers about why her skirt was at home rather than folded neatly in the bottom of her workout bag. "You get up early and go work out before a big confrontational meeting so you can be nice and healthy and laid back, instead of nervous and stressed out, and where does it get you? Trying to figure out how to decently get from the dressing room to the parking lot, that's where."

She briefly considered putting her leotard and tights back on, but because of their sweaty state, it wasn't a very alluring alternative. With a flash of inspiration, she turned to the locker labeled Lost and Found and began to sort through its contents. Luckily there was no one else in the dressing room to witness her foray. "If only I needed deodorant, I'd be in luck," she muttered to herself, as she sorted through the items that had been left in the locker room and never claimed.

It pushed the limits of probability that someone would have left behind a skirt to match her blouse. A pair of shiny black nylon work-out shorts appeared to be the only functional possibility. And they weren't even Umbros, a fact her son would have immediately pointed out to her if he had been present. She cautiously gave them the sniff test. She was in luck. Either they hadn't been worn before they'd been left behind, or they'd been abandoned so long that they'd had a chance to air out.

Tory pulled off her slip, pulled on the shorts, and took another critical look in the mirror. Combined with her panty hose, black high-heeled shoes, and her silk blouse, the effect was somewhere between that of a highly paid cocktail waitress and a hooker who charged by the hour, she decided. But it should do for a trip through the waiting room to the parking lot. It wasn't like she was going to get cold or anything like that. Murmuring a private apology to the unknown person who would not be finding her shorts in the Lost and Found that day, she packed up the rest of her stuff and walked out.

It was unusual for someone to be in the lobby of the Las Cruces Women's Fitness Club so early on a Friday morning, and it was even more unusual for the person to be male. It was really unusual for that person to rise and address Tory by name on the one day she was minus fifty percent of her intended outfit. If she was going to be beating the laws of probability this morning, she would a lot rather have found a green and black skirt in the Lost and Found locker.

"Uh, Tory Travers?" the slight young man standing in front of her repeated his question. He started to drop his eyes, as people usually do after initiating a conversation, but obviously thought better of it. The fact that she was a good bit taller than he was didn't give him a lot of places to look without dropping his eyes. It certainly made for an intense eye-to-eye encounter.

Against mounting evidence to the contrary, Tory decided to act as if this was an everyday encounter. "Yes, I'm Tory Travers," she replied. "Do I know you?"

"No," he said nervously. "We've never met, but I've talked with some of your employees. I'm Billy—Bill Hartman. I'm the Quality Control tech for the El Paso Precast Concrete Company."

Tory knew that she was unconsciously gearing up for the approaching morning meeting when the first response that came to mind was "Oh, yeah, those assholes." The booming international metropolis of El Paso, the western-most Texas city, lay to the south of the small New Mexican town of Las Cruces. Only forty-five minutes away by car, it was another city, another state, another world. But for all its size and industrial character, it was not necessarily a better place for getting precast concrete. Of all the construction-related industries in the two states, Tory had decided that El Paso Precast Concrete was the lowest of the low, but she had thought she would be postponing confronting this issue until her ten o'clock meeting. Until after she retrieved her skirt.

She censured her initial response and changed it to a mild, "Oh, yes, El Paso Precast. You all are doing the precast work for the University stadium project. Well, what can I do for you?"

"I want to talk to you."

That much was obvious. The question was, did she need

to talk to him? She gravely consulted her watch. "The project status meeting is at ten o'clock over at the University Facilities Planning Division. I'll be there and I'm sure we'll all be talking about the project at great lengths then." Hopefully in a more complete outfit, she thought to herself.

Hartman cleared his throat. "Uh, I'm involved with the stadium project, but I'm not here for the ten o'clock meeting. I really need to talk to you about something else." He glanced furtively around. "Privately," he added.

Tory stifled an impulse to blurt out "Give me a break." A private conversation, and her in panty hose, work-out shorts, and high heels? Who ever said that clothes didn't make the man, or woman, or person? The situation was getting more ludicrous by the moment.

Then she thought, maybe this guy was looking to change jobs. In that case, experience had taught her that she could talk to him now or spend a lot of time later trying to avoid him. Besides, it would be a new experience. She had never talked to a prospective employee before while wearing panty hose and workout shorts. It made her grateful her company didn't have a dress code that she'd have to explain.

"Okay," she said. "But I'm curious. How did you find me?"

"Your secretary told me where you were."

Ah ha, Tory thought to herself, Sylvia must have thought this guy was up here about the stadium project, the same as I did. The office nickname for her in-step-with-the-latest-fashion secretary was Chicana Madonna, but Tory mentally referred to her as the Dragon Lady when Sylvia was on her high horse. Neither love nor money could pry information out of Sylvia when she made up her mind not to release it. Everyone in the office was aware of the problems with the stadium project, and everyone, including Tory, fully expected the lid to blow in the project status meeting scheduled for later that morning. Sylvia must have sent Hartman over here because she thought he had some technical information to impart before that happened. Too bad she hadn't dug a little deeper.

"So how did you figure out who I was out of all the people coming in and out of here?" Tory asked curiously.

Hartman cleared his throat again. "Well, your secretary told me that you were tall, had dark brown hair, and would be dressed for the meeting later this morning." He heard what he was saying, but there was no choice between looking down or keeping his gaze focused on her face, so he continued to look directly at her. God, that must be hard to say with a straight face, thought Tory. "She said that most of the women working out this time of day were people that didn't work, who wouldn't be dressed to go into the office," he concluded miserably, unable to restrain himself from completing his ill-timed explanation.

Tory cleared her throat, and realized that she was beginning to adopt his mannerisms. This prompted her to action. "Let's go next door," she said decisively. "There's a coffee shop there, and I'll be able to sit down with you for a few minutes." She gestured to the door, and refused to budge until he preceded her out. She was damned if she was going to give this guy an opportunity to evaluate her professional attire from behind.

Once seated, they went through the preliminaries of getting coffee. Now that she was actually sitting down with this guy, Tory was more than a little curious about what he might have to say. It was hard to believe that his presence really had nothing to do with the stadium project. That would be entirely too coincidental.

Hartman engrossed himself with preparing his coffee after they were served, and she refused to help out by asking any conversational questions. She figured she had up to an hour to waste. Retrieving her skirt before the project meeting had become a big goal for her this morning. After all, one had to maintain some kind of standards.

"I never really wanted to be an engineering technician," Hartman blurted suddenly. This was not exactly the kind of opening statement that Tory had anticipated, and it rapidly got even stranger. "I always wanted to be a writer," he continued.

"Okay," said Tory. She waited for more explanation, but none was forthcoming. "What does that have to do with me?" she asked after a while. Was this guy a conversationalist or what? There was no point in wasting a whole hour if this wasn't, after all, job-related. She was already beginning to regret agreeing to this conversation.

"I've been doing freelance writing," Hartman started speaking again slowly, and then began to pick up speed.

"Political and legal stories are my specialty. I've been doing a series for the *El Paso Times* on the abortion issue. You know, it's a really hot subject now, in light of the recent Supreme Court decisions."

Tory nodded, to indicate that just because she was an engineer didn't mean that she wasn't aware of national political developments. She even read books totally unrelated to engineering once in a while, but she didn't feel compelled to expound upon the fact. She was beginning to feel distinctly uneasy about this whole conversation, and it had nothing to do with what she was (or what she wasn't) wearing.

"The theme I've been using is that different political factions have been drawn together by this issue. One of the most conservative and fanatical is the Christians in Government group that's headed by Mason Barkley out of Florida. They're having a rally in El Paso in three weeks. I'll bet you're surprised to hear that El Paso was selected as the site."

Tory wasn't surprised, she was dumbfounded. It had been a long time since she'd heard the name Mason Barkley in any conversation she was a part of, although forever wouldn't have been long enough for her. She felt her stomach automatically clench in anxiety. With an effort she resisted an urge to grip the table. She supposed she was now going to have the chance to discover why this person was talking about Jameson Barkley to her. She felt very sure that whatever the reason was, she wasn't going to like it.

"They chose El Paso for their rally to try to emphasize the international nature of their efforts to eliminate abortion," Hartman continued. "Even if it's restricted or out-lawed in the US, they're concerned about border communi-ties where women will still have access to abortions. Barkley is the leader of this group, which has strong stands on a lot of other issues. He seems to inspire fanatical loyalty from his followers. And that's how I found out about you."

"Exactly how did you find out about me?" Tory's voice sounded flat and unemotional to her own ears.

"I found out that you were Vicky Wheatley, the teenage girl who had an affair with Barkley and ruined his political career years ago."

"No, Mr. Hartman. I am the person who enabled Jim Barkley to rise from the ashes, phoenix-like, transformed into a new and powerful entity: a repentant, well-publicized, born-again Christian politician. But you didn't listen to my question. I didn't ask you what you found out, I asked you how you found this out."

"Oh," he swallowed audibly, nervous again. "That was pure coincidence. There have been all those problems with our part in the stadium project, and Mr. Lester, the owner of our precast plant, figures that you're probably going to come down pretty hard on us. Anyhow, he had heard that you'd published a couple of articles in some professional journals about quality control programs for structural integrity. He figured that if we researched the articles and adopted some of your recommended procedures, it might help out."

"You mean, he thought that if you made a few cosmetic changes to your operation, especially after what happened during the last pour, I might be so flattered that you had considered me an expert that I would let bygones be bygones."

"Well, I wouldn't exactly put it that way."

"I'm sure you wouldn't. I still don't see the connection between quality control of precast concrete structures and Jim Barkley."

"You really are Vicky Wheatley, aren't you?" Hartman started to look animated again. "Up to this point I've had a hard time believing it myself. But I just realized that you called Barkley 'Jim'. Not many people remember that Barkley's real name is Jameson, and that he used to be called Jim. He's known as Mason now, not Jim. Probably part of him putting his past behind him, don't you think?"

"Mr. Hartman, I am trying very hard to understand the point of this conversation. It might help if you would finish answering my question. How did you find out about this connection between Barkley and me?"

"Well, when I went to dig up the articles you had written, I went to the University library. The one in El Paso, that is. They have a computer system for literature searches. You enter a name, and the system pulls up all the articles or books written under that name. For women, it cross-references and searches for publications under a maiden name, which is displayed on the screen. So I got a screen which displayed your maiden name, which stuck in my mind for some reason. Later I was doing some of my own research for my newspaper series, specifically on Mason Barkley, the man. I started scanning some old news clippings, and you were in all the headlines, seventeen, eighteen years ago, as Vicky Wheatley."

"The wonders of modern technology," said Tory drily. "So what do you want?"

"An interview, of course. Preferably an exclusive one. How you felt about Barkley then, and how you feel about him now. Whether or not you agree with the political principles that he endorses. Whether, after all this time, you think he's really changed." Hartman's voice rose with the last statement.

This was probably as close to exhibiting excitement as this guy ever got, thought Tory. "Absolutely not."

"Why not?" He actually looked dumbfounded at her refusal.

"Because I have no desire to have anything to do with resurrecting that part of my past."

"But how have you managed to keep it quiet for so long?"

"Keep what quiet? The events that you're talking about happened over eighteen years ago, to a very young girl and a very minor politician, in another state half a continent away. When I came here to college, some people were aware of the connection, of course. But two years after I came here, I gave everyone something else to talk about. I married one of my professors. I was nineteen and he was forty. How's that for a human-interest angle? But since then, I've proceeded to live a rather ordinary, mundane life. I doubt that there are more than three or four people around here who still connect me with the man you say is coming to El Paso."

"What can I do to change your mind?"

"Mr. Hartman, I've negotiated a lot tougher situations than this. What part of no is it that you don't understand?" Tory doubted if Hartman would realize that this was one of the main negotiating phrases she used in dealing with her fifteen-year-old son.

"You can't expect me to keep quiet about this." Hartman's face had gone all splotchy, and he was looking really upset. Tory briefly wondered what she would do if he broke into tears. This simply couldn't be happening, at least not on a morning that she was supposed to be obsessed with her ten o'clock meeting. Surely things would be going differently if only she had all her clothes on.

Tory gave Hartman a long, considering look. "No, Mr. Hartman, I don't expect you will keep quiet about this. But I will never, with you or anyone else, consent to talk about Jameson Barkley and the person I was eighteen years ago. You'll have to excuse me now, I have real work to do."

"You'll be sorry if I have to write this without your input. You have to talk to me. I'm the one that found out about this first ..." Hartman actually started to rise, but sat back down quickly when Tory got to her feet. She looked down at him and shook her head for emphasis.

Later, when she was asked if she had been threatened by Bill Hartman, she would only remember feeling upset, and disgusted, and saddened that his need was so great, and so base. And later she would remember her last glimpse of Hartman's pale, disappointed face and sloping shoulders.

But at least one thing had been accomplished. She didn't think once about what she was wearing all the way back to her car.

CHAPTER TWO:
ALL IN A DAY'S WORK

"**I** don't know what the hell all this bitching and moaning is about. The stadium project is going fine. It's meetings like this holding us back, and all because the inspectors on this job are on some goddamned kind of witch hunt. If it's progress you want, I suggest you throw them off the job and find someone who is capable of doing inspections without generating all this hysteria."

The large, sun-burned man who was speaking paused and looked at Tory, who was sitting at the other end of the conference table from him. "Excuse my language, ma'am," he said, in a tone of voice that was far from apologetic. Tory had long ago grown tired of such apologies, which were, after all, only an effort to demonstrate she didn't belong there with the rest of the "guys." And she really didn't like being called ma'am.

"Harold, don't apologize for your language on my account," replied Tory. "You've said a lot worse when we've been alone together. I actually think you're being admirably restrained." Her comment elicited a few discreet chuckles from a couple of other people sitting around the conference table.

But her comment didn't slow down Harold Kemp any.

He continued to expound upon his particular viewpoint, which was that his exemplary construction company had never, ever made a mistake. Tory felt like telling him to give it a rest, everyone in the room knew that for anyone involved in construction to make that statement was bullshit. But Harold was kind of like one of those wind-up toys her son had when he was smaller. It was easier to let it run down than to try to interrupt it.

It was actually a pretty typical construction project meeting, although tempers might be running a little hotter than usual. But then, today the stakes were a little higher than usual. The contractor was giving the client assurances that everything was going okay, the inspectors were trying to convince the client that their concerns were serious enough that the contractor should be forced to address them, and the client was listening to it all and trying to decide how much of each version to believe.

The thing that charged the air, of course, was money. Just as the promise of potential profits drew numerous people to construction, there was the ever-present reality that even larger sums could be lost, virtually in minutes, in meetings like this. All the University project director had to say to the contractor to drain his profits (and the blood from his face) was "Tear it out and do it over." And, if you happened to be the inspector on the project, as Tory was, there was always the threat of being thrown off the job if the project director was convinced that her company wasn't doing its job appropriately.

Tory leaned back in the plush swivel chair and tried to

remember the details of the article on aging that she had read a few weeks ago. It was something to the effect that anxiety-producing brain cells died off as one grew older, contributing to the mellowing associated with age. Certainly the phenomena must be well advanced by the age of thirty-five, she reflected. Maybe it was ongoing even at this very instant. If she could only get her earlier conversation with Hartman out of her mind. She wondered how long it would take him to resurrect the scandal of her past, and what kind of effect it would have on her present life.

She rolled her head around to ease some of the stiffness in her neck, and to convey to Kemp that she was relaxing during his tirade. Actually, it was a matter of priorities. She had a hard time being absolutely nuts about two things at a time, but what Kemp didn't know wouldn't hurt him.

She tried to visualize a void in her brain where the anxiety-producing cells used to live. The comfort of this vision was minimal (after all, she had been accused before of having a hole in her head where the common sense portion was supposed to reside) and didn't succeed in obliterating the on-going sound of Harold Kemp's angry voice. And how could Harold go on ranting and raving if the aging theory was correct? He was certainly a lot older than she was.

And then she picked up on the word "hysterical" for the second time. With a sigh, she gave up the goal of detachment, and decided she would be doing well if she could just achieve some restraint.

"These have got to be the most hysterical set of inspection reports I have ever encountered in all my years in the construction industry. And I would like to remind you, sir, that my years of experience in this field are many." Harold Kemp leaned across the table and stared at Tory to emphasize his point, although he was supposedly speaking to the man in charge of the meeting, the New Mexico State University Director of Facilities.

As Tory tuned in again, she sensed, rather than saw, the small wiry man at her side tense for action. While trying to keep her upper body totally motionless, she managed to negotiate a resounding kick under the table to the shin of the man seated next to her.

"If Jazz loses his temper and gets into a fight with Harold Kemp," she thought, "there will be blood shed in this fancy conference room, and what will the next group of well-heeled alumni football fans make of that?" Kicking her colleague prevented her from jumping right in with a heated retort.

She could still, after all these years, conjure up her deceased husband's voice at will. He had always been the cool one, and he had tried to teach her that she didn't have to fight every fight herself. "Nine times out of ten, Tory, when you are accused of something in front of a group of people, someone will come to your defense, or diffuse the situation, if you are in the right. The point is, you have to wait long enough to give that someone a chance to do it. It's always more effective to wait and see what will happen instead of jumping in first thing to defend yourself."

"Okay, Carl," she said to herself. "I'm waiting."

And then, sure enough, it was the Director of Facilities himself, who finally broke the silence with his polite Texas drawl. "Mr. Kemp, I'm sure that we can all appreciate your feelings in this matter. However, the point is that the inspection reports that we have been receiving in this office have been a matter of grave concern to my engineering staff. Grave concern, Mr. Kemp. It's not everyday that we build a new football stadium at this University. Along with it being a high visibility project, it is also an intense-usage facility. We don't want any structural instability in a stadium that's going to contain some seventy thousand jumping, stomping, screaming Aggie fans."

Not to mention the numerous ones who won't be stomping because they've passed out and become part of the dead load on the structure, rather than part of the live load, Tory thought to herself before she resolutely censored that train of thought. Being part of a drunken crowd watching grown men chase and tackle each other had never been her idea of a good time, but she had had the sense through many sports-related projects never to voice that opinion.

"Director Henderson is right," chimed in a University Planning Engineer, who had spent a good part of the meeting covertly studying Tory's legs. "These inspection reports don't merely record the problems normally associated with a job of this type; there have been errors and mistakes noted which cast doubt upon the integrity of the whole project."

Well, score one for the good guys, thought Tory. It had been a good decision to go home and retrieve her skirt. Had she shown up in her stockings and work-out shorts, this guy might have been so distracted he would have never made his statement. Tory shamelessly flashed him her brightest smile. She firmly believed in encouraging signs of technical competence wherever and whenever encountered, no matter how fleeting.

Harold Kemp glared at Tory before pushing himself heavily to his feet to reply. "You don't have a problem here, you have hysteria and overreaction. Kemp Contracting has built over twenty-five projects on this campus and there's never been a problem with any of them." That was enough like going out on a limb that he glanced nervously at Tory before continuing. "Well, not any significant problem, that is. I suggest that you look at the people," and he heavily emphasized the term *people*, "that are providing the inspection services that have everyone around here so all-fired worked up." And with one last glower at Tory, he sat down amid the three Kemp foremen that had accompanied him to the meeting. Sitting together like that, obviously perturbed, sunburned and well-muscled from years out on construction sites, they looked rather like the redneck branch of some Mafia family, Tory reflected.

Well, you can outwait some of the people some of the time, but you can't outwait all of the people all of the time, Tory thought to herself, as all eyes in the conference room turned to her. All except Jazz's. He was furiously staring down at his hands in his lap, and she had a momentary pang of remorse about kicking him in the shin.

Jesus Alfonso Rodriguez was more commonly referred to as Jazz. He had once broken the jaw of a man in a bar fight who had called him Jesus, instead of the Spanish pronunciation "Hay Suse." He was one of the best field technicians Tory had ever come across. There had been a brief time after Carl had died, best forgotten, when Travers Testing and Engineering Company had consisted only of Jazz and herself. But Jazz was unrelenting about the correctness of construction practices, fiercely loyal, and even less tactful than a younger and ambitiously determined Tory had been, so the kick to the shin had been warranted after all. Which just went to show that not all valuable business skills are verbal ones.

Tory elected not to stand, discarding the dramatic gesture of the contractor as being of no use to her, but she did elect to address the Director, Charles Henderson, as if no one else in the room mattered. Because, actually, no one else really did.

Henderson, shrewd and direct behind his slow Texas drawl, had the authority to shut down construction on a multi-million dollar project, to throw the current contractor off the job and replace him with another, or, more to the point, to replace the firm providing inspection and testing services. Tory resolutely tried not to think about how important the stadium inspection contract was to her firm.

"Mr. Henderson," she said carefully. "I have listened to the discussion about the inspection reports submitted by my firm. I have heard the term hysterical used more than once, and I don't like it. There are certainly some terms I could use to describe the current quality of construction management on this project."

Careful, she thought. You're indulging yourself and drifting into dangerous waters. Name-calling in these meetings never stood anyone in good stead. She knew, because she had certainly resorted to it from time to time. If even an old dog can learn new tricks, so can a female in a traditionally male field. And that concept would sure be a surprise to some of the people in the room.

"But I won't," she continued. "The point is that my company stands behind each and every report that has been submitted, behind the recording of each and every problem that has led to this meeting today. Certainly we're aware that there are no perfect projects. Just like Harold and his people, we're not novices in this field. Mistakes will be made, and the purpose of inspection and testing is to minimize the amount of mistakes that go uncorrected. But it has come to a point where some action needs to be taken. We all know that this project was not funded for full-time inspection. Unfortunately, in my opinion, even instituting full-time inspection at this time would not solve the problems we've got already."

That had certainly gotten everyone's attention. "Please explain," the Director requested.

"Director Henderson, I know that you haven't had time to read every inspection report on this project, and that's certainly not your job. But in this case, I would strongly suggest that you do so. Besides the on-site deviations from good construction practice, we have found serious problems at the precast yard that far outweigh the other problems."

"Like what?" the Director asked.

Tory carefully tried to choose her next words, but the effect of the kick had worn off, and Jazz could no longer contain himself. "Like finding one of the major supporting columns ready to be poured, with half of the main reinforcing bars missing," Jazz burst out. He glared at Harold Kemp and his foremen. Well, I couldn't have put it more succinctly myself, Tory thought.

Everyone said "What?" more or less simultaneously, but Kemp was the only one who roared to his feet. Must be an ingrained habit of his, Tory thought. "Why wasn't I informed?" he bellowed.

"You were," Tory answered sweetly. "The inspection report was hand-delivered to your office yesterday." But maybe you decided that it was just another hysterical document to be dismissed, she thought to herself. That was progress. Just a few years ago she would have probably spoken that thought out loud.

The last exchange had effectively broken up the meeting, and the Director had no intention of wasting further time listening to everyone's exclamations and disclaimers. "I intend to study this whole file myself," he said, effectively negating the existence of his attending staff. "I want to have Ms. Travers and Mr. Kemp in my office at two this afternoon, by which time I will have come to a decision. No one else need attend." He looked sternly around the room, silencing the general outcry. "Good morning." And he exited.

Still standing, Kemp drew himself up to his full six feet

and glared at Tory. "Well, little lady, you've certainly put a bee in his bonnet. I just hope you have a leg to stand on when this whole affair is said and done."

Tory stood slowly, unfolding herself to her full five-feet ten-inches, plus two-inch heels. She looked Kemp level in the eyes and smiled sweetly at him. "Your concern is touching. See you this afternoon," she said, and using the Director as her role model, exited the room.

Jazz scrambled to his full five-feet five-inches and followed her, but there were no more polite leave-takings. Scowling at the floor, muttering as he passed Kemp, the word *pendejo* was fully distinguishable amid a stream of Spanish epithets. There were few job-related issues about which Jazz didn't have passionate feelings. Tory doubted it would be much comfort to Harold Kemp to know that *pendejo* was indeed one of his more benevolent terms. After all, one could be called worse things than a pubic hair.

Tory stepped outside the administrative building and put on her sunglasses against the bright New Mexican summer glare. The air was hot and dry, and the campus was almost deserted. Not only was it the break between summer classes, anyone on campus would have taken refuge in some air conditioned building during the mid-day hours unless there was some pressing reason for being out in the scorching sun. A reason like working construction on a stadium that was being built at breakneck speed to accommodate the fans for the first fall football game, Tory mused.

Descended from a race indigenous to the New Mexican desert, Jazz refused to make concessions to the heat. He leaned against the building and lit a cigarette. "*Qué creo*, boss lady?" he asked.

"*No se*," she answered, falling easily into the Mexican/English slang that had become a part of her vocabulary during the years she had lived in New Mexico. "It's a pretty political job, with lots of good-old-boy relationships that go way back, things that we'll never even know about, much less understand. The funding is a combination of private endowments and state money, which makes the whole situation even more complicated. Henderson hates controversy, but he's a pretty straight-forward guy. He realizes what a nightmare of publicity it would be for the University if there was some question about the safety of their stadium, much less an actual collapse. We've stirred up a hornet's nest, that's for sure."

Jazz drew one knee up under him and pressed the heel of his dusty boot into the wall, exhaling a cloud of cigarette smoke. "You need to let them know we aren't going to let that *cabrón* Kemp get away with the shit-assed things they've been doing."

So, Kemp had been elevated from being called the Spanish equivalent of pubic hair to the title of goat. "There are so many subcontractors on this job that it's hard to tell who is directly responsible for letting things get so shoddy. I don't mind you riding them to let them know what's not acceptable, but we don't have to go out of our way to antagonize them. We can get this project whipped into shape. We've done it before."

"If we don't get our asses thrown off this job," Jazz replied, flicking cigarette ashes to the ground.

"Well, we'll know this afternoon."

"You want me back at the site?"

"No, it's lunch time and I don't think there'll be too much going on right now. Why don't you get some lunch? I'm going to go on over there and take a look around and then get some lunch myself. I'll give you a call after the meeting with Henderson."

Jazz took off and Tory walked over to her personal company vehicle, a white Mazda RX7. It was one of her few concessions to the fact that after some years, Travers Testing and Engineering Company was no longer quite the shoestring operation it had been initially. She usually wasn't averse to walking, but even after eight years, she avoided walking around campus if possible. It still brought back too many memories of her life here as a student, taking a class from Carl, getting to know Carl, falling in love with him, becoming his wife, the mother of his child, his business partner, and finally, his widow.

Just as she had predicted, the stadium construction site was deserted when she drove up. She grabbed the hard hat she always kept in her car and stepped out, walking past the construction trailers and the **HARD HAT AREA** signs. This was how she liked construction sites the best, deserted so there was no distraction of busy crews, and just at the beginning of the time when a project became identifiable.

The site work, clearing and layout, had been done weeks

ago, and the stadium foundations had been poured soon after. Utilities were going in now, construction activities indiscernible to the untrained eye. Stretching toward the sky were the five-story-high concrete columns that would serve as the backbone of the structure. Never again would they be so clearly visible, standing naked and alone on the site. Soon they would be connected to and covered by the other elements and components that would come together to form the finished stadium. Tory could see the bleachers in her mind's eye, the press box, even the yelling, screaming fans.

Ideally, they would never even be aware of the stadium itself except as a destination. No public attention would be focused on the design drawings, load calculations, selected safety factors, evaluations of conformance to building code criteria, selected materials, and construction practices. At least not if the architects, engineers, contractors, materials suppliers, and Tory's staff all did their jobs correctly.

After checking the general progress on the site, Tory stepped into the Travers Company site trailer to see what the latest schedule changes were. She called her office to check for messages, and got a recording of Sylvia's voice. Since most of the staff was out at various sites, Sylvia relied on an answering machine when she left the office for lunch or to run errands. Tory activated the messages recorded on the machine and was informed that her son was going swimming and that she was urgently requested to return a call to one Emmett Delgado, who was calling long distance.

That's one return phone call that can wait, she thought

to herself, and checked her watch. There was just about enough time to get lunch and make it back to Henderson's office by two. Another productive day to be spent in meetings, she thought. The things they don't teach you in school when you pick your profession and try the label on for size.

The wait to see the Director was mercifully short, for few things are as uncomfortable as sharing limited space with a proclaimed adversary. While construction sites allow plenty of room for posturing, gesturing, and swearing, there are few acceptable behavioral options in a hushed and carpeted waiting area. Kemp, looking exceedingly uncomfortable, still in his suit donned for the morning meeting, made a pretense of leafing through a magazine. Tory tried to imagine his reaction to reading a glossy exposé of her affair with Jameson Barkley eighteen years ago, and decided it was not a comfortable fantasy. So she contented herself with studying, in minute detail, the paintings hanging on the walls.

Henderson opened the door and motioned them inside. Tory and Kemp both seated themselves in front of his massive desk and awaited his judgments, much like Moses awaiting the Ten Commandments, Tory thought to herself.

He didn't keep them waiting long, or dance around the subject. "I am extremely concerned about the type and frequency of problems documented in these construction inspection reports," he said. "However, that in itself would not lead me to do more than issue warnings to you, Mr. Kemp, and direct the Travers Company to give me frequent updates on your subsequent performance. But this incident at the precast yard is critical. Frankly, this was not something that we anticipated when we drew up the contract for inspection services. The inspections at the precast yard were intended to be infrequent visits to become familiar with the procedures and personnel and to monitor overall progress on casting the parts for the stadium. Are you absolutely sure about this incident where a column was missing the reinforcing bars, Mrs.—uh, Ms. Travers?"

Anyone else that Tory had worked with for years would have called her Tory, and eliminated the need to choose between Mrs. and Ms., but that was part of the Director's style. Tory had sometimes wondered what he called his own wife in the privacy of their home. She herself had a hard time remembering that Henderson's first name was Charles, and not Director.

"Yes sir. My foreman was going over concrete mix specifications with the plant foreman when they asked him if he would like to see one of the main columns poured. My foreman was the one who stopped the pour and pointed out the problem. Of course, they claimed that his action was premature, and that their own quality assurance people would have caught the problem. But what else could they say when they were caught with their pants down?"

The Director looked at her sharply, but Kemp missed the chance to gloat over the Director's disapproval. For the first time that day, the contractor looked concerned rather than angry. "Damn it," Kemp said, "what's their problem?

If something like that happened, how are we going to be sure about the integrity of what's already out there? I've had problems with El Paso Precast before, but only with things like schedule and price bargaining. A column without reinforcing steel can crumble like sand."

"That's exactly the point that I've been trying to make," said Tory quietly.

"Are there other columns that have already been fabricated? Was there any independent inspection when they were cast?" asked the Director.

"Yes, and no," answered Tory. "Four of the six columns had already been cast before we caught the problem with the fifth. Those four are already on site. The fifth, the one that my foreman saw poured, will be placed on site Monday, and the sixth is scheduled to be poured late next week."

"What do you recommend?"

"Authorization to access all in-plant data at El Paso Precast concerning the pours of those four columns that are already on site. If the evaluation of that data does not satisfy our concerns, I want authorization to do on-site testing to assure ourselves that those columns were fabricated the way they were intended to be."

"What type of testing will you need to do, and what will be the effect of what you're suggesting upon the construction schedule?"

"Our evaluation in itself shouldn't have to delay construction. If I can get the data from the precast yard on Monday, we should know by Wednesday whether we need to do on-site testing, which will consist of X-raying the existing columns to verify that the correct reinforcing is present. The on-site testing could be completed in two to three days, to coincide with the placement of the last column, and construction can proceed as planned. Of course, that's assuming that we don't detect any problems."

"And if you do?"

"You take down the unacceptable column or columns and have them recast."

"And what would the impact of that be?" the Director asked Kemp, because he would be the one that knew the potential impact of such delays.

Kemp was back to looking angry rather than concerned. "If that happens I'll have the owner of El Paso Precast, Petey Lester himself, out there pouring columns, and they can shut down whatever other projects they have going on. That's the whole problem here, they've gotten more work than they can handle and they're cutting corners to get it done. I don't give a damn what they do on their other work but if they screw up my job—"

"Harold," Tory interrupted gently, "we're all sure you'll do anything you can to keep this job on schedule. After all, as the prime contractor, it's your company that will bear liquidated damages if the deadlines aren't met."

She saw Kemp wince almost as if she had struck him. For contractors, liquidated damages, a penalty for non-performance, were something to be avoided at all costs. In addition to the immediate economic penalty, companies facing liquidated damages were looked upon askance by their bonding agents. And the level at which a construction company could be bonded affected the size of jobs that it could bid on.

"How would it affect the construction schedule if one or more of those columns had to be replaced?" Tory asked Kemp.

"Ten days per column to be replaced, maybe twelve," Kemp answered tersely.

They all sat for a moment in silence. Tory imagined Kemp envisioning dollars sprouting wings and flying away before his very eyes, and the Director phrasing diplomatic explanations to a bunch of fanatical alumni about why their promised stadium wasn't ready for football season. And if it weren't for the "hysterical" inspection reports issued by her company, none of this would be happening right now. Not for the first time, she reflected that construction inspectors rated right up there with dogcatchers and child abusers in general popularity.

The Director cleared his throat. "Consider authorization granted for evaluating the columns already in place," he said to Tory. "And I want your people at the precast yard when the sixth column is cast. Document this in a proposal to me, and make sure that Mr. Kemp receives a copy. I am sure that Mr. Kemp and I will be able to work out something agreeable to the University about who will bear the costs of this added effort."

With the implied threat of no more University construction projects, there was no doubt that he was right. "In the meantime, I am not going to increase the inspection activities on site. But please be aware that I plan to personally monitor the situation, and I will revisit that decision as I see fit. Is there anything else that we need to discuss?"

"Yes," said Kemp flatly, and Tory's fantasies of escaping unscathed disappeared. Kemp placed an envelope on the Director's desk. "I am lodging a formal complaint about the lack of safety procedures followed by Travers Company personnel. All individuals on the construction site must wear hard-toed shoes and hard hats at all times. At various times, recorded in the complaint on your desk, Travers' foreman has been on site without a hard hat. We are giving notice that this is not acceptable, and if he or other Travers personnel do not immediately conform to standard safety requirements, we will bar them from the site."

There was an appropriate pause following this announcement. "This is very serious, Ms. Travers," said the Director soberly, even though all three of them knew it really wasn't. "I expect you to take whatever steps are necessary to eliminate these problems immediately."

"Yes sir," Tory answered. She had been around long enough to know when to roll over and play dead. Kemp was making sure that Jazz would pay for his surly behavior earlier.

The Director stood to indicate that the meeting was over. "I'm sure that I'll be seeing both of you tomorrow night at the reception for the new theater department chair. It would certainly reassure me about cooperative relationships on this project to see you two on the dance floor for one dance."

This was the point at which Tory's son would have said,

"Oh, intensely gross. Get a grip." Tory didn't have the latitude to voice those sentiments exactly, but she felt she could get away with objections couched in humorous sarcasm. What was definitely needed was a light touch.

"I'm sure that Petey Lester, the owner of the El Paso Precast Concrete Company, will probably be there, too," Tory said. "Would it reassure you to see both of us dance with him, or will having him dance with just one of us do? Since Harold has met Mr. Lester before and I haven't, I nominate Harold for the honor of making this noble gesture of good will."

The Director almost smiled. "We must keep our sense of propriety. What I find reassuring might disquiet others. So I will leave the matter up to your professional judgment, Ms. Travers. I myself have had the opportunity to witness it improving over the years."

And after that, there was no question in anyone's mind that the meeting was over.

Sylvia was peering at a computer screen when Tory walked in, trying to get a new spreadsheet for project scheduling to work. Sylvia always dressed up even more than usual to celebrate the weekly advent of Friday. With her frosted hair, red mini-dress, and spiked heels, she looked like anything but the competent secretary, bookkeeper, and office manager that she was. It was Jazz that had christened her Chicana Madonna, and the name had stuck. Most of the staff was in the habit of calling her Maddie as a result, a practice from which Tory, with some effort, refrained.

Sylvia continued peering intently at the screen as Tory entered her office. The messages and reminders would come, but not until Tory had had time to settle herself at her desk and give them the attention that Sylvia thought they warranted. And they would be given in the order that Sylvia deemed appropriate. Equipment vendors that had gotten on Sylvia's bad side had long given up the hope of ever getting their messages passed on to Tory.

"So, Sylvia, what's been happening?"

Sylvia didn't look up from her screen. One of her more outstanding talents was the ability to carry on a conversation and process data simultaneously. "Not much, boss. Jazz is checked out to the stadium site for the rest of the afternoon. He wanted you to get in contact with him as soon as you get back in so he'll know if he's still being paid to give Kemp grief."

There was little that went on in the office that Sylvia didn't know about. Meeting with the University's Director concerning one of the firm's larger jobs was not an everyday event, and Sylvia's curiosity was understandable. And the sooner that Tory answered her unspoken questions, the sooner she would divulge her own information concerning the events during Tory's absence.

Working in a volatile profession and performing a frequently unpopular review function fostered a certain cohesiveness among Tory's workers. Her staff was used to backing each other up under stressful conditions. And to Sylvia, each individual employee was like a family member under her care, to be nagged, prodded, and scolded at times, but to be defended to the last breath against outsiders, namely clients and contractors.

"Well, the University plans to keep on paying us to keep Kemp's people on the straight and narrow. No one seemed to agree with his opinion that our inspection reports are hysterical. As a matter of fact, they've authorized an additional study to verify the adequacy of the steel reinforcing bars in the columns already on site. It's going to be a real rush job. I'm going to sit down and price it and draft a proposal as soon as I take care of whatever else needs my immediate attention. I'll need you to run a final copy and hand-carry it over to Henderson this afternoon before five."

"No problem. Things have been pretty quiet this afternoon. Mike is out doing a house inspection, Sara is working on logging inspection reports, and Bruce is in the lab working on our backlog of soils tests. Juan and Jimmy have gone to the dog track."

One of Travers' on-going projects consisted of providing soils testing services to Sunland, a greyhound track just on the New Mexico side of the New Mexico-Texas border. Travers Company provided weekly soils sampling and testing during the racing season, to ensure that the track moisture content and density remained as consistent as maintenance practices could make it. Hitting one hard spot on an otherwise loamy track could shatter a greyhound's fragile leg, which impacted the track at greater forces per square inch than the leg of any race horse.

"Well, sign me out for Monday morning. I'm going to drive down to El Paso first thing to get the precast yard data on the stadium columns. If everything goes smoothly, I should be able to get back into the office by eleven. Schedule Juan in the office for the afternoon to do the data evaluation for me. Is there anything else I need to take care of before I start pricing this study for the University?"

"Call Jazz. Call Cody. Call Lonnie." She paused dramatically to save the most unsavory directive for last. "Call Emmett Delgado." It was no secret that Emmett's company desired to acquire Travers Testing and Engineering. And it was no secret that to know Emmett Delgado was virtually universally to loathe him.

"Do I have to?" Tory asked. They all depended to a great extent on Sylvia's definition of what had to be done and what could justifiably be put off. But today she wasn't cutting Tory any slack.

"If you don't, you know that he'll just call back every hour. So if you call him now, it will save me having to talk to him again. Which is just fine with me." She flipped her hair behind her shoulders with long blood-red nails, to show just what she thought of Emmett Delgado.

"The things I do to make your job easy," Tory replied, closing the door to her office and preparing to do her duty. But some pleasures could come before duty, and besides, calling her son always came before anything else.

Carl's death when Cody was seven had been no surprise, for his fight with cancer had begun several years before Tory had met her husband. Both Tory and Cody had been aware that in many ways their relationship with him was merely a long preparation for the final parting. They learned early to rely on each other in difficult times, and the closeness built by shared loss had so far survived Cody's adolescence. Much of it was based upon humorous tolerance of each other's differences, coupled with the knowledge that each had to shoulder dual roles. Tory was both mother and father to Cody, and Cody was both son and companion to Tory.

Even as a small child, Cody had fiercely defended Tory's right to the type of life she had chosen. That had made many things easier, since she had never had the option to be a more conventional type mother than the owner of an engineering firm. The nine years she had had with Carl had barely given her enough time to finish her degree and become a registered professional engineer.

After graduating from college, Tory had worked with Carl to establish Travers Testing and Engineering Company when he no longer had the strength and stamina to continue teaching, and when they both realized that it was paramount to establish some type of income source that Tory could depend upon after he was gone. They had been given just enough time to accomplish their goal, and no more. Tory worked with Carl for the four years that were required before she could take the examination to become a registered professional engineer. She received the results of her successful completion of the exam just two weeks before he died. Her first action as the sole owner of the company had been to hire Jazz. The ensuing struggle during the next few years to run the business and keep it from going under had probably helped her cope with her grief as much as anything else.

At first, she survived on projects already under contract at the time of Carl's death, and the work she picked up from people who came to her out of respect for Carl or sympathy for the young widow and child. But gradually, and with a lot of assistance from Jazz, Travers Testing and Engineering Company became an established firm under the direction of a no-nonsense female engineer who was as much concerned with quality as with budget, and who won the reputation of refusing to back down when her inspection reports or test results were under fire.

In the last five years, business had progressed beyond the two-person office that had struggled for survival after Carl's death. Her firm now had a healthy portion of the larger projects around the state, and a respectable amount of business across the state line in the sprawling metropolis of El Paso. As with any small engineering firm, the profit margin remained unrelentingly narrow and the potential liabilities loomed large. But each year, the Travers Company clientele continued to expand.

Which was why Emmett Delgado was trying to pressure her into letting his large El Paso architectural and engineering firm acquire the Travers Company. Such an acquisition would allow his firm to offer a whole new market of expertise to an expanded geographical area of established clients.

Which was not part of Tory's game plan. Which was one of the reasons she was calling Cody and putting off calling Emmett. Which didn't last long.

Cody was merely reporting in from his morning swimming expedition on his way to his afternoon job working the dinner shift at McDonald's. This habit of checking in with each other several times a day had evolved from the early days after Carl's death. Tory had had to hold their lives together with frequently changing childcare arrangements and she had felt a need to repeatedly check Cody's emotional state of well being. However, as he had grown older, it was sometimes difficult to discern who was now checking up on whom.

Deciding to procrastinate no longer, Tory dialed Emmett Delgado, starting to draft the proposal to the University on her personal computer while she waited for him to come on the line. She and Emmett went way back, having been engineering freshmen together during her first year at college. He had pursued her, fascinated by the Floridian girl engineering student, a doubly exotic combination in those days when the females in each engineering department could be counted on one hand, and out-of-state students were few and far between. After one disastrous date in the pre-Carl days, she had refused to go out with him again. She had then proceeded to outdo him in every class they had together, and neglected to slouch to disguise the fact that she was a good two inches taller than he was. It had not made for a perfect relationship.

"*Qué pasa, mi corazón?*" "What's up, my beloved?" was the type of exchange that made Tory's jaw clench. Emmett had never stopped coming on to her, not before Carl, not during Carl, and not after Carl. And over the years, the nasty undercurrent to his banter had steadily increased.

"I'm returning your call," Tory replied evenly.

"Oh, you're right. And for a moment there, *chica*, I thought you were actually calling me just because you wanted to talk to me. *De nada.* I wanted to see how the stadium job is progressing. I hear you got pulled on the carpet this morning to answer for all those nasty, nasty reports that you're in the habit of writing. What's going on?"

"Good news travels fast." It was just Tory's luck that with everything else that was going wrong with this particular job, Emmett's firm was the designer of the stadium and Emmett was the structural engineer for the job. So he did have a perfect right to inquire about its status. Tory explained as tersely as possible the outcome of the day's meetings.

"*Pobrecita*" was Emmett's reply. "If you had the backing of a big firm like Webb, you wouldn't have to go through all these things by yourself."

"I wasn't by myself. I had Jazz with me, and that was just about all the company I could handle."

"Ah, Jazz," laughed Emmett. "Just as hot-headed as you are, only you've learned to hide it better over the years. That's the problem with corporate takeovers—sometimes it's just not possible to find a place for every person on the original staff. And I must confess, I don't see a place at Webb where poor old Jazz would fit in. Now you, I can always think of a place I can fit you in. I just wish that you would return the favor— you know, think of a place where you could fit me in—"

"Emmett, I've answered your questions. And discussing what Webb would or wouldn't do with my employees is ridiculous. I have work to do." It had been a long day, and Tory was tired. She flagrantly ignored her standards of self-restraint. "Why don't you go play with yourself?"

His reply was immediate, and his tone was ugly and urgent. "Don't hang up on me, Tory. I have things to tell you, things you're going to have to listen to." There was a pause, and he changed his tone again. "Are you going to the fund- raiser tomorrow night, the one to introduce the new theater department head?"

"Emmett, I have said everything I have to say. Try to hold that thought."

It was if she had never spoken. "Of course you'll be there. It's practically a command performance. Anyone having anything to do with the University will be there because it will be too big an opportunity to miss out on. I'll be there, and I'll look for you, Tory. We have a lot to talk about."

Obscenities only incited Emmett, Tory reflected wearily. She really should simply hang up. But she indulged herself one last time. "I'm too tall for you, Emmett," she said, and ended the phone call.

She tried to shake off the unpleasant exchange and refrain from wondering what Saturday night conversation topics Emmett had in mind. The idea of seeing Director Henderson,

Harold Kemp, Petey Lester, and Emmett Delgado all at the same time boggled the mind. The only thing missing would be to have Bill Hartman show up and follow her around, asking for an interview.

Tory was sure that one of the reasons Emmett had first shown an interest in her stemmed from the talk of scandal surrounding her when she started school. If that part of her past did indeed get resurrected, he would probably find it some kind of sick turn-on. She sincerely hoped she would never have to find out. She resolutely turned her thoughts to the business at hand, and dialed Jazz at the job site.

Tory launched directly into Kemp's complaint about a certain foreman's lack of safety procedures on the site, and read him the riot act to the extent that was credible. It was expected of her. And he cursed and complained that he had to take his hard hat off to beat some sense into some of those *estúpidos* at the site, and she replied that that was no excuse, his job description required him to be able to beat sense into them while keeping his hard hat on. Complaint and protest having been duly registered by each party, she was then able to give him the news about the Director's decision. And he was glad, but it wasn't accepted form for him to come out and say so.

"This is going to be one of those typical no-win situations," she told him. "If we hold up construction because we find that one of those columns is faulty, there'll be schedule problems and everyone will be screaming. But if we hold up construction merely to verify that the columns are all right, everyone will say they knew that already. There's always the outside possibility that we could be sitting on a lawsuit if the contractor is assessed penalties because of a delay that we're responsible for. So we've got to do this study as quickly as possible, but we've also got to be really sure about our conclusions. I'm driving down to El Paso to get the precast yard records on Monday morning. By late Monday afternoon we should know if we have to test the columns already on site. If we do, I promised the Director that we could be done with the testing and evaluations by the end of the week, or the following Monday at the latest. Do you see any problem?"

"Just an impossible schedule, that's all. We'll need to make sure we get all our instruments calibrated the first time and we'll need to run on overtime to develop the film and evaluate the shots. You just keep telling them whatever makes them happy and don't worry about us peons who actually have to do the work."

"Glad to know you have such a can-do attitude," Tory said.

Before she could say goodbye, Jazz interrupted her. "Hey, boss. That complaint business that Kemp pulled—it won't happen again." That was as close to an apology as she was going to get. But Jazz was as good as his word, and if he said it wouldn't happen again, she knew it wouldn't.

She didn't look up until two hours later, after she'd turned the proposal over to Sylvia and used the uninterrupted time to catch up on other paperwork. There was a knock at her door. "Got a minute, Tory?"

Lonnie Harper was the only non-staff person besides Cody allowed direct access to Tory's office by Sylvia. Everyone else had to satisfy Sylvia's criteria of whether or not they really deserved some of Tory's time. Not only did Sylvia bestow this unusual privilege upon Lonnie, she remarked at least weekly that if Tory had any sense she would marry the man. Since it was a choice of replacing Sylvia or learning to put up with her unsolicited advice, Tory had become an expert at the latter. Especially since there were times when she secretly reflected that Sylvia might be right.

Just looking at Lonnie was enough to make Tory feel better. Tall and lean in jeans and a workshirt, dusty from a day which had doubtless involved cotton fields and cattle, he had changed little since he and Tory had been in school together. There wasn't much in his appearance to suggest that he was heir to the holdings of one of the largest established ranching families in southern New Mexico, and that his name was known and respected throughout the valley.

"Lonnie, come in and sit down. I got your message, and I'm sorry I didn't get back to you. Time just got away from me. Yours is about the first friendly face that I've seen all day."

"One of those days, huh?" Lonnie asked, as he eased his frame into one of the chairs in her office. "Tell good old Lonnie about it, Tory."

"Good old Lonnie" was a joke between them, but it went far to describe their relationship. Lonnie's wife, his sweetheart since high school, had died in a hit-and-run accident six months after Tory lost Carl. His tragedy had been all the harder to bear, since the loss had been so unexpected and his wife had been joyously pregnant at the time. Well-meaning friends kept throwing Tory and Lonnie together after their respective losses, and it became easier to keep company with each other than to buck the popular opinion that everyone must have a partner. A mutual respect had deepened into a close friendship, with neither of them critical of the other's need to talk endlessly about the lost spouse, a practice that the non-bereaved seem to find perverse after the first six weeks, much less after the first two years. If Lonnie's feelings for Tory had deepened over the years into something that Tory could not reciprocate, they were too attuned to each other's needs to let it get in the way.

Tory felt the burden of the day lighten as she related the recent events to Lonnie, heightening the comic aspects and acting out the various exchanges. Laconic to the point of silence in certain situations, Lonnie always appreciated Tory's ready tongue, although he was aware that it often landed her in trouble that could just as easily have been avoided. And because he felt a need to look out for her, Tory omitted Bill Hartman from her discussion. The stadium project and the upcoming fund-raiser were immediate enough realities to deal with. There was always the outside chance that a problem that was not staring her in the face might resolve itself. Hartman might, after all, develop a conscience. Or the printing presses for the *El Paso Times* might burn down. Or something.

"Saturday night sure sounds like it's shaping up to be some affair. Are we still on? How about I come over at eight and we head over there about nine? That would give me a chance to see Cody."

"Of course we're still on, though I admit I feel guilty about having you escort me to something that isn't going to be very recreational."

"I don't know about that. With all the various players expected to attend, it sounds like the biggest circus to hit town in a long time. I'll have to go whether you stand me up or not, so I can watch you wise-crack yourself into deeper trouble with these people than you're in already."

"You're just hoping that I'll put you on the payroll for escort service."

"Only if you agree to hazardous duty pay. Hey, it's past quitting time. Even Maddie has deserted you. She told me that it was after five so she was using the time to paint her nails while she loyally guarded your door. When I showed up she said that I was welcome to the job. What do you say we get some dinner? Where would you like to go?"

"McDonald's."

"Somehow I thought you'd say that." And Friday was finally over.

CHAPTER THREE: PARTY TIME

"**M**om, Lonnie's here!"

Tory finished toweling her hair and shook it back from her face. "Okay," she shouted back. Someday they would have to stop shouting at each other and learn to act a little more civilized, she reflected. But if carrying on conversations from different rooms made the house noisy, it had also made it seem a little less empty.

"Mom, we're going to my room" was the next communication, and then there was silence. Tory knew no one would be breathing down her neck for her to finish getting ready. Cody and Lonnie would be sequestered together in Cody's room, engrossed in the latest computer game. Cody amazed his mother by being all-round good at almost everything— good grades in school, a natural athletic ability, and a usually sunny disposition. As he progressed into his teens, she sometimes felt from all the horror stories she had heard of personality transformations, that she was waiting for the other shoe to drop.

She pulled on her dress, a simple sheath of electric blue, and surveyed herself critically. The dress brought out the blue of her eyes, and made her hair look darker than usual. She turned sideways to the mirror. "Eat your heart out, Emmett," she thought. If she was going to have to spend the evening with distasteful people, she at least wanted to look good to do it.

One of the advantages of being so tall was that she could eat most everything she wanted without gaining weight. Her natural body build, plus the exercise she got in her job, had kept her at the same weight since she was sixteen, except for the traumatic times in her life when her weight had dipped alarmingly and she had become gaunt and drawn. Like when her brother had died, and when Carl had died. And when the affair with Jameson Barkley had made the press and she had left home, never to return. Outwardly she had appeared composed and independent, but inside she had been deeply hurt and frightened.

Tory always thought of that period in her life as simply The Scandal. She found it humorous that for a time there were others who had applied that label to her relationship with Carl. As if it weren't perfectly normal for a freshman student to fall in love with, and then marry, one of her college professors. She smiled to herself as she put on long, gold hoop earrings, a present from her deceased husband.

But she found her thoughts returning to that earlier time. As much as she tried to dismiss her conversation with Bill Hartman, she couldn't help wondering how her life would be affected if he reopened that part of her past for public consumption. Her past had never been a secret in New Mexico, although of course it had never been of as much interest to people here as it had been to everyone in Florida. A few people had made a point of drawing an analogy with her past reputation when she started dating Carl. In a way, that new relationship had eclipsed the other, for it was much more entertaining for people to talk about something occurring right before their very eyes, rather than rehash something that had happened a couple of years earlier in another state.

Then, after providing so many conversation topics, to everyone's absolute amazement, Tory and Carl embarked on a routinely conventional marriage. She had gone on to finish college in spite of taking a brief break to give birth to Cody the summer between her junior and senior year. In spite of everyone's predictions, she and Carl had lived and worked happily together for nine years, until his death had put an end to it.

The other, The Scandal, was so long ago, she mused. As unpleasant as it would be to have it unearthed again, she had a fatalistic certainty that she would live through it relatively unscathed. It would probably have a lot more effect on Jameson Barkley than on her. She now lived a life that could withstand scrutiny. She kept no secrets, save for one, and she had already paid the price for that one long ago.

She resolutely turned her thoughts to the evening to come, but that wasn't much of an improvement. She was still worried about Emmett. She hoped that he wouldn't be such an asshole tonight that Lonnie would feel pressed to come to her defense. And there was no way that Harold Kemp wouldn't be feeling antagonistic toward her. He was probably computing the interest on the money she might end up costing him. And Petey Lester was bound to be pleased to meet the person who had publicized his firm's mistakes to the University. All in all, it was shaping up to be an all-around peak social occasion. And Princess Diana thought she was under a lot of pressure.

She combed out her hair and put on some lipstick and was done. She looked in the mirror to give herself a brief pep talk, for she didn't like the fact that she was allowing herself to anticipate problems. Enough problems arose in her daily life without going around anticipating them. "Maybe Emmett Delgado has caught the flu," she told her reflection, "and maybe he's home this very minute, in his plush bathroom, in his plush condo, barfing his guts all over his plush rug." She winked approval at herself and went down the hall to wrest Lonnie, protesting, away from Cody's devices.

Tory and Lonnie walked outside and stood a few minutes admiring the beauty of the night before getting into her car. The relentless heat of the day had been replaced with the cool briskness of a New Mexico summer evening, containing just a hint of mountain chill. To the east rose the majestic Organ mountains, dramatic with their stark towering slopes, appearing from a distance like vertical sheets of sheer rock. These mountains tended to look more imposing than their northern counterparts because there was little natural vegetation to soften their stark, steep peaks. These were the vertical spires which resembled the organ pipes after which the mountains had been named. Only upon intimate contact, penetrating into their interior and climbing high above the plain from which they rose, did one discover pine trees, fresh water springs, and in the right season, snow.

Through these imposing structures was a highway to eastern New Mexico, following the natural space between the ranges that composed one of the passes through which early explorers, and then settlers, had been able to journey. El Paso del Norte, or The Pass of the North, had been named after just such an opening in the mountain ranges to the south of Las Cruces.

Las Cruces, on the other hand, was named after a man-made landmark. Either some pestilence or Indian raid had taken a heavy toll on an unfortunate party of settlers. Before moving on, the survivors had erected several crosses in their memory, perhaps to also serve as a warning to the ones that came after them. The names of both the deceased and the living had been lost to history, but their tribute lived on in the name of the town that grew up where the crosses had been placed: Las Cruces.

Tory's house, a sprawling frame structure, was on the outskirts of Mesilla, which, in turn, was on the outskirts of Las Cruces. This small town, mainly populated by Mexican-Americans, had only recently awakened to a booming tourist industry around its central plaza. The tourists were rediscovering that Mesilla was the site of both the signing of the Gadsden purchase and the trial of Billy the Kid. The central plaza was now bounded by shops on two sides, by St. Albino's Catholic Church on one end, and by Padrino's on the other. The latter was known among the tourists and college students as a "real dive," a place to get Mexican food and drinks in an authentic native atmosphere. Only the native residents realized that the *real* dive was two blocks farther away, down a narrow dirt road: a small adobe building with a nondescript sign proclaiming it as the El Palacio Bar. Students, tourists, and Anglos in general did not know of El Palacio's existence, and those that did found no reason to frequent it. Its clientele was mainly Mexican laborers and the language spoken there was Spanish, full of border colloquialisms not taught in foreign language classes. Tory had been there twice, both times with Jazz.

Tory loved the contrasts of Mesilla. Large, modern adobe houses stood on the outskirts of the town, interspersed with older adobe structures that in many cases were barely more than hovels. Some regional artists and authors of significant acclaim had made their home in Mesilla during the last decade, alongside the Mexican-American residents who in many cases had resided there for generations. Tourists frequented Padrino, exclaiming over its quaintness, unaware of El Palacio's existence only a few hundred feet away.

Lonnie lit a cigarette and leaned against the car. As a concession to Tory's fanaticism about smoking, he never lit a cigarette in her house, office, or car, but she had reluctantly acquiesced to his right to smoke outside. His contention was that all the men in his family had smoked, and none had lived long enough to die of it.

"What a panorama of contrasts. Out there," he gestured toward Las Cruces, "is a state university with famous faculty and state-of-the-art research projects. And down here, in lots of ways, it's like time has stood still. And over there," he gestured in the general direction of the Indian town of Tortugas, "it's the same thing, only with a totally different culture."

"Carl used to say that this is a land of contrasts and compromises," replied Tory. "Do you know that in the old graveyard down the road from the Mesilla plaza is the grave of a *bruja*—you know, a Mexican term for a witch? She died in the early nineteen fifties, and her family wanted her buried in the graveyard, which is hallowed ground. The Catholic priest at St. Albino's refused to grant his permission, and the family kicked up a big fuss. So they used modern technology to come up with a compromise. They put her body in a slab of concrete above the ground and placed it in the graveyard. That way she was in the graveyard, but not actually in the hallowed ground. Or, as an engineer would say, she was 'on site' but not 'in the subsurface.' Presto, everyone is happy."

Lonnie looked at her in wonder. "Sometimes I think you know more about this place than I do, and I've lived here all my life."

"I was an adopted child of New Mexico, not a natural one, so I had to work harder," she smiled at him.

"Maybe we can sneak out early tonight and you can show me the graveyard you're talking about. It couldn't be any more ghoulish than the group you're to see tonight."

She frowned at him. "I wish you hadn't reminded me. What a zoo. What a way to earn a living."

"I've offered to stake you forty acres any time to let you experience first hand the luxurious joys of ranching," Lonnie replied.

"Listen, you work with cows and horses. I seem to spend a lot of time working with asses. Who do you think has the better deal?"

"Cattle, Tory. You simply can't ranch if you persist in saying cows. No self-respecting rancher ever says cows. You're probably better off being an engineer."

It was a fifteen-minute drive from Tory's house in Mesilla to the foothills where the sprawling campus of New Mexico State University lit the night. Originally a land-grant university known as New Mexico Agriculture and Mechanical Arts, the school had leaped into the twentieth century, boasting an enrollment of over 20,000 and four branch campuses around the state. Yet it was still one of the few places where a parent could send a child off to college accompanied by their horse, especially convenient for those who had ambitions of making the school's intercollegiate rodeo team.

"I'm a little concerned about the people you're getting involved with on this project," Lonnie said above the hum of the car.

Tory looked at him in surprise. He seldom commented on her activities unless she asked his opinion. "Lonnie, don't worry about Emmett. He was a pain when I first knew him, he's a pain now, and he'll likely be a pain to someone when they make arrangements for his funeral. It's unpleasant to deal with him, but it's no big deal."

"Emmett is an alcoholic," said Lonnie flatly. Lonnie's father-in-law had been pushed over the narrow line dividing hard drinking from alcoholism by his daughter's death, so

Lonnie had more first-hand knowledge than Tory of the subject. Still, Tory was surprised by the statement.

"He certainly can be obnoxious when he's had too much to drink, but I don't know if I would classify him as an alcoholic."

"Well, it's only a matter of time before more people realize he has a problem, unless by some miracle he decides to get help. Talk has it he's blown several major deals by insulting potential clients. His projects always bid over budget, and his own subordinates are floundering around without sufficient direction, trying to wing the technical design without any kind of real supervision."

Tory looked at Lonnie in surprise a second time. It sounded like he knew more about Webb than she did. Lonnie had brothers and uncles, cousins and aunts, friends of his parents and even a few friends of his grandparents, dispersed around the Southwest in various walks of life, many in important positions. Tory had often wondered if there was anything in a five-state area that transpired about which Lonnie didn't know something.

Lonnie slanted a look toward her unasked question. "I have a nephew that's doing a student internship at Webb, drafting."

Tory let out a low whistle. "That's a really scary thought, for an engineer of record to be essentially nonfunctional. There are design disasters even in situations where everyone is on their toes. Something still gets overlooked or miscalculated, or someone makes a wrong assumption. Webb designed the university stadium, and Emmett is the structural engineer in charge. Are you telling me that in addition to all the construction problems, there may also be significant design flaws?"

"No, that's not what I'm telling you, although I hadn't thought about it in that light. You would know more about the possibility of those things than I would. I guess what I'm telling you is that I think for the most part you can dismiss Emmett. This effort to get you to sell your company is really a personal obsession, and once he's gone I don't think that anyone else at Webb is going to pressure you. So just try to wait it out without letting him get to you."

"Okay, I'll just keep trying to remember what a lady I am. So how come you're concerned about the people I'm getting involved with if you're telling me to write off Emmett? Are you really worried that I can't handle the flack from Kemp? I've got an ace up my sleeve. If he gives me any serious problems, I'll take him aside and proposition him. I figure he'll drop dead from shock and outrage on the spot, and that will solve that problem."

The thought of Tory propositioning Harold Kemp was enough to make Lonnie laugh. Tory had once told him about a meeting in which Kemp became so outraged at her that he was purple with apoplexy. But helpless before his own conditioning of a previous generation and time, Kemp had still compulsively stood and held the door open for her when she left. Of course, that didn't mean he would lose a chance to exert pressure in other ways.

"If you proposition Kemp," said Lonnie, "you better

be prepared for the possibility that he could take you up on it. You have this weird sense of humor, and other people don't always recognize it. But it's Lester and Colliney who concern me."

Tory glanced sideways at him. "I don't even know anyone named Colliney," she said. "At least, I don't think I do. Sounds like a good Irish name, though."

Lonnie sighed. "I really shouldn't be telling you this."

"Okay, so don't. Wait 'til I know something juicy and develop scruples."

"Don't be so touchy. When you told me about your meeting on Friday, the name Lester rang a bell. I couldn't figure out why, so I made some phone calls this morning."

"Busy little bee," commented Tory. "And all this time I thought you'd spent the morning out on the range, punching cows—I mean cattle—playing your guitar and singing old cowboy songs."

"Do you want to hear this or don't you?"

"If it concerns one of my projects, of course I want to hear it. I just don't want to be the cause of you compromising your sterling morals by passing on gossip."

"Your concern for my morals is touching. Okay, you've wormed it out of me. It's not really gossip, it's just something that needs to stay confidential between you and me. Petey Lester has run El Paso Precast for twenty years, and he's been successful at it. From what I hear, he's no better and no worse than one would expect him to be. About ten years ago he started getting into some development work, mainly building low-income project housing. And from what I hear, what he supplied was substandard, and there was talk about an investigation when the project began to experience cracking. But the matter got dropped, and fault was never determined."

"Wake me up when we get to the confidential part."

"Anyway, Lester only has one child, a daughter named Tiffany. About five years ago, she married Kent Colliney."

"Enter the mysterious Colliney."

"Colliney is a rather despicable individual, but as Tiffany is the apple of Lester's eye, he had no choice but to accept him into the family."

"And into the family business."

"Ah, you're sharp."

"And I thought you loved me just for my pretty face."

"No, actually I love you more for your sweet disposition. But in any case, you're right, with no sons—"

"An absolute necessity in any family business, with all the incompetent daughters running around in the world—"

"Do you want to hear this or don't you? With no sons, Lester took his son-in-law into business with him. Now he has a hard time controlling him. The good news is that El Paso Precast went from being a medium-sized firm to being one of the largest in west Texas. The problem is that they're over-committed and under-managed. It's all Lester can do to keep up with the projects that Colliney commits to at low-ball prices, and try to cope with the process modifications that he's made. Like buying all of their materials in Mexico."

"Ah, so Mr. Colliney likes to travel in exotic foreign lands, playing the part of the big American buyer."

"Exactly, and talk has it that he can't wait for Lester to retire and get out of the picture, so that he can run the whole show himself."

"Very interesting. But I don't see where this affects me. We're going to give the job the same type of evaluation that we would whether Lester's daughter married a Kennedy or Attila the Hun. Once they started to make that pour with reinforcing bar missing, they were under suspicion as far as I'm concerned. Maybe it was a once-in-a-lifetime mistake. Maybe not. That's what we intend to find out."

"I haven't finished."

"Are we finally getting to the juicy part?"

Lonnie laughed. "If I'm going to spill the beans, there's just no way that you're going to let me get away with acting like this conversation is on some type of higher plane, is there?"

"No." Tory pulled into a parking place. She turned off the car, doused the lights, and set the emergency brake. "If you're going to talk, 'hombre,' do it now. I feel a party in the air."

"Yeah, if there was ever a party animal, it's you, Tory. We both know you wouldn't be caught dead here if there weren't potential clients and you couldn't smell the possibility of new work. I know what turns you on."

"I just love it when you talk dirty to me. Listen, talk now or forever hold your peace. I have places to go and people to see."

"Here it is. I have a cousin in the Public Health Department in El Paso. It seems that Tiffany Colliney went to her doctor for a pregnancy test and turned out to have syphilis. Her only sexual partner was her husband, and the doctor had to report his name to the Health Department. Colliney wasn't very anxious to cooperate, but the Public Health Department has ways of persuading people. His list of sexual contacts was quite long, and included ladies from some of the ritzier establishments of ill repute across the border. He's just lucky it wasn't AIDS."

"She's lucky it wasn't AIDS. Tough break for Tiffany. So Colliney not only likes to wheel and deal, he likes to play around on the side."

"What I'm trying to tell you is he didn't pick up his medical problem in Boys' Town."

"What's Boys' Town?"

Lonnie looked at her with glee. "You mean there's a local expression that you don't know about? Boy's Town is a low-rent red-light district on the Mexican side of any border town. There's one across from El Paso, one across from Laredo, and so on. I'm really surprised you never heard the term before."

"I can hardly wait 'til the question comes up on the next game of Trivial Pursuit. When I answer it correctly to a cheering crowd of thousands, I'll be sure to give the credit to Lonnie Harper for opening my eyes to this special knowledge. I wonder what category the question will be under."

"In any case, what I was trying to say is that Colliney's intimate contacts weren't from Boys' Town. The places he frequents are run by drug dealers for entertaining their business associates, not the kind that are run by pimps for profit.

The point is, Colliney is not just someone whose greed may be indirectly responsible for the problems with the infamous column pour. He may be into other types of business dealings, like bringing drugs across the border. All of which I'd prefer for you to steer clear of."

Tory was genuinely touched by his concern, as well as impressed anew by the breadth of his contacts. "You never cease to amaze me. And all this time I've thought the only two things that you knew about were cattle and cotton. Notice, please, that I didn't breathe the word cows."

But Lonnie had one more piece of information to impart before they closed the subject. "My cousin told me one other thing. The doctor that filed the report on Tiffany said that due to the syphilis, it was extremely unlikely that she could ever have children. I wonder how that news is going to affect the family business dynamics." He looked seriously at Tory. "Which is something you'd be better off not finding out about."

Tory smiled at him. "Lonnie, I assure you, if it doesn't affect the stadium project, I won't go poking my nose into the reasons why El Paso Precast Concrete is having quality control problems. Now, let's go see who needs some engineering done."

Lonnie shook his head. "Let it never be said that Tory Travers isn't a dynamic Saturday-night date."

Corbett Center, the University Student Union, was not the most elegant place in town to hold a dinner dance/reception/fund- raiser. The large open room on the top floor was euphemistically termed the ballroom. Tasteful decorations aside, it was still the same institutional facility at which Tory had attended freshman ice-breaker dances many years ago. Then, she had stood in fascination, watching as the bands alternated between western and rock music. Depending on the selection, the group on the floor had been totally different than the group on the sidelines, waiting their turn for the "right" kind of music.

For the last few years the trend in such functions had been to hold them in one of the town's hotel reception halls. However, some ambitious souls had proceeded from there to hold a couple of University functions across the state line in El Paso, where the choice of facilities was luxurious and plentiful. The press had picked up on these instances of University money being spent out of state, and all of a sudden the people responsible were doing a lot of explaining.

It was not merely a case of public desire to have local funds spent with local businesses. For the past decade, New Mexico had been engaged in a feud with El Paso over water rights, with the water-hungry metropolis eager to sink wells which would draw from New Mexican aquifers. The fight had been fought furiously in the courts, touching on every pertinent aspect from interstate commerce laws to age-old Indian water rights. And much of the New Mexican populace was right there in the trenches, emotionally involved in the issue. There had been boycotts of Texas facilities and businesses. Many a New Mexican pickup sported a bumper sticker which stated "If El Paso wants our water, then piss on them!" And in this land of contrasts and compromises, Tory had seen the same bumper sticker on more than one Mercedes.

In any case, not only had University functions come home to Las Cruces in the last year, once-bitten-twice-shy administrators were embarking on a new era of watching budgets. Tory could only hope that they had not gone so far as to have the campus food service cater tonight's affair.

The fund-raiser, at a hefty price per attendee, was to benefit the theater department and introduce the new chair who was to assume his position in the fall. Hosted by the Alumni Association, the attendees were by no means limited to theater buffs. Tory doubted that more than a third of those present had ever attended a performance on campus, the status of nationally famous playwright Mark Medoff, a member of the University faculty, notwithstanding. There were faculty members present because they were expected to be, influential alumni and members of Las Cruces society there to see and be seen, and representatives of companies that served the University there to show their support, but also on the lookout for the opportunity to do business. It was among the latter group that Tory could be counted.

Besides being an institute for higher education, a university of any size is like a small town, a consumer of products and services at the multi-million-dollar level. As Tory walked in the door, she could identify, without effort, a manufacturer's rep for paper products, a sales rep for IBM computers, and the owner of a local automobile dealership.

And then there were the construction-related attendees, including architects, engineers, surveyors, contractors, and material suppliers.

As Lonnie and Tory flashed their tickets, she checked out the room much as a commando would check out the terrain for an expected skirmish. She needed to say hello to the right people (read Henderson into the script) and avoid others (read Emmett, Kemp, et. al.). Then she would seek out the faculty involved in defining facility needs and the administrators involved in managing new construction and renovation projects.

Typically, a project was years in transition from planning to construction, and the selection of design professionals was governed by state regulations intended to eliminate competitive pricing of services as the main selection criterion. However, there were emergency situations, like flooding or cracking, that could result in hiring a consultant in a matter of days. Information about project priorities and perceived selection criteria could be invaluable, and Tory had seen deals made and broken at functions like this, without any formal selection committee playing a part.

The band was set up at one end of the ballroom, playing popular music, and toned-down versions of established rock hits, in an effort to offend no one. Tory gave a passing thought to Cody, whose passion was classical guitar music. A product of the 'sixties generation, if it wasn't rock and roll, it was lost on Tory. She had tried listening to selections suggested by Cody, but she had always found herself poised on the edge of her seat, unconsciously waiting for a beat and some catchy lyrics. Finally even Cody had despaired of her, informing her with resignation that he supposed there could be worse fates than having a heavy-metal mom.

Along one side of the room stood a dinner buffet, complete with a salad bar and a bar of another kind. Lonnie obligingly went to fetch a club soda for each of them, their drink of choice. His line was that he didn't drink to make up for the fact that he smoked, and Tory's was that she didn't drink so she would always have at least one virtue to hold over a teenage son. The truth was that Tory didn't drink during business, and she considered the evening's activities to be business every bit as much as the hours that she spent in her office or on a construction site.

"Good evening, so nice to see you here." Henderson had appeared like magic at Tory's side. "You are looking lovely, as always." Tory wondered if that was supposed to mean that she always looked wonderful, or if her appearance tonight was no big improvement on standing hot, sweaty, and dusty on a construction site, wearing steel-toed boots and her hard hat. "Let me introduce you to our new theater department chair."

She allowed herself to be led smoothly into the throng of people and introduced to the guest of honor. What followed was a brief, stimulating conversation between the three of them, for Henderson was definitely a man of culture, and Tory had a passion for theater second only to her passion for rock music. She felt that any entertainment which combined the two bordered on the sublime.

Ever aware of proper etiquette, Tory and the Director were careful to keep their conversation at just the right length, wary of monopolizing the individual that supposedly everyone present had come to meet. They said their goodbyes and walked away. Tory noticed to her amusement that Henderson escorted her back to the exact spot where he had encountered her, where Lonnie stood waiting with their drinks, ready to accept the transfer of escort responsibility. She stifled an unprofessional urge to giggle.

"I had no idea that you knew so much about theater," remarked Henderson approvingly. "I'm sure the new department chair is very encouraged to meet an engineer with such a love of the performing arts."

"It's encouraging that you think so. But I'm still wondering how I'm supposed to encourage Petey Lester to do his job right within a social context, assuming he's even here tonight, or that Harold hasn't already cornered him somewhere. I was wondering if you might have any suggestions."

Unflappable as ever, Henderson smiled: "Subtlety, Ms. Travers. Small talk. Genteel suggestion. I'm sure you get the picture. Try not to step on any more toes than you absolutely have to, or, at least if you do, try not to attribute any of the wounds to me. Now, I must make sure that some other people here tonight have a chance to meet the guest of honor. Excuse me." And he was gone.

"Boy, Tory, you were smooth. I hope you do better than that at the negotiating table," said Lonnie mildly.

"Give me a break," replied Tory. "At least I have on all the required articles of apparel tonight."

"I beg your pardon. What's that supposed to mean?"

"Forget it. It's an inside joke."

He gave her a puzzled look, and changed the subject before he got in any deeper. "I've been keeping a lookout for Emmett for you."

"Lonnie, I am capable of taking care of myself, you know."

"Are you Tory Travers?" Tory turned to find a short, powerfully built man at her side. Standing almost directly behind him was a petite blond woman, shifting nervously from foot to foot. "Harold Kemp pointed you out to me. I tried to get him to come over and introduce us, but he told me just to come up and introduce myself. He's quite a joker, Harold is. Muttered something about wanting to wring your neck if he got too close to you. I'm Petey Lester, and I'm pleased to make your acquaintance." Caught unawares, Tory had to stop herself from flinching at the strength of his grip. "This is my daughter, Tiffany." Tory wondered if the omission of his daughter's married name was intentional.

Tory introduced Lonnie, who shook hands and then began watching the dancers with studied concentration. Tory immediately regretted having informed him seconds before that she was capable of taking care of herself, because it sure would be nice to have a friendly participant in this conversation. But Petey Lester appeared to be as friendly as a fat wriggly puppy. Just a lot older and larger.

"Harold called me Friday afternoon about the stadium project and the extra study you want to do on the columns. It's a bad business, all this problem with the columns. Of course, I'm certain the problem with the reinforcing bar was just one of those things that your inspector happened to see before it would have been rectified by my people. My foreman gave me a detailed briefing about the situation."

"Columbo, isn't that his name? My foreman gave me a detailed briefing about the situation, too." Tory decided that it wasn't stretching the truth too far to describe Jazz's ranting and raving as a briefing. "We feel the situation definitely warrants whatever effort is necessary to make sure there's no problem with the rest of the columns."

The smile on Lester's face never wavered. "I certainly don't agree with you. You know, everyone is under a lot of pressure to look good. I think my Mr. Columbo and your Mr. Rodriguez got caught up in a situation where each of them wanted very much to be in the right. Personality conflicts like that tend to aggravate an insignificant problem. But in any case, my staff and I will be happy to do whatever we can to help put your mind at ease about the situation."

Insignificant problem? You nincompoop, she wanted to say. Instead, she said evenly, "That's very cooperative of you." Lonnie continued to be totally engrossed in watching the dancers, as if he had been struck mute. If only they were sitting next to each other at a conference table, she could have had the satisfaction of kicking him in the shin. Hard.

"Yes, well, we certainly plan to be cooperative." As if he had a choice, Tory thought. "We want to do whatever we can to simplify your efforts. I understand that your study will involve an evaluation of the concrete pour data."

"As a starting point."

"But I understood that was all that was necessary if everything was found to be in order."

Strictly speaking, that was true, but Tory was hesitant to let it go at that. For the first time Lester's tone of voice had started to sound a little less than friendly. Was this what Henderson had in mind as social persuasion? Tory wondered. Lonnie and Tiffany continued to do their pillar of salt imitations. "Frankly, Mr. Lester, I really can't say at this point what all may be required." Let him chew on that.

Almost as if he could read her mind, Lester tossed a piece of ice into his mouth from his empty glass and crunched it. Was this body language or what? He swallowed and looked at her consideringly. "If the paper study doesn't satisfy your concerns, I would imagine that you'll want to do some actual testing of the other columns already on site."

No shit, Sherlock. "Yes, we'll probably X-ray the columns to make sure the reinforcing bars are present and aligned according to the design documents."

"Isn't that expensive? Have you considered other alternatives?"

So Kemp has hit you up to share the expense if he gets stuck with it, thought Tory. "I want to go with X-ray because it's the quickest. The costs will depend on how easily we can calibrate our instruments, and how many anomalies we have to resolve. But if this was just a one-time mistake like you seem to think, then we don't have anything to worry about." Tory thought that was an exceedingly generous statement for her to make. "But on the other hand, I plan to do whatever is necessary to make sure that the stadium that's erected out there is a safe one."

"Without a doubt. Will your concern cause you to also undertake a review of the design?"

That was unexpected. "Mr. Lester, I'm sure that you know that's out of my area of responsibility. What are you trying to say?"

"I'm only trying to make the point that sometimes the aspects of a construction project that get the most attention are not the ones that most warrant it."

"I'll certainly bear that in mind." What's that supposed to mean? Wondering if concerns about Emmett's design capabilities had reached other ears besides Lonnie's, she said, "We plan to conduct a rigorous evaluation of those stadium columns in any case. And you can rest assured that if we become aware of any design deficiencies while we're doing it, we will not hesitate to bring them to the attention of the appropriate officials."

"No, I'm sure you wouldn't hesitate to do that," replied Lester, with just the slightest emphasis on the word *you*. "But, I feel certain that once you have a look at the data, the matter will be resolved."

Tory took a sip of her drink. She studied him for just an instant longer than necessary over the top of her glass, and then turned to his daughter. "I'm sorry, I didn't catch your name."

"Tiffany. Tiffany Colliney." Tory had to bend down to catch her nearly inaudible reply.

"Oh, you must be married to Kent Colliney. Is he here tonight? I'd really like to meet him. I've heard so much about him." Tory had the satisfaction of seeing Lonnie choke on his drink. "Harold Kemp has told me about how involved he is in helping your father run the precast yard," she added smoothly, as Lonnie raised his eyebrows at her warningly.

Tiffany looked miserable and made no effort to answer. Initially, Tory had thought that she was just uncomfortable with their conversation, but now that she turned her full attention to the woman, she recognized all the signs of someone who was just going through the motions, whose thoughts were definitely somewhere else.

"I'm afraid Kent isn't here tonight," Petey Lester answered smoothly for his daughter. "He's in the habit of taking off on buying trips and not being real definite about his itinerary. I keep telling Tiffany that it's all part of the business, and that she had better get used to it. I brought her with me tonight, rather than leave her pining at home."

"In that case, may I ask you to dance?" Tory shot a look of pure amazement at Lonnie, who carefully avoided looking at her. Tiffany looked nervously from her father to Tory and then back again, and seeing no guidance there, acquiesced. She and Lonnie disappeared into the group of people dancing, and Tory and Lester stood watching them in what she supposed was meant to pass for companionable silence.

But before they had decided whether to move politely away from each other or resume sparring, Tory felt a hand on her arm and turned to face Emmett Delgado. "Tory. Aren't you looking fine tonight? We need to talk."

"Emmett, what a pleasure. No companion with you to-night?" It was common knowledge that Emmett was in the middle of his third divorce. Reportedly the present wife was proving to be the most difficult of the three, refusing to vacate their joint residence until various financial affairs had been reconciled to her liking. "Let me introduce Petey Lester, the owner of the El Paso Precast Concrete Company. Or perhaps you two have already met ..."

"Yes, we have," said Lester curtly, without offering to shake hands. All vestiges of the friendly puppy dog had vanished. "Good evening, Mr. Delgado. The two of you must excuse me, I see someone I must talk to."

Tory looked at his retreating figure regretfully, reflecting that Lester might have made a charming conversation partner after all, particularly considering the present alternative. She indulged herself with one fleeting fantasy of Lonnie staked out on an ant hill, and then turned back to deal with the inevitable.

Emmett grabbed her arm again. "I mean it, we really need to talk."

"If that's what it takes to get rid of you, I'll give you exactly five minutes. But take your hand off my arm. Let's go out in the hall so we don't have to have this conversation complete with an audience. I can hardly wait to hear what you have to say."

Tory slipped through the groups of people surrounding the dance floor, nodding hello to the many that she knew. Emmett followed close behind, until they were finally standing together in a deserted hallway.

"I meant what I said. You look real fine tonight, Tory." Tory noticed for the first time the empty glass in his hand, and the slight slur to his words. Emmett sober was no joy, but Emmett drunk could be a force to be reckoned with. Maybe she should have stayed in the ballroom

"Okay, Emmett, what is it?"

"Your company, Tory, your little company that will be such a shining addition to Webb."

Tory kept a careful rein on her temper. "I've told you repeatedly that I have no intention of selling, to Webb or anyone else."

"You've always thought you were better than everyone else. Do you really think that you have what it takes to make that business grow? For that you need contacts with the big boys. Contacts you'll never have, Tory. No matter how good you are, you'll always be an outsider to the groups I'm talking about. Webb needs a better toe hold in the New Mexico market, and your company is going to provide it. And I'm the one who's going to deliver it."

"Emmett, you've become obsessed by this. It's not going to happen."

"I need this. The positions above me at the main office are filled by people who will stay there 'til they die, and all the branch office manager positions are filled. If I could deliver your company, they'd have to let me run it."

Over my dead body, Tory thought to herself. "Emmett, it's really not as much fun to run my company as you seem to think it is," she said without thinking.

"Always joking, aren't you, Tory? Why come up with a straight answer when a wisecrack will do as well? You tell me no, and you think that's going to be the end of it. You can't expect me to leave it there."

It struck Tory that his words were almost identical to the ones used by Hartman. You didn't have to be too intelligent to figure out that a threat was going to follow. Was she in demand or what? One amateur reporter wanted her memoirs to further his fantasies of a journalistic career, and this asshole wanted her company to feed some personal egotistical obsession. Maybe later Harold Kemp would ask her to meet him in a dark alley.

"Let's see if you can wisecrack your way out of this, Ms. Travers," continued Delgado. "Take the term 'lawsuit' and see how much humor you can find in it."

A lawsuit was the nightmare of every professional design company. In a construction-related suit, everyone got drug into court, including the inspector. From the defendant's point of view, the result of a lawsuit could be devastating, whether or not guilt was ever determined.

Most lawsuits were incredibly time-consuming, taking years to resolve. For the defendant, this involved endless demands to prepare statements and reply to depositions. Whether guilty or innocent, the resulting legal fees could be staggering. And then there was the matter of professional liability insurance, known as errors and omissions insurance.

This was the type of insurance required of design professionals by many public agencies, governing bodies, and some private clients. In the 1980s, these premiums had skyrocketed, often doubling or tripling in a twelve-month period. Depending on who was doing the explaining, this was due to increasingly complex construction projects, new public awareness of potential environmental impacts, losses sustained by the insurance brokers over a period of years, and several catastrophic structural collapses that had occurred in the early '80s.

Doctors had historically had to deal with astronomical insurance premiums. But whatever the doctor's speciality, his mistakes only affected one person at a time, or in the case of an obstetrician, possibly two. But when something went wrong with a building, from a structural collapse to unintentional dispersion of asbestos particles, potentially hundreds of people could be affected. And hundreds of them could sue. And, unlike doctors, engineers didn't get to bury their mistakes, or send them to jail, like attorneys did. Catastrophic engineering mistakes made headlines and remained permanently entrenched in public perception.

The insurance premiums for a design firm depended upon the coverage, the amount of business done annually, the types of projects undertaken, and the past history of the firm. Those in high-risk specialties, such as structural design, paid more than firms whose specialty was landscape architecture. Firms with no history of litigation paid considerably less than ones that had been involved in court cases.

So a law suit, seldom a small matter to anyone, could be the kiss of death to a firm such as Tory's. It could sap profits both directly and indirectly, and drive insurance premiums to the point where coverage was no longer affordable. More insidiously, it could affect a firm's reputation to the point of driving it out of business. And all of this could easily occur before a judgment was ever made.

Avoiding being named in suits required providing quality services, good business sense, an unfailing commitment to documentation, and a lot of luck. Travers Testing and Engineering Company had only twice been the subject of lawsuits. Due to early defensive action, excellent legal counsel, and the ability to produce key documents refuting the claims, both suits had been dismissed.

Even as she cursed herself for continuing to participate in the conversation, Tory couldn't resist asking, "What are you talking about?"

Emmett smiled triumphantly, "El Paso Savings and Loan. Remember that job, Tory?"

"Yes, I remember. It was a fourteen-story structure. Webb did the design; we did the soils testing. I don't remember who the general contractor was."

"Well, you'll get to know him real well. The owner has a cracking building. A cracking building that's only two years old, and they want somebody to burn. They think we walk on water, Tory. They consult us at every turn. And they've come to us for recommendations on how to proceed."

"We're clean on that project."

"But that's not really the point, is it? This is going to be a big one, Tory, really big. And I can decide whether or not you're drawn into the middle of it."

"You do what you need to do."

"That's it, Tory. Act like you're above all this. Act like it doesn't scare you. All the design and the testing took place over three years ago. I don't care what kind of documentation you have, Tory. I may remember recommendations that your firm made a lot differently than you remember them. And I may just find that I happened to document all those conversations. In fact, whether or not I documented them may depend on the outcome of our conversation tonight. Telephone memos are admissible in court, Tory, and all the judge is interested in is the letterhead and the date on the memo. They don't carbon date that type of thing, you know."

"Emmett, I always knew you were a real lowlife, but even I can't believe you're saying this. You're talking about fabricating documents. That's fraud. As a special favor to you, Emmett, I'm going to forget that we ever had this conversation."

"Oh, we had this conversation all right. I've wanted you for a long time, Tory. And getting your firm is going to be almost as good as getting you. And I figure that if I play my cards right, I may end up with both. If you start acting real nice to me, I may let you go ahead and accept Webb's offer for your company without dragging you into this other business. Otherwise, I may just sit around and bide my time until the price has gone down."

"Why don't you go somewhere and sober up, Emmett?"

That stung him. She turned to walk back to the ballroom, and he followed close on her heels, furiously. "Don't you walk away from me like that!"

She had miscalculated. She had thought that being back among the crowd would bring Emmett to his senses, but her walking away had enraged him. Lonnie was nowhere in sight, and as luck would have it, neither was any other familiar face. She walked to the buffet, accepted a plate from a server, and gave the selections her studied attention. None of which did any good.

"You've got ice water in your veins, you bitch. No wonder you married someone twice your age who was too sick to ever be a real man. I've always wondered who fathered that little bastard of yours, probably some—"

Tory's self-control snapped and she turned around and slapped him.

In the movies, when a woman slapped a man, he took his medicine without flinching, and immediately turned his head back so the two antagonists could enjoy a long eye-to-eye stare. But in this case, as happens so often, reality was very different from the movies.

When a tall, physically active woman slaps a man who is several inches shorter than she is, his head doesn't whip back so he can confront her with a long meaningful stare. When the man in question has had several drinks too many, none of him remains in place. Emmett followed the general direction of Tory's blow, slowly but surely falling back into the salad portion of the buffet. Reaching out unsuccessfully to try to save himself, his left arm dislodged a large bowl of cherry tomatoes, which hit the floor just milliseconds before Emmett did. Slumped against the table, holding his jaw, he looked at

Tory with pure hatred, while she regarded the scene with horrified disbelief.

The last of the cherry tomatoes were still rolling to their final resting places as he yelled, "You'll regret this, you bitch. I'll get even with you."

Appearing out of nowhere, Henderson was suddenly at her side. Two of his staff members were magically right behind him, helping Emmett up and smoothly ushering him out of the room. Before Tory could even begin to phrase her apologies, the Director began to apologize to her.

"I'm so sorry, Ms. Travers. Mr. Delgado seems to have gotten out of hand. Do accept my apologies; it won't happen again. And do excuse me, I must see to the other guests."

And he was off, smoothing inquiries in his wake, a comment here, a wry joke there, successfully turning people's attention away from the debacle. Standing with her mouth literally hanging open, mortally embarrassed and in the middle of an expanse of cherry tomatoes, Tory was vaguely aware of Lonnie approaching from across the room. But before he could reach her, Kemp appeared magically at her side.

"I believe you had saved this dance for me?" Was Harold Kemp asking her to dance? Maybe she was dreaming. Not questioning her good fortune, Tory successfully maneuvered through the cherry tomatoes to join him in a stately two step. They danced in studied silence for a few minutes. Over his shoulder, she could see the caterers putting the table to rights, and Lonnie gallantly offering his arm to Mrs. Kemp and leading her onto the dance floor. He seemed to be on a roll in exercising his social skills, she reflected.

"Don't think I'm going to cut you any slack just because you got me out from the cherry tomatoes, Harold."

He looked at her in irritation. "Let's get something straight, little lady. The feeling is mutual." She wanted to tell him to stop calling her little lady but she didn't feel up to it right at the moment. "You've pushed things too far this time, Tory. My subcontractors are about to revolt over the time that's been lost reworking items because of your damned inspectors. This project was bid on a schedule tight as a witch's ass to begin with. A lot of people stand to lose a lot of money if we don't finish on deadline, and I'm at the head of that line. You better tell your people to start cutting us some slack, lady."

"You better tell your people to start doing the work right the first time," Tory replied sweetly. People always said that trouble came in threes. Lester, Delgado, and now Kemp. She sincerely hoped she was done for the night. Even the possibility of more business wouldn't lure her to another one of these human sacrifices for a long time. Jumping into a live volcano instead didn't look so bad, in comparison.

Kemp glowered at her while he continued to guide her around the dance floor. She didn't think it likely he would let her lead. "You've been in this business too long not to realize that you're setting yourself up for some trouble if you don't slack off. We can make things hard for you, too."

The music ended. "What a lovely dance. We must do this more often," she told Kemp. While continuing to give her a stare that would have turned lesser mortals to stone, he bowed formally to her from the waist, turned on his heel, and was gone.

It was a while before she met up with Lonnie again. People that she only vaguely knew made a point of coming up and talking to her, as if to assure her that she was not being held at fault. Many of the men asked her to dance, including a few with whom she had professionally adversarial relations. Either people were nicer than she had expected, she reflected, or Emmett had offended more people than she realized. She stuck it out for an hour to keep up appearances, but by the time she was alone with Lonnie again she was ready to go home.

"Well, if it isn't the gallant cowboy. For someone who is supposedly tongue-tied, you sure managed to make the rounds tonight. Want a ride home with me, or have you found a better offer?"

"You sure have an original way of taking care of yourself, I'll grant you that. You should consider yourself quite a lucky lady."

"I'm dying to know why. Because you're letting me give you a ride home?"

"No, because talk has it that Emmett made a pass at one of the servers this evening before he turned his attentions to you." He lapsed into one of his characteristic silences, and Tory decided to take the bait.

"So?"

"So, she was Henderson's niece."

CHAPTER FOUR:
ALWAYS ON A SUNDAY

Senior Detective David Alvarez of the El Paso Police Special Case Force was just getting ready to relax with a beer and the TV when the call came. He stowed the beer back in the refrigerator on his way to the phone, because the odds were against anyone but the Department calling him on a Sunday evening. He wasn't currently dating anyone, and most his friends were from the Job. They weren't likely to call on a guy's afternoon off. Any getting together was arranged ahead of time; no one liked the phone ringing during time off.

Actually, it wasn't the Department dispatcher calling, but Alvarez's partner. Given a choice, the dispatchers preferred to call Scott Faulkner, his easy-going partner, and let him relay messages on to Alvarez. The dispatchers seemed to believe that Faulkner was much less likely to tell them to go to hell and find someone else to handle the problem. Why some of the people on the receiving end of those conversations should take it personally, Alvarez couldn't figure. After all, he always showed up, one way or another. Were people really expected to be pleasant about canceling plans?

"David—it's Scott. There's been a m-m-murder out in the Anapra area, and the Chief wants us to check it out." Alvarez had worked with Faulkner for so long that he no longer noticed his partner's intermittent stutter. It had taken him a while longer to overcome his instinctive distrust of Faulkner's monied WASP background. Eventually, though, he had come to realize that it was just as difficult for someone to become a cop when their family ran to doctors and lawyers as it was when your grandmother didn't speak English and fewer than half the kids in your neighborhood finished high school.

Like some individuals that are stutter-free when they sing or recite, Faulkner's stutter disappeared completely in an emergency. Alvarez knew from first-hand experience that Faulkner could yell "Watch out!" or "He's gone down that alley" as plainly and as quickly as anyone else. Sometimes he could get through whole conversations without a single hesitation. Which still didn't mean that Alvarez wanted to be talking to his partner on a Sunday evening.

"Hey, *cabrón*, it's the end of the weekend in a border town. That's when everything turns ugly. Too much Monday morning on the horizon. So someone has a stiff on his beat—what else is new? What's so special about it that the boys in blue can't take care of it? I'm off duty, man. And by the way, you're supposed to be off duty, too. Or does that get too boring for a family man like you?"

One of the reasons that the two of them worked so well together was Faulkner's ability to let a good portion of what was said to him go right over his head. If it wasn't a fact worthy of inclusion in a report, or a discrepancy between one witness's testimony and that of another, Faulkner tended to brush it aside. Not so Alvarez, who had been known to brood obsessively over the subconscious meaning behind a choice of words, or the nuance of tone in a certain conversation. One with a nose for facts, and the other one on a constant lookout for shades of meaning. Taken together, they were a formidable detective team.

"For st-starters, there doesn't seem to be a motive. This guy was a technician for a company out in Anapra, found dead in the office. It looks like he was murdered while doing some extra weekend w-w-work. Nothing of value was taken, and no one has found any signs of vandalism."

"Let's see if we can't solve this one over the phone. If robbery wasn't the motive, either it was something personal or your random murder event. Maybe it was just your friendly neighborhood sociopath out for a Sunday evening romp."

Faulkner always responded literally to his partner's suggestions. "That's part of the problem. No signs of break-in, either. According to the watchman that discovered the b-body, the door to the office automatically locks from the inside unless someone goes to the effort to unlock it, like they do during working hours. And the watchman had to unlock the d-door to get in tonight, like always. He says that for security reasons, when someone is out there after working hours, they tend to leave the door locked."

"A crime of passion, then. The guy ran around with the wife of the boss, and the boss came out and put an end to it."

"Maybe. We're just now starting to get some background on the victim. But there's something else."

To warrant calling in Alvarez's ad-hoc department, there was usually "something else." There was a dark side to the city that came with its border location. This darker side included drugs, organized crime, kidnapping, industrial espionage, and smuggling, all with potential international political ramifications. It was with these types of cases that the Special Case Force dealt, and it was these applications that made Alvarez's Mexican heritage and fluent border Spanish invaluable.

"So what else can you tell me about what went down?"

"The night watchman says that part of the company records are g-g-g-gone."

That must be what had tripped their involvement. "So what kind of company are we talking about? Stolen records implies a law firm or an investment company. Or maybe one of those high-tech industrial research outfits. But wait. You're talking Anapra. They don't have that stuff out there ... Oh, shit." Alvarez realized that in the space of less than five minutes, he had been sucked into the challenge of solving the riddle. Now there would be no turning back.

His partner had never had any doubt about that. "Wrong on all three counts. The outfit is a m-m-manufacturing firm. They make concrete pipes or something like that. Definitely not your white collar type operation."

Alvarez was silent, simultaneously turning several possibilities over in his mind, already sifting for the connection, the payoff, the benefit that had driven one human being to eliminate the life force in another. There were lots more questions to ask and ideas to bat around, but the trail would be growing colder by the minute. "Okay. I'll pick you up in ten minutes," he said, all thoughts of a quiet evening at home already history.

"Okay. I'll be ready. My in-laws are visiting this weekend."

"I guess that means you'll be waiting out in the yard. You didn't volunteer us for this gig, did you? Even a sheltered white guy with your upbringing should be able to figure out that the way to avoid having in-laws is to avoid getting married in the first place."

"This is a conversation that's two years too late, so you might as well give it up. I'll be w-w-walking down the street to meet you."

Alvarez and Faulkner both lived in the southern foothills of Mt. Franklin, one of the two huge mountain ranges that rose in the middle of the El Paso metropolis. The other was named Sugarloaf, after its South American counterpart. For a long time the mountains had actually bordered the city, but now the city encircled them. In the last ten years, developments had begun gradually creeping up the mountainsides themselves.

Alvarez got a kick out of some early resident actually naming a desert mountain after some place in Brazil. Perhaps it had been an unconscious retaliation against the blatant Texas patriotism that had pervaded the naming of most early landmarks. Without any effort, he could think of numerous older schools, some of which he had attended, named after Texas heroes: Crockett, Travis, Bowie, Austin, Houston, and of course there was an Alamo street, and the central plaza downtown was named after a famous battle for Texas independence: San Jacinto.

Alvarez was thirty-eight, and he could remember when "The Eyes of Texas Are Upon You" was sung in school rather than the national anthem, and when Texas state history was a complete year of required high school curriculum, equal to the time required for studying United States history. Texas history came before national history in the curriculum, the philosophy being that if a student dropped out before completing both, the important one would have been taught first.

But the area that was their destination, Anapra, had a name of Spanish derivation and a population that had historically consisted of poverty-level Mexican-American workers and illegal aliens. When Alvarez had been growing up, the Anapra area had been known as Smeltertown, taking its name from the industry located in the area. Some of the residential areas clustered around the industrial yards resembled their poor Mexican counterparts, or "barrios," which were in plain sight just across the Rio Grande River. Recently, more industrial businesses had begun to swallow up some of the shabby Anapra residential areas, hungry for inexpensive land on which to locate their facilities.

In the midst of this mixture of heavy industry and poverty rose the unlikely majesty of the huge statue of Christ by Urbici Soler. Atop Mount Cristo Rey and visible for miles upon approaching El Paso from Las Cruces via I-10, this was a shrine to which the people of the area had attributed miraculous qualities. It was approached by a footpath marked with the fourteen stations of the cross; the climb took about an hour for the physically fit. Alvarez remembered climbing

up there numerous times as a child. His paternal grandmother, who had helped his mother raise him and his sister,
had been very fond of shrines.

Now, few but the totally devout or totally desperate visited
the shrine. Isolated upon a mountain which was only a few
feet from the Mexican/American boundary, it had become a
site of vandalism and robbery where the stronger preyed upon
the solitary and infirm. So, reversing a trend where works of
art are taken from the poor to places where they may be enjoyed by the affluent, this majestic Christ had been abandoned by the local dilettantes and tourists. It had become the
property of people too poor to worry about the added element of crime that it introduced into their environment.

Unlike the south, the southwest had not had formal
desegregation in the 'sixties. A lot of this stemmed from
the fact that there was not an established history of Anglo
majority in the area. But this didn't mean that there hadn't
been de facto segregation, and it didn't mean that there
weren't bitter efforts to resist the changes brought by the
Civil Rights movement.

When Alvarez was in high school, some well-meaning
bureaucrat had seen fit to investigate the fact that there was
glaring racial imbalance in many of the El Paso public
schools. The residents of the Anapra area were a scarce two
miles from a brand-new high school in an affluent suburb,
yet they had been zoned to attend Alvarez's school, the second oldest in the city, primarily attended by Mexican-Americans and located a good ten miles from Anapra. In the press

wake that followed, Alvarez and his contemporaries learned the meaning of a word coined in another time and in another place: gerrymandering. Today, at least on the face of it, things were different.

And Anapra today was different than it had been in those days of awakening ethnic heritage. For a time, in the 'sixties, the area had been home to the hippies as well as the poor. It had even become, for a brief time, a trendy place for certain celebrities to appear during their tours to El Paso. There had once been a ramshackle nightclub called Free Holy, a play on the Mexican name for a staple of life: frijole beans. It was a place for the El Paso hip to see and be seen. Supposedly Joan Baez had once played there until the early morning hours, leaving her formal concert for paying fans early, and entertaining for free those lucky enough to be at Free Holy that night. At least, that was what Alvarez had heard. His past did not include hippiedom.

As water settles to its lowest level, so interracial marriages tend to settle to the level of the member on the lowest rung of the social totem pole, unless there is some interceding factor, such as wealth, to prevent it. There was no wealth in Alvarez's family, and he had been raised in every way as a low-income Mexican-American. Only his lighter skin and his uncommon height hinted at his Anglo parentage, provided by his farm-bred Kansas-native mother. Imported to the area by her military family, which had drawn a stint at Fort Bliss, she made the mistake of falling in love with Alvarez's father. He was dark and reckless and heartbreakingly handsome, and as ill-prepared as she to handle the result of their relationship, which was Alvarez himself.

Her family stuck around long enough to make sure that the honorable thing was done, and then abandoned their newly married daughter and all ties to their grandson when their next post conveniently turned out to be in Germany. Alvarez's sister made her appearance the next year. When it became apparent by the time she was five that she was mildly retarded, the whole situation proved too much for his father. Deciding that his wife's family had arrived upon a solution that seemed to work, Alvarez's father joined the army when David was seven and was never heard of by his family again.

Perhaps it was the early responsibility of being the only male in his family that drove Alvarez to be a little bit different than most of the children that he grew up with. He ran with the wild kids in high school, fought, drank, smoked dope, and shoplifted with the most reckless of his contemporaries. But with no father, he was forced early to be responsible for bringing home money to his family. And with his mother and sister literally worshipping the ground that he walked upon, there was always something holding him back from the most dangerous temptations—the hot-blooded violence of gang fights and the easy money of drug dealing. In an almost conscious decision to remove himself from these possibilities, he decided to graduate from high school and become a cop.

Surprising himself as much as anyone else, he proved to be a success at his chosen career. He was courageous, he was quick physically and mentally (qualities his father had pos-

sessed), and he was level-headed (thanks to the genetic con-
tribution of numerous generations of midwesterners on his
mother's side). Perhaps more important than anything else,
his dual heritage had given him a talent for playing the
chameleon. A department scholarship had sent him to college, and by the time he finished his degree in criminal
justice and law enforcement at the University of Texas at El
Paso, he could play the sophisticated intellectual almost as
well as the crude street-wise "greaser," and many more roles
in between. And, ultimately important to his line of work,
he could think like each of the roles that he could assume.
More than once, an uncanny identification with a murder
victim or suspect had enabled him to catch the killer.

There wasn't enough information yet to begin charac-
terizing the victim in his mind, much less start to get a
hazy outline of the killer. But that wouldn't stop Alvarez
and Faulkner from trying. A good portion of their time
together was spent trying out hypotheses on each other, no
matter how early in the game, no matter how farfetched.
Alvarez had once told someone that police work consisted
of fact gathering and storytelling, and a successful detective just kept gathering facts and spinning stories until
there was a perfect fit between the two.

Which still didn't mean that he wouldn't have enjoyed
his beer and the ball game. Throwing open the door to his
partner, who, true to his word, had been walking up Savan-
nah to Alabama Street to meet him, Alvarez felt called upon
to continue his protest. "I still don't understand why we're

being called in on this case," he grumbled, visualizing the six-pack on the bottom shelf of his refrigerator. His partner was blond and stocky, with tell-tale skin that broadcast news of any recent exposure to the sun. It was obvious that Faulkner had been outside this weekend, most likely on some wholesome family-type activity. For some inexplicable reason, that disgruntled Alvarez even more. He just hoped the in-laws had been included.

"He obviously wants his best minds on it," said Faulkner, unruffled. Integral with his literal interpretation of life was his unshakable opinion of his abilities and those of his partner. "This is an election year, so the politicians are paranoid about showing that we're winning the war against crime. N-no murder left unsolved, and all that."

Alvarez glared at him, unmollified, so Faulkner decided to elaborate on his explanation. "And maybe the Chief decided to call us because you were right and he was wrong about the Jemez case, and maybe he's still mad about it. If that's the case, you're responsible for ruining my evening off. You're lucky I don't hold a grudge."

"Yeah, maybe you're right. Did you ever notice how much your stutter improves when you're not around your in-laws? Anyhow, now the Chief has to approve my travel expense claims for that trip to Las Vegas where I nailed the Jemez gang's major buyer," replied Alvarez, savoring the memory of sweet victory.

"It still would have been good form to have gotten his approval before you took off." Faulkner was still slightly disgruntled about the inconvenience of having to cover for his partner for those two days. The souvenirs that Alvarez had brought back for him had done nothing to soothe his irritation.

"Listen, man, I won fair and square. You had your chance to go and you blew it."

The outcome of this particular decision had been determined by the high score on a pinball game. Although Alvarez had vowed he'd never seen that particular machine before, much less played it, Faulkner still had his doubts. But he was prevented from voicing them once again by their arrival at their destination.

Alvarez pulled his bronze Corvette past the sign that identified the El Paso Precast Concrete Company, and parked next to the two police cars outside the prefab building that he assumed served as an office. Although it was close to 8:30 PM, it was still essentially light. In mid-summer, dusk didn't come until 9:00 PM or after.

"Let's go," he said to his partner, the heightened awareness that he always felt at the scene of a crime driving away all thought of other matters.

A uniformed officer was roping off the building, using a yellow plastic tape similar to surveyor's tape, but which had "Crime Scene Do Not Enter" printed on it. Alvarez flashed his badge at the officer, and then he and Faulkner were inside.

They walked through a small reception area, past what Alvarez assumed was the secretary's desk, and down a hall with one small office and two larger offices opening off it. At the end of the hall was a door which opened into a large room obviously used as some type of laboratory. It was filled with broken pieces of concrete, bags of materials, and a lot of equipment that Alvarez didn't recognize. The body was slumped against the wall across the room, the face in profile. A uniformed police officer and an individual in civilian clothes, who Alvarez assumed was the medical examiner on call for this beat, stood waiting by the body.

The introductions were brief. Alvarez was assured by the uniformed police officer that all proper procedures had been followed: the area and all exits and entrances dusted for prints, the body examined to the extent that it could be without being moved, photographs taken, and all readily observable, pertinent facts recorded. Someone from the company had been notified and was on the way to make a positive identification of the victim to corroborate the preliminary identification by the watchman, who had seemed to know who the victim was, but not his name. Now, all that remained prior to moving the body was to let the Special Case Force detectives take a look at it.

"Glad you could come," said the uniformed officer as Alvarez bent down to get a better look at the body. If some wiseass wanted to make an issue out of territoriality on Alvarez's time off, he could be up for it. Alvarez looked up sharply and scanned the officer's face for signs of sarcasm, finding none. The guy looked young, and he looked green, the latter observation more a physical fact than a judgment regarding lack of experience. His face, Alvarez noticed, was covered with a sheen of perspiration. And it was anything but warm in the overly air conditioned office.

"First murder case?" Alvarez asked noncommittally.

"First as officer in charge, sir," the policeman answered, fixing his eyes somewhere above and behind Alvarez's head.

Alvarez raised one eyebrow in acknowledgment. If the guy hadn't barfed, he was doing good, and he didn't need Alvarez to comment on it. Alvarez turned his attention to scrutinizing the body, something that Faulkner, oblivious to the young officer's discomfort, had already gotten a good start on doing. Relieved not to be the recipient of some patronizing chin-up-you-get-used-to-it speech, the officer relaxed some as Alvarez bent down to get a closer look at the victim.

The man on the floor was obviously dead, and would appear so even to the most novice observer. Alvarez was sure the night watchman would have found no reason to touch the body before reaching that conclusion and calling the police. The right arm was twisted behind the body in a most unnatural position, the face had the swollen, discolored look of strangulation, and there was a thin line of dried blood snaking down the exposed nostril to the man's shirt. The victim was dressed casually in jeans, tennis shoes, and a T-shirt, and appeared to be between twenty-five and thirty years of age.

"How long?" Alvarez asked the doctor.

"I understand the night watchman's call came in at 7 p.m.," he replied. "I'd say he'd been dead between two and six hours, by then. I can tell you more after the autopsy."

"Did you know that the doctor on the scene says that in every single murder mystery I've ever read?" Alvarez asked conversationally, straightening up. There was no comment forthcoming from the doctor. He would probably rather be home watching the ball game, too, Alvarez deduced. He wasn't an ace detective for nothing. "Cause of death strangulation?"

This time he got a response. "Most likely. But there was a serious blow to the head." The doctor pointed to a swelling on the victim's head, partially disguised by a thick head of dark hair. "We think that's the instrument that was used." He pointed to a short steel rod lying on the floor by the body. "But, then again, we'll know more after the autopsy." If this guy's wit got any more dry, they'd be dealing with a freeze-dried body, Alvarez reflected.

"Whoever did it certainly had their choice of w-weapons," remarked Faulkner. He was right as usual. Alvarez looked around the room again for the first time since he had walked over to the body. Almost every available space was filled with a whole assortment of heavy items, including concrete tubes, steel cylinders of different thicknesses, and various steel rods. In addition, there were numerous mallets and hammers hanging on the walls. It was hard to walk around without literally tripping over something that could serve as a weapon.

"How does anyone know that there are records missing?" he asked the uniformed cop.

"The watchman says that some kind of company records were in a large black binder that is always kept on that bench.

The guy works for a private security agency, and he signs in at various points on his patrol. His sign-off sheet for this company was kept in the back of that binder. He says that the victim was a technician here and that he was often working with the records. So whenever the dead guy was working and the watchman made his rounds, he handed the binder over to the watchman to sign. They were on a speaking basis, but the watchman didn't know his name."

"Where is the watchman?" asked Alvarez, finally putting his finger on the thing that had been bothering him since he walked in the room.

The doctor was the one that answered this time. "He's old—about seventy, and with a heart condition. He was very upset. He gave his statement to the officer here and I let him call his daughter to come get him and take him home."

Alvarez frowned and gave the doctor a long look. The doctor looked right back at him. "Well, I guess we all better hope that he's around tomorrow when we start to want to ask some questions," said Alvarez mildly.

"I don't think a seventy-year-old man came in here, hit this guy over the head, physically overpowered him and strangled him, then decided to call up and report the whole thing to the police," said the doctor.

"Stranger things have happened," said Alvarez pleasantly.

"Yes, and quicker things have happened than this investigation, too. We've been sitting around here almost an hour waiting for you two hotshots to show up."

As suddenly as Alvarez could decide to make an issue

out of something, he could decide to drop it, too. It was one of his more endearing traits, he always thought. He flashed a genuine smile at the doctor. "Keep your shirt on, doc. If my hotshot partner says that it's okay, you can move the body now. He's the expert. I just come along to try to keep the flow of conversation going. But if I have to trace that watchman to some god-forsaken place over the border tomorrow, you come keep me company. Deal?" The doctor merely sighed in exasperation. Alvarez decided that they were never going to be close friends.

Faulkner agreed he had seen all there was to be seen. But before they could start to remove the body, the other beat officer was at their side. "The foreman for this outfit is here," he said to no one in particular, for he wasn't really sure to whom he should report this fact. "His name is Jack Columbo. He's waiting outside the door."

"Well, by all means, invite him to join us," said Alvarez congenially.

Of all human reactions, shock is the most difficult one to successfully fake. And Alvarez would have bet his last dollar that Jack Columbo was experiencing genuine shock. It was even a little worse than the shock that resulted from absolutely unforeseen circumstances, because in Columbo's case, he had had a chance to think about what he would be seeing before entering the room, and had found that imagining it was not the same thing as actually being there.

Columbo stood frozen in the doorway, staring at the

body as if he couldn't tear his eyes away, his heavy breathing audible in the silence. Alvarez took the opportunity to take a good look at him. He was a big man who obviously made his living through physical labor. His arms and legs were heavy and muscular in his white T-shirt and worn jeans, but he had a significant roll of indulgence hanging over his western tooled belt. His skin was tanned and his face was wrinkled with squint lines. Alvarez guessed his age to be somewhere on the far side of forty.

"Can you tell us who this is, sir?" asked Alvarez quietly.

"Yes, it's Billy Hartman, our quality control technician."

"Are you absolutely sure? I can t-turn the head so you can get a full look at the face." This, of course, from Alvarez's helpful partner.

"No, no. That's not necessary. I've worked with the guy for three years. I know who it is." And, almost as an aside, "Poor bastard."

"Thank you, Mr. Columbo. That's all that's necessary in here. Would you step out to the front office with me?" Jack Columbo gratefully followed Alvarez out of the room to the front reception area.

"Mr. Columbo, have a seat. Have a smoke. Relax. I'd offer you a drink if there was one to be had here. I need to ask you a few questions, but I would venture to say that the worst is over for now. Okay?"

Jack Columbo took a deep breath and seated himself at the secretary's desk. Alvarez leaned against the wall, extracted a small notebook from his jacket, and watched as Columbo lit a cigarette with shaking fingers. He noticed with satisfaction that Columbo didn't seem to question the "for now" part of his reassurances.

"You are the company foreman?"

"Yeah."

"Who is your boss?"

"Petey Lester, the owner, and his son-in-law, whenever he's around."

"The son-in-law have a name?"

"Kent Colliney."

"You said 'whenever he's around.' Where is Mr. Colliney now?"

"How should I know? Off on a buying trip, off wining and dining prospective clients, off sleeping off a hangover, I don't know."

"It sounds as if Mr. Colliney doesn't keep a very regular schedule."

"You can say that again."

"And Petey Lester? Do you know where he might be found? Or is his whereabouts as big a mystery as Mr. Colliney's?"

"No, man, I know where Lester is. He's up in Las Cruces at some type of fund-raiser talking to the New Mexico State University people about future construction projects."

"And when is Mr. Lester supposed to return?"

"Tomorrow. He's almost always here every Monday no matter what else is going on, to review the week's output and revise scheduling to make sure everything runs smoothly. He'll be in sometime before noon, at the very latest."

But it would be unlikely that Mr. Lester would be able to make the upcoming week run smoothly, no matter how early he got in, thought Alvarez, and switched tracks. "This Billy Hartman, got any idea why anyone would want to kill him?"

"No, man. He was a quiet guy. Got along okay with everyone, not really one to hang around with the other guys, but okay. He did his job okay, too. Really took it hard when something got messed up, but then you can't run an outfit like this perfectly. Mistakes happen. If anything, maybe he was a little soft on the guys in the yard. Always hated to make them do anything over again. Always asked, you know, instead of told them what to do."

The way Columbo said it left no doubt that he knew the difference between asking and telling people what to do. "So he didn't have any enemies here at the yard that you know of?" Alvarez used his chameleon talents to pick up Columbo's lingo, feeding it right back to him. Repeating people's speech patterns and slang back to them tended to make them feel more at ease, almost like conversing with a buddy instead of a cop.

"Not that I know of."

"Were your bosses happy with him?"

"Yeah, man. He did a really bang-up job with the paperwork end of things, something nobody else around here wanted to mess with. Things were in real bad shape as far as record-keeping goes before he got here. A company like ours got named in a lawsuit a few years back and didn't have any documentation to back up their claims. Ended up going down the tubes. Really shook everyone up, and that's when they hired Billy. He has, I mean had, an engineering technician associate degree."

"It looks like he was out here doing some work after hours. Is that normal?"

"Not routine, if that's what you mean. But yeah, he'd come out here sometimes on weekends to get caught up if we'd had a really heavy week. And we've been running overtime shifts once or twice a week for the past month, so yeah, it makes sense he was out here running tests or pushing paper."

"It appears that his records were taken by whoever killed him." Alvarez watched Columbo closely, who, in turn, looked back at him in surprise.

"Why would someone do that?"

In interrogating witnesses, it never ceased to amaze Alvarez that many of them seemed to think that he knew the answers, like the procedure was some game show and they were trying to come up with the correct response. "I don't know. That's why I'm asking you."

"Well, I don't know either, man." Columbo stubbed out his cigarette and looked back at Alvarez defiantly. Anger was always a good mechanism to avoid shock and fear.

"Does Hartman have any family?"

"Yeah, a wife and a mother-in-law that lives with them."

"Did he run around on his wife?"

"How should I know, man?" The anger was really kicking in now and subduing the shock. Alvarez wondered how

Columbo would react to knowing he was a textbook model of the reaction of an uninvolved witness. The tough-guy act could keep the confrontation with his own mortality at bay for a little longer. "I don't know if he ran around. I don't know who would steal the process records of a precast yard. And I sure as hell don't know who killed the guy. But I'm beginning to think maybe I shouldn't talk to you anymore unless I get a lawyer, or something."

"Take it easy, Columbo." Alvarez had been down this path so many times he knew when to back off, and exactly how to do it. Put the emphasis on the everyday, the normal. Make the guy feel like an expert. Talk about things that have nothing to do with that body down the hall that's as dead as you and I will be someday, he thought. The time to play hardball might come later, but for now all he wanted was more facts to help him fill in the picture that was forming in his mind. "Tell me what you do here. I don't even know what a precast yard is. Do you make cement pipe or something like that?"

The question immediately distracted Columbo from his other concerns. "Man, if you're going to talk precast, you gotta get one thing straight. Cement is what comes in bags, and concrete is what you make outta it when you mix it with sand and gravel and water. Got it?" Alvarez nodded his understanding without interrupting the flow of information.

"We don't make pipe here, but some yards do. We've always been in the business of making things that go into holding up buildings or structures, like beams and columns. Some of the stuff we do is called 'off the shelf.' These are things that people use all the time, like standard-size beams. We make a certain quota of items like that and sell them on demand. The other things we make are specialty items for contractors. Huge things, little things, weird things. If a guy can put dimensions to it, Jack Columbo can build a form to cast it."

"So you build a mold, and mix up the concrete, I mean cement, and—"

"Listen, the cement is in the bag, remember? It's the glue that holds the concrete together. Once you mix it up, it's concrete, man. Concrete."

"So you use bags of cement to mix up the concrete and pour it into the mold and make whatever thing it is that you're supposed to make?"

"Yeah, except it's not as simple as you make it sound. First you gotta build the form, what you're calling a mold. Then you gotta get the mix right, and add reinforcing bars or connection plates or whatever else might be called for to go inside the concrete. The pour and the cure time depends on the temperature and the humidity and the mixture itself. And if you screw it up and the whole thing doesn't pass quality tests, you start all over. Of course, that doesn't happen very often. I make sure it doesn't."

"So Hartman's job was to verify that everything was done correctly?" Working it back to Hartman, keeping it in the context of the job, all textbook procedure in interrogations, like one, two, three ...

"Yeah, essentially."

"So what exactly were the records that he kept?"

"All kinds of things, man. Sources of materials used, product test results, records of pours, who was in charge, what the weather conditions were, what crew made what pour, sketches of the form and placement of reinforcing bars, things like that."

Several things in this last description interested Alvarez, but they were items that would likely cause Columbo to balk now and could be pursued later. Alvarez felt that Columbo would be around tomorrow every bit as strongly as the doctor felt the watchman would be. Besides, it looked like the business of moving the body was over, and it was time to make another request.

Alvarez flipped his notebook shut. "I want to ask you to do something for me. It won't be pleasant, but it's important. These officers are going to have to go inform Mr. Hartman's wife that he's been killed. It would help immensely if there was someone there who knew her husband, so we won't have to go through the whole business of how it might be someone else."

Columbo started to protest, but Alvarez cut him short. He had noticed that the foreman wore a wedding ring. "If it were your wife facing two police officers with this type of news, you'd want someone there to kill any false hopes right off the bat." Columbo couldn't come up with a way to wiggle out of that one. After he grudgingly agreed, Alvarez thanked him for his cooperation and decided to hit him with the last piece of bad news.

"See you in the morning."

=======

Now there were more immediate things than the outcome of the last case or a lost Sunday evening to discuss. They had not even pulled out of the precast yard before Faulkner initiated the storytelling. "What do you think?"

"I think we need a make on the guy who got stiffed. Also on the owners. I think we can let the watchman and Columbo ride for now—they smell squeaky clean to me."

"I agree. I'll dig up what I can about Hartman and put a rush on working up background info for b-b-both Hartman and the company." Faulkner was such a genuinely likable guy that it was likely the techs in the office would drop whatever they were working on and prioritize his requests. Which was why they divided the work between them the way they did.

"I'll show up bright and early tomorrow back at the precast yard, hang around and talk to some of the guys. I want to get a good look at the owner when he shows up tomorrow. If no one gets word to him tonight, he should come in fresh as a daisy. If someone does get word to him tonight, that will be interesting, too. Columbo sure didn't give the impression that he knew how to reach him."

"Did you get a look at all the supplies in the yard?"

Alvarez gave his partner an admiring glance. It was typical that while he had been talking to a co-worker of the victim, his partner had been checking out the physical surroundings. "No," he answered frankly.

"There were s-supplies and materials all over the place. A lot of it from across the b-border."

"Drugs?"

"Well, if there's something besides cement in some of those bags, I'm willing to bet it's not d-diamonds."

Alvarez wryly noted Faulkner's correct use of the term "cement," and then dismissed it as being the result of a privileged background. A hypothesis he wasn't about to test by discussing it with his partner. He certainly didn't want to hear that every Joe Blow instinctively knew the difference between concrete and cement.

"Columbo mentioned another firm that had gone under when they were named in a law suit and didn't have any documentation to defend themselves. Maybe this is something along those lines."

It only took Faulkner a few seconds to consider this. "I see t-two possibilities. A rival firm wants to d-d-do them in, so they break in and steal the refuting evidence. Hartman gets in the way, so he gets clobbered."

"How did the killer get in the locked door?"

"He dropped by the office earlier in the week for a friendly chat and stole a key."

"Okay, but not great. I'd give it a four out of ten."

"I said there were two possibilities. The records d-d-documented a total screw-up for some job that was going to end up in c-court. The owner is the only one who knows about the suit so far, so he c-c-came in to destroy or alter the records, was discovered by his own quality control tech who threatened to squeal. So he had to kill the guy."

"I like it better because it gives access to the victim without a lot of extra effort. Or maybe the guy that was directly responsible for the screw-up wanted to cover it up, so he took the records and wasted Hartman. That makes all the employees involved in the actual manufacturing potential suspects." Alvarez mentally tried this scenario on Columbo and discarded it. The shock, verging on distaste, had been too genuine.

Faulkner thought over the latest scenario. "I give that a three out of ten because it makes more suspects, which m-makes m-more w-w-work for us. Have you ever noticed that all your ideas seem to work out that way?"

"Good point. In any case, unless we find some evidence of an active or pending suit, liability as a motive is probably a dead end. Of course, if some guy did make a big screw-up and was real paranoid about it, that doesn't rule my idea out. Damn. I'll up yours to a six, access or not." They both rode in silence for a few minutes, out of stories.

"Columbo said that they've been working a lot of over-time lately, and that one of the things the records contained was a list of the crews that made the pours."

"Illegal alien labor," said Faulkner instantly, without a single stutter. The guy never ceased to amaze Alvarez.

"Yeah, but that's not really something to waste some-one over unless really big bucks are involved. And in any case, you would think that Hartman would have to be in the know about it."

They pulled up at Faulkner's house. Alvarez saw Faulkner's wife, Donna, wave from the front window. She and Alvarez had instituted an uneasy truce when she had married his

partner two years before, and so far it was still working. So
was the marriage, it seemed. Alvarez didn't really see a need
for marriage in general, and for police officers in specific he
thought it was extremely unwise. But what else were you
going to do when you were an All-American boy like Faulkner?
He must be bound by birth to procreate his gene pool, which
was a responsibility Alvarez didn't subscribe to. Alvarez waved
back. Let it never be said he wasn't doing his part in the
relationship. Having done his duty there, he turned his attention to his partner. "Hey, old buddy, old pal ..."

This was the accepted prelude to asking for a favor.
Faulkner shook his head in disbelief. "Not after that Las
Vegas c-caper, don't old-buddy-old-pal me.

"Seriously, man. If we get into this hot and heavy I need
you to cover for me on Wednesday. It's Anna's birthday, and
I promised her I'd go up to Las Cruces to see her. There's
going to be a little party or something."

"What a weasel way to get me to c-cover for you again."

"Man, I use any way I can get." Alvarez never cut Faulkner
any slack about his stutter, feeling free to comment on it at
will. And Faulkner never tried to make Alvarez feel better
about having a mentally retarded sister, and he never tried to
pretend she didn't exist. Faulkner accepted without comment the unconditional love that Alvarez exhibited for his
sister. If, in many ways, she had always been a weight around
his neck, she had also been his anchor to reality and responsibility. Ever since he could remember, it had always seemed
like him and Anna together against the world.

"Okay. You take Wednesday and I'll cover for you. But I get next S-Sunday off. No matter if someone slaughters the whole s-s-staff of the El Paso Precast Concrete Company. My in-laws are leaving on S-S-Saturday."

"Deal. Have you noticed how you've started stuttering more since we've pulled up here? Is it the proximity to your in-laws or marriage in general that makes you nervous?"

Like the doctor at the scene of the crime, Faulkner disdained to answer. But Alvarez had already deduced that he wouldn't.

CHAPTER FIVE: MISERABLE MONDAY

Tory had spent most of Sunday in solitary seclusion at her office, ostensibly catching up on some work. Actually, she spent a great deal of nonproductive time stewing over recent events. She immediately pulled the project file on the El Paso Savings and Loan job to make sure everything was in order. She soberly left a note directing Sylvia to copy the file so there would be a back-up if the original somehow got "lost." Perhaps Emmett Delgado would wake up with a raging headache and no recollection of his threats from Saturday night, but Tory wasn't counting on it.

After such a disquieting social event, Tory didn't sleep well on Sunday night. She was already awake when the alarm went off, even though she had set it an hour earlier than usual to make the trip to El Paso. She felt the first twinges of a tension headache behind her eyes, never a good sign. But, inspired by the need to get an early start, she forced herself out of bed and into the shower.

The promise of the day's coming heat was enough to make the thought of anything hot for breakfast unattractive. Tory grabbed some juice and yogurt on her way through the kitchen to Cody's room. The sight of his tousled head on his pillow was comforting, although she was jealous that he remained dead to the world. "To be fifteen again," she thought, and then immediately reconsidered, shaking her head at herself. "I wouldn't be fifteen again if you paid me."

She sat down with the paper long enough to note that another day had passed without her name appearing in the front page headlines. She sincerely hoped that she would have no problem in limiting the subject of her meeting with Bill Hartman to the stadium project. She would need to keep it clear that she was there to ask the questions, not the other way around.

She also wasn't looking forward to meeting the foreman that Jazz had confronted over the column pour. Jack Columbo, she thought Lester had said his name was. She was relatively sure about the Jack part, since Jazz had repeatedly referred to him as the Jack-Ass of the El Paso Precast Concrete Company. It was extremely unlikely that Mr. Columbo would be kindly disposed toward her or her requests for information, especially since his reputation might be on the line. "Engineering," she mused to herself. "What a way to make friends and influence people."

She picked up her briefcase and her car phone from the kitchen table. Cody wouldn't have to get up for another hour to make it to work, so she wouldn't get to see him again until evening. Another inconvenience because of other people's mistakes. But that was the wrong attitude, she chided herself. If people didn't make mistakes, there certainly wouldn't be a need for inspectors. And then she might have to design buildings for Emmett Delgado. She locked the door behind her.

The drive to the precast yard took exactly forty-five minutes. Although Tory was reasonably good at distracting herself from problems when there was work to be done, driving left idle time for her to mull over her encounters with Hartman and Delgado yet again. So she was relieved to reach her destination on schedule, at least until she noticed the police car parked in front of the office, and the bright yellow crime scene tape around the building.

Some of the tape was across the steps in front of the entrance to the office building. Tory ducked under it, ran up the steps, pulled open the door, and stepped inside.

A middle-aged Mexican-American woman was sitting glumly at the front desk, looking up at a uniformed policeman who was standing beside her, taking notes on a pad. Both looked up at Tory in surprise. "Ma'am, are you an employee?" the officer asked.

Well, most everyone is an employee someplace, she thought, but refrained from pointing that out. Willing herself to remain optimistic, she earnestly addressed the officer.

"My name is Tory Travers, and I'm here to look at the pour records for the stadium project. I need to talk to Bill Hartman and copy the records that I want to take back with me. After that, I may need to talk to Jack Columbo for a few minutes."

Both the officer and the secretary continued to stare at Tory. She ran a mental replay of her words, and decided that they had been clear enough for anyone to understand. The secretary continued to stare at her in silent amazement, but the officer blinked and came back to life. "You stay right here," he told her. He started down the hall and then turned back anxiously. "You make sure she stays right here," he admonished the secretary, who momentarily turned her look of wide-eyed amazement from Tory to the disappearing officer. Then Tory and the secretary waited in expectant silence.

He was back almost immediately, followed by a tall, lanky Mexican-American man dressed formally in a short-sleeved shirt and tie. Tory wondered if Columbo's style of dress was due to an order from Petey Lester to polish up their image for her visit. It wasn't routine to come across a foreman in a tie at a precast yard.

"Hello, I'm Tory Travers," said Tory, and handed him a business card. "I assume you're Jack Columbo. I need to talk to Bill Hartman and see your pour records for the stadium project. I'll copy the portions that I need to take with me. When I'm done, then I'll know if I have any questions for you. The whole thing shouldn't take more than an hour and a half, and then I'll be out of your hair. I can tell you've had some kind of problem out here, but I need to get my information as soon as possible."

The tall man leaned against the wall and took his time as he studied Tory's business card. Then he slowly proceeded to look Tory up and down. His demeanor definitely was not one of a helpful employee, so Tory decided to forge on. She had found that it was preferable to face insolence head on rather than ignore it. "If you can't help me, or won't help me, I would like to see whoever is in charge," she said, all friendly earnestness gone from her voice. "Like I said, I'm in a hurry."

He put her business card in his pocket. "Yes, I can see that you are. I am 'whoever' is in charge. Please, step into this office." He motioned toward one of the doors behind him.

"No, thank you. That's not necessary. I just need to get into your lab records and go over the details with Hartman. Then I'll get back to you if I have any questions."

"No," he contradicted her firmly. "We need to talk first thing, not last."

Tory looked at him in exasperation. The last thing she wanted was for this jerk to throw a wrench in her schedule. "I really don't want to discuss the situation further with you until I've had a chance to look at the records," she replied. "It doesn't really matter at this point who was responsible, so don't give me a hard time about accessing your records. You can call Henderson or Lester or Kemp or whoever, for approval. And you can do that while I'm talking to Hartman."

"You're not listening to me." The even tone didn't change. "I already told you that I am the one in charge here. Not Lester or the other two that you mentioned. Which I will want to ask you about, along with your urgent desire to see this company's records. See, we do have a lot to talk about."

Tory could feel the pressure behind her eyes change from a warning dull pain to a full-fledged headache. This was going to cost her even more time, and time was a precious commodity. She could feel a loss of temper coming on. She addressed the man blocking her path in a very quiet voice. The secretary would have had a hard time making out what she was saying, but that didn't matter. This was between her and Columbo.

"Listen, don't give me any shit about this, Columbo. I don't care if your nose is out of joint because my foreman caught you with your ass hanging out. That's your problem, not mine. I'm here to take a look at those records and you're not going to sidetrack me, so give it up now. Let's be real clear on the situation here. If you have anything else to say to me before I go see Hartman, say it now and say it fast. I'm not going to be intimidated and turn around and go home without the information I've come for. So get it out, and then get out of my way."

Tory's speech hadn't had its intended effect. The man didn't even stand up straight to answer her, but continued to lean comfortably against the wall. He deliberately considered a moment before answering. "I have three things to say. First, you cannot talk to Bill Hartman. Second, we are going to have our little talk."

Tory took a deep breath to reply, but he casually held up a finger admonishing her not to interrupt. "I can see it's hard to get you stopped once you get started, but I said that I had three things to say. I want to introduce myself. My name is David Miguel Alvarez, and I am a detective with the

Special Case Force of the El Paso Police Department." And, finally standing up straight, he extended his hand.

Tory simply stood there. The man standing in front of her had effectively silenced her, but they both knew he'd deliberately let her run on, assuming that he was someone else. She might have to talk to him now, but she'd be damned if she'd shake his hand.

It wasn't often that someone refused to shake an officer's hand at an initial meeting. It admittedly took some nerve to stay resolved through the awkward moment and refuse to acknowledge the gesture before it was withdrawn. Although he was too experienced to let it show, her refusal to formally acknowledge his identity irritated Detective David Miguel Alvarez and in the end, that made all the difference in the world.

As Tory preceded him down the hall, Alvarez took advantage of the opportunity to look her over unobserved. So she wasn't going to change her demeanor just because he was a detective. Was this a case of dramatic bravado covering up a guilty conscience, or was she just to the manor born? She certainly didn't like being set up, but then no one did. She wasn't going to back off just because of his authority, and that was a little more unusual. But those who came from a privileged background often considered themselves immune to authority. Alvarez had seen it often enough.

In his line of work some of the people who ended up bothering him the most weren't the ones who came from the gutter. In many cases, they were only continuing the types of criminal behavior that they had observed around them since birth. The wealthy, the privileged, and the disdainful were another story. And Alvarez could smell a privileged background emanating from Ms. Tory Travers.

Still, he had to give credit where credit was due. Those were some of the longest, nicest legs he had seen in a long time, even if they were partially obscured in a plain straight skirt, paired with no-nonsense flat leather shoes. Let others have their cute, petite versions of femininity. Alvarez preferred tall women, and the legs that came with them. The rest of this package wasn't bad, either. Maybe a little flat-chested, but it was hard to tell with the type of tailored shirt she was wearing. Alvarez had been fooled before about such things, and was therefore not willing to commit to a judgment based on current information.

Her skin was the creamy translucent kind that did not belong in the Southwestern sun, although right now it was flushed with anger. He definitely concluded that her best feature was those eyes, those heart-breaker eyes, bluest of blue and outlined with long, thick lashes, as dark as his own.

His observations were not strictly those of the male connoisseur of attractive women. He considered such things an integral part of his job. He tried to imagine how those eyes might have looked as she brought the steel rod down on Hartman's head. If she had managed to knock him out with the initial blow, she looked perfectly capable of strangling him. And if not, well ... maybe still capable. It looked to him as if she could have been a match for a stunned Hartman.

Tory walked into the office he had indicated and sat down without being asked. He noticed her glancing at the chair behind the desk, but it seemed that she didn't quite have the guts to claim it, although he was sure the thought had occurred to her. He decided to keep her a little off balance, so he also neglected to take the seat behind the desk, and instead sat down in a chair right beside the one that she had chosen. Sure enough, that violated her sense of personal space right off the bat, and he was rewarded by seeing her draw back somewhat. Encouraged, Alvarez leaned back in his chair and stretched out his legs to take up more of the available space. Score one for Mexican Management Maneuvers, he thought.

He watched her take a quick look around the office. That was cool, waiting for him to be the first one to speak. After all, he wasn't the one in a hurry.

Actually, Tory was using the time to try to get her temper under control. She didn't want to know what was going on, but she had a feeling she wasn't going to have a choice. She could almost feel the passing minutes eating into her projected schedule. But more than frustration, the main feeling she was experiencing was one of resentment. She felt she had been purposely set up by Alvarez's tardy identification, and she didn't want to start negotiating for what she needed at such an embarrassing disadvantage. But the damn man next to her looked like he was willing to sit there all day.

"This is Petey Lester's office," she finally said, after looking around. She made it sound like an accusation.

"Yes, it is. But I'm using it now. Mr. Lester has not yet

returned from a business trip, but he is expected to be here shortly," Alvarez answered pleasantly.

"I want to see some ID."

"Certainly, Ms. Travers. Why didn't you ask before? You know, people just never ask to see badges the way you see it on TV all the time, and after all the trouble it takes to get one, it certainly is a pleasure to have the opportunity to flash it once in a while." Tory refused to rise to the bait while he fished his badge out and handed it to her. She studied it intently, and then handed it back to him. And said nothing more.

Alvarez let the silence become a little heavier, and then made his move, watching her every expression while he spoke. "You wanted to talk to Bill Hartman. I'm afraid that won't be possible. He was murdered sometime yesterday afternoon or early evening."

She just stared at him. And then said, "You've got to be kidding."

He reached over to the desk, picked up one of the photographs there, and handed a close up of Hartman's head to her. She looked at it for a measurably shorter time than she had studied his badge, and handed it back. "I'm sorry," she said. She was amazed to find that she actually was. But along with the shock, feelings of relief washed over her, shocking her even more than the news of the murder.

Well, her response sounded honest, more believable than some horrified disclaimer on how terrible the whole thing was, thought Alvarez.

But Tory couldn't let it lie. It would take something more than Alvarez's news to make her forget her purpose in being there. She waited what she considered a respectful period, and then jumped right back in.

"But the fact that there's been a murder doesn't have to affect what I'm doing. I need to look at the recent pour records. I won't get in your way, I won't touch anything I'm not supposed to, and I won't even have to be here very long." Alvarez was astonished when she actually started to stand up, ready to go, having dispensed with all the necessary explanations from her perspective. This one had balls. Or great acting skills. Talk about a one-track mind.

"Sit down," he said curtly, abandoning his congenial, pleasant persona. He was finally getting impatient. It was time to take control of the interview. "There has been a murder committed here. You don't seem exactly overwhelmed with shock and sorrow. Did you know Mr. Hartman?"

Tory sat back down in exasperation. "Would you be more impressed if I threw myself on the floor and pounded the carpet with my fists?" she asked. That just kind of slipped out, and garnered a raised eyebrow and a frown from the man sitting next to her. Tory took a deep breath and took another stab at answering his question. "My office staff communicated with him on various projects. I met him once, briefly. Listen, Detective Alvarez, nothing I say or do is going to change the fact that he's dead, or that I still have a job to do."

Alvarez decided to cut to the chase. "It appears that the person who committed the murder also took the company's quality control records. The records that you so adamantly and urgently insist on seeing. As far as I am concerned, you are under suspicion merely for showing up here this morning, wanting to talk to the deceased and wanting to see the stolen records. What we're going to discuss now are the answers to some questions I want to ask, not what you thought you had scheduled for this morning. We can do it here or we can do it down at the station."

Tory glared at him for a moment, obviously thinking. "What a great theory, Detective. I come down here yesterday and kill Billy Hartman and take the records. Then I come back this morning and ask to see him and the records just so no one will think I killed Hartman and took the records. Do they pay you extra to be stupid, or do you do it voluntarily?"

"It has been done before," said Alvarez evenly. He noticed that since she had been effectively thwarted in getting what she wanted, she was no longer making much of an effort to keep her temper under control. "Can you account for your whereabouts between noon and six p.m. yesterday? With witnesses?"

That took more than a moment for her to think through, and Alvarez could tell as he watched her face that the answer to his question was no. "Exactly," he said. "Let us stop fencing and get down to business. I want to know who you are, what you're doing here, what you know about Hartman, what you needed to see Columbo about, and who Henderson and Kemp are. I want to know all this in detail, no matter how long it takes. And then, if I am satisfied with your answers, I may let you leave."

If looks could have killed, Alvarez had no doubt that he would have been as dead as Hartman. But she sat in the chair and told him what he wanted to know with icy precision.

After all the effort he had gone to, he was disappointed in the information that she could give him. There was only one exception. He noticed that she hesitated ever so slightly before answering his questions about her relationship with Hartman. But that might be attributed to her reluctance to reveal any information that would involve her further in the case. It was amazing how acquaintances never wanted to own up to knowing someone once they turned up murdered, Alvarez reflected. A real killer to popularity.

According to Ms. Travers, she had met Hartman only once, on the Friday before the murder. Their conversation had concerned quality assurance procedures, something that Alvarez frankly found of little interest. She had never been at the precast yard before today, so she could shed no light on Hartman's relations with his fellow employees. And Henderson and Kemp, once their identities had been explained, did not interest Alvarez much, either. Victoria Travers appeared to be exactly what she said she was, an engineer looking for some records having to do with a football stadium being built in Las Cruces.

"All right," he said finally. "You can leave. If we need to ask you any more questions, we'll get in touch with you."

"I can leave?" she asked incredulously rather than gratefully. "What do you mean—I can leave? I've already explained and re-explained to you what I need to do. I need to see Jack

Columbo, and talk to the people on the crews that poured the stadium columns. Lots of times individuals keep informal notes that are incorporated later into the company records. And I need to get into that lab to see if there's anything there that Hartman was working on that has to do with my project. I may be able to reconstruct what I need. And I sat here and did what you asked," she said as if accusing him of not keeping some bargain.

This lady just didn't quit. "I showed you the picture of Hartman. His death was the result of a criminal act. You either don't seem to understand that, or it doesn't seem to be important to you. My job here, my only job here, is to catch the person who committed the murder. For you to think that you're going to be given access to this place is stupid. Do you get paid extra for that or do you do it voluntarily?" Now she had him saying these things. This was not part of interrogation theory, but he was getting damned tired of this lady and her attitude.

"Do you think I'm going to faint and then quietly disappear because you showed me a picture of one person who has been killed? I'm sorry that it happened, and I do understand what your job is. But you don't seem to understand mine. Have you ever seen pictures of scores of dead people, killed because of a structural collapse? I have. And it's criminal not to do whatever can be done to assure that something like that doesn't happen. You are keeping me from information that's vital to my job. And I have a feeling that you're doing it just because I mistook you for the yard foreman."

Neither of them was exercising any restraint now. "I wouldn't let you into that lab if you'd mistaken me for Jesus Christ himself, lady. What do you think I am, crazy? As far as I'm concerned, you're still a potential suspect."

"You're reaching."

"*Y tu también, señorita.* I may just be a poor dumb Mexican cop to you, lady, but I actually understand what you've been talking about. Is that a surprise or what? Listen to this. From what you've told me about this whole deal, you can always go and X-ray these columns to find out if they have the reinforcing rods that they need inside them."

"Bars. Reinforcing bars. At least try to get the terms right," Tory snapped. "My tests can only be as good as my preliminary information. I need the records of the placement during the pour to give us an indication of what we're looking for, and exactly where to find it. Without those records, I won't be able to conclusively test everything in the time that I have before they go on with the construction of the stadium. If the preliminary indications don't show anything doubtful, the University may decide to pass on those columns without ever really knowing for sure if they're exactly like they're supposed to be."

"So life is full of many small imperfections. You're talking theory and what-if's, and I have a murder on my hands. Take an educated guess which is going to have priority. Use your engineering judgment you keep talking about."

Tory shot him a look of pure dislike. "You're impossible. When Petey Lester gets here, you tell him I was here and what I need."

Alvarez momentarily adopted his thickest Mexican accent. "Yes, *señorita*. Right away, *señorita*. You want I should do anytheeng else?" And then he said in his most serious voice, the one that a number of people had come to regret ignoring, "I hate to tell you this, but you are not exactly 'numero uno' on my list of the things that I want to discuss with him."

"Cut the act, Detective. This isn't a racial thing with me. Some of my best friends and all that shit. Is it racial with you? Or is it something else? Would things have gone differently if I'd come in and batted my eyelashes at you and admired what a powerful guy you are, and said pretty please real nice? And I am not a *señorita*, I'm a married woman."

"I'm sure he's a real lucky guy."

"He's dead."

"I'm sorry. But let me point out that I've known you less than two hours and you're already associated with two dead men. It's not exactly an outstanding character reference."

"You just never quit, do you? You showed me a photograph of one poor, unlucky, dead bastard. If you came to my office I could show you how little is left when hundreds of tons come crashing down on a group of human beings. I plan to get access to the information that I need, Detective Alvarez. I plan to talk to certain individuals who will be more far-sighted than you, and who certainly have more power than you do. And if the process makes life a little miserable for you, so much the better. This is not the last that you will hear from me. Happy hunting." She walked out the door.

She didn't slam the door, but he was sure the thought had occurred to her.

Y tú, thought Alvarez. Yeah, if you'd batted your eyelashes and shown a little respect, things might have been a lot different. Then he turned his attention to his impending conversation with Mr. Petey Lester, if he was indeed going to show up later in the morning, and what he would do if he didn't.

Tory spent part of the drive back to Las Cruces replaying her conversation with David Alvarez, appalled that she had lost her temper and simultaneously trying to think of even more biting, intimidating things that she could have said to him.

After getting nowhere with that, she had no excuse to avoid confronting her mixed feelings about the death of Billy Hartman. As horrified as she was about his murder, she had to admit that the news brought a certain amount of relief. It had been an automatic decision to omit telling the detective anything about Hartman's request to interview her. Alvarez had asked her what they had talked about, and she had answered him. Just not very accurately or very completely. If interest in her connection with a prominent visiting politician died with Hartman, so much the better. One less thing that she had to worry about, and for right now she had enough worries about trying to meet the deadline for the column study.

She spent the remainder of the drive back planning what to do about the whole sorry situation. A call to Charles Henderson was high on her list of priorities. And after that, a talk with Lonnie Harper might not be such a bad idea. He might well be able to suggest someone in the El Paso Police Department to whom she could talk directly about her problems with a certain detective.

She caught Jazz in the office filing some inspection reports before heading out to the stadium site. She pulled him into her office and explained the situation at the El Paso Precast Concrete Company to him. "I want you to go ahead and start X-raying the columns today. If I can't get my hands on any records, and if the University holds us to our schedule, we need to start site-testing right away."

Jazz nodded his agreement. "What a tough break, boss. Who could have guessed that those records would up and disappear on us, *que sí?* Poor Hartman. I only met him once, but he seemed like a decent guy. Too bad it wasn't that asshole Columbo instead. Hey, you don't suppose someone killed him to cover up the mistake that they made on pouring that column?"

In spite of her lengthy conversation with Alvarez, this was the first time that it had gotten through to Tory that the murder might, in fact, not be totally unrelated to her concerns. She considered the concept and then rejected it. "I don't see how, Jazz. You witnessed the situation and documented it. It's been brought up before the people in charge, and they have accepted the possibility that there may be something wrong with the other columns. So all of it's out in the open. I don't see how killing Hartman could have anything to do with the stadium project or with us."

"Yeah, I can't see it either. But the timing is real funny."

"So funny I spent my whole morning laughing. You'd like the detective that I met this morning. I ticked him off so much by insisting on seeing any remaining records that he's decided to include me on his official list of suspects."

Jazz looked nothing but stormy at this revelation. "You've got an alibi with me, boss, anywhere, any time."

Tory was embarrassed at such a sweeping statement of loyalty. "Thanks, I think. I'll remember that the next time that you're pissed off at me. I'm sure it won't come to that. The only times I've been tempted to kill someone have been in broad daylight in front of a dozen crew members on a construction site, and so far the sheer fact of being outnumbered has saved me every time. Let's get busy on those columns."

"You're sure you're going to be okay, boss?"

"Why wouldn't I be okay?" And because she was still a little embarrassed, she couldn't just let him just leave like that. "And Jazz, don't forget to wear your hard hat."

"You told me once already, okay? And I told you it wouldn't happen again. I won't even get out of the truck before I put my hard hat on. You want I should wear it on the drive over there?" And everything was back to normal with Jazz.

After he left, Tory spent a few minutes getting through to Henderson. After listening to her explanations, he promised to see what he could do about the situation. Tory was wondering how forcefully she could count on him to follow through, when she looked up to see Sylvia at the door to her office, appearing extremely unhappy. Anything that made Sylvia appear unhappy was bound to be serious.

"Can I talk to you a minute. Privately?"

This was not a good sign. Tory and Sylvia did not usually need to have private conversations. The sign of everything going well in the office was normally proportional to the amount of banter going back and forth between Sylvia and everyone else. Tory nodded, and Sylvia came into her office and shut the door behind her, all of her usual bravado and good spirits gone.

"For five years I've worked for you, Tory, and just like you told me, I've always opened all the mail. No matter who it's to, no matter how it's addressed, I open it and date stamp it just like you told me to when I first came to work for you."

"Right. So what's the problem? Did someone here get a torrid love letter, or better yet, a package that ticks?"

But Sylvia refused to smile. She handed Tory a legal-sized sheet of paper. Tory had seen pictures of ransom notes, made from words cut from printed matter. This was just like one of those. And there was no way that whoever opened this communication could have avoided reading it. While Sylvia sat watching her, Tory digested the message:

YOU ARE CAUSING TOO MANY PEOPLE
TOO MUCH TROUBLE TORY TRAVERS GET
OUT OF TOWN TWO WEEKS LET THINGS
COOL DOWN YOU WILL BE PAID TO DO

THIS DON'T TELL POLICE OR ANYONE
ELSE ABOUT THIS DON'T STICK AROUND
OR PEOPLE WILL GET HURT AND YOUR
BUSINESS TOO THIS IS NO JOKE I'VE
KILLED BEFORE

Alvarez perched himself on the corner of the desk that his partner was occupying, and waited more or less patiently for him to complete his phone call. With Scott's stutter, sometimes that took quite a long time. It was close to 5:00 PM, and the department headquarters was about as quiet as it ever got, since the shift formally changed at four. Alvarez had finally caught up with his partner in the open bull-pen area. Government-regulation green steel desks, showing their many years of wear, had been crowded into the area until there was little room to walk around. However, this was the main setting where preliminary information on a case was usually gathered and exchanged.

Some of the initial procedures in any investigation were formal ones—checking with the coroner's office, requesting official background information on the victim and involved subjects, and getting reports from the analytical laboratory. But other related procedures were informal—bargaining with the coroner's office to see if your body (so to speak) could be autopsied before someone else's, checking through the police grapevine and with their informers to see who knew what about whom, and pressing a laboratory guy to give an opinion about what the tests really might mean, versus what they could be counted upon to show as evidence in court. Formal or informal fact-finding, Scott Faulkner was as good as they came.

"*Qué pasa, amigo?*" Alvarez asked when Faulkner had completed his phone call.

"Not much, unfortunately. N-not much we didn't already know, and n-no b-breaks on anything we didn't. The d-d-doctor has n-narrowed down the t-time of death to between t-t-two and s-seven p.m." Scott stuttered his way through his response with no embarrassment. His stutter always got worse when he was tired and he had been talking a lot. Alvarez didn't ask how he had managed to get their subject processed so quickly; it was a cardinal rule in his book never to look a gift horse in the mouth.

Faulkner took a resigned breath and continued more slowly. "The night watchman didn't leave for parts unknown, so the doctor was right about that. But the guy has virtually n-nothing to add to his original statement. He's really t-t-torn up about the whole thing. Seems he makes the rounds for several businesses in the area. He t-told me it had been his usual routine to check on the precast yard about five-thirty p.m. and every three hours after that, until eight a.m. But his company had just had a s-s-seminar and it seems that they really emphasized frequent changes in routine. So last weekend he switched his rounds to make his first visit at six forty-five p.m. He k-keeps saying that if he had only been there earlier, maybe Hartman wouldn't have been killed."

"Yeah, well, did you tell him that if he had been there

earlier we might be dealing with two bodies now instead of one?"

Fact-finding, not comforting witnesses, was Faulkner's forte. "That's a good idea. I'll try to remember to t-tell him that the next time I see him. Anyhow, Hartman seems clean, at least from what we can tell at this point. No history of c-c-crime or drugs, apparently a happy home life, and he wasn't in debt any more than your average g-guy on the street. No record of a current suit against the precast company either. And we struck out on the m-m-murder instrument. That rod was used to hit Hartman, but if anything, it takes prints too well. There are full and partial prints all over it, and most are Hartman's. It looks l-like it may have been wiped, but they can't tell anything conclusive. That's all."

Alvarez regarded his partner with admiration. All this, and on a Monday, too.

"So t-tell me about your constructive day," said Faulkner. "Got it solved yet?"

"Everyone at the yard echoes Columbo. Can't imagine why Hartman got stiffed. Most of the employees seem to think that they can come up with alibis if they need to, or at least no one seems overly upset about the possibility."

"What about the owner and his son-in-law?"

"Lester showed up around eleven and exhibited the ex-pected regret and remorse, not to mention a lot of concern that production will be down for a few days. He didn't act overly shocked, but then I got the feeling that he's been around enough that walking in after the deed was done and cleaned up wasn't going to shake him up that much. Not quite the same thing as Columbo being called from home on a Sunday evening and having to come out and look at the body. Lester was pretty cool, all in all. Whether he's hiding something or not, I can't tell. Yet. There's something about him that just doesn't ring true, so I definitely want to check out his alibi."

"So he's got an alibi?"

"But of course. He took his daughter to a fund-raiser at New Mexico State University on Saturday night and stayed over Sunday and Sunday night for some more socializing. Sunday afternoon he attended a private pool party at the Hilton Inn where he and his daughter were staying. Then he attended an Alumni dinner at the University again, stayed Sunday night at the Hilton, and returned this morning. He says his daughter and various other individuals can account for his whereabouts all of Sunday until late evening, when he went to bed in his hotel room."

"What about the absent son-in-law?"

"Ah, yes, the traveling Kent Colliney. According to Lester, he's somewhere south of Juarez buying materials and equipment. No one knows exactly where he is, or exactly when he'll return. Or even how to get hold of him, which is interesting."

"That sounds pretty vague."

"No kidding. But according to the crew members that I talked to, his behavior is par for the course. And when I pushed Lester about it, he as much as admitted that he didn't like it either, but he couldn't control the guy. I pushed him a little more about it and he unwillingly put forth the opinion that his daughter and son-in-law were having marital problems. He thinks these disappearing acts are Colliney's way of getting even with her."

"Sounds cozy."

"Women. You can't live with them, and you can't live without them. Of course, you wouldn't understand that, being happily married and all. But I, poor bachelor that I am, did manage to find a foxy woman while working hard in the field today. Talk about cozy. We ended up chatting for almost two hours. You would have liked her, Scott. She's just your type: something like five ten, looks healthy and strong as a horse, and a real ball-breaker to boot." Donna was five two, looked like she would be blown away by a strong wind, and seemed to be unceasingly sweet to everyone, including her husband's partner, even when they worked weekends or forty-eight hours straight. It was enough to make you wonder if the marriage was going to work.

Alvarez handed Tory's business card to his partner, who studied it with all the attention that a piece of physical evidence deserved. "Victoria Travers. P-president, Travers Testing and Engineering Company, Las Cruces, New Mexico. What's the connection?"

"This lady is so hot to trot to get her hands on the stolen records that she actually threatened me with the intervention of Big People, if I didn't let her sashay her classy little ass into the laboratory where Hartman was stiffed. Not only that, she wanted free rein to sift through any remaining records to her heart's content."

"I'm glad to see that you stood up to the intimidation so well." The problem with having such a literal partner was that you were never quite sure if your leg was being pulled. "You think there's a connection b-between this Victoria Travers and Hartman's murder?"

"Probably not, although the whole thing is damn coincidental. Her intense desire to get those records could be due to the professional reason that she claims it is, or it could be something else. She can sure be one tunnel-visioned broad. Let's run a background on her. If it turns up anything interesting, I'll drop by on Wednesday when I go up to Las Cruces and hassle her a little on my way to see Anna. Then you won't really be covering for me, because I'll actually be on the case."

"What dedication to d-duty. While you're there, why don't you do some checking on Lester's alibi?"

"Good idea, but I already thought of it. If we don't come up with some obvious reason that Hartman got iced, we're going to have to start looking into more convoluted motives."

"Drugs, smuggling, impending lawsuits, a clearing house for illegal alien labor," Faulkner recited, stutter-free. He had obviously rehearsed the list in his head a few times. "M-maybe fabricating a sideline of products with faulty materials to sell to disreputable contractors at rock-bottom prices."

Alvarez shook his head wearily. "Any of those are going to be really hard to get a handle on unless we just happen to get a lucky break. Just for today, let's pretend it was some simple motive, like good old garden variety maniacal hatred. Give me a story."

"Lester's daughter was secretly in love with Hartman, and it was ruining his m-marriage. His wife followed him out to work Sunday because she thought he was meeting his lover, not knowing that the lady was in Las Cruces with her father. Hartman's wife tried to reason with him, but he refused to give up the love of his life. So she k-killed him."

"I kind of like it."

"Only problem is, Hartman's wife was home all Sunday with her ailing mother. I ch-checked."

Of course. "So, they were in it together."

"The mother's in a wheelchair."

"Minor problem, man. It was like this ..."

CHAPTER SIX: TERRIBLE TUESDAY

Tory was determined that Tuesday was going to be better than Monday had been. A good deal of Monday afternoon had been spent trying to reassure Sylvia, who wanted Tory to go directly to the police with the anonymous threatening letter. Not only did Tory feel vaguely foolish about such an action, in the back of her mind was the conviction that the letter was the latest episode of ugly dramatics from Emmett Delgado. She wasn't sure she wanted to get the police involved in the situation, especially after her unpleasant episode yesterday at the precast yard.

After Sylvia gave up trying to get Tory to call the police,

she lobbied to have Tory tell Lonnie about the letter, or even Jazz, on the basic sexist premise that letting some male know about the situation was bound to make it better. Tory finally managed to convince her to keep quiet about the whole thing and to adopt a wait-and-see strategy. Even then she wasn't able to put the whole thing behind her, for Sylvia's reproachful and worried gaze followed her for the rest of the day.

When Tory had a chance to talk to Lonnie on Monday evening, she asked for suggestions concerning how she might gain access to the lab at the El Paso Precast Concrete Company. He wasn't much help. It didn't seem that his list of immediately accessible contacts extended to the El Paso Police Department, at least on the face of it. She felt he wasn't giving her problem the attention it warranted. Cody had been given three days off from work, Lonnie was tired of the summer heat, and between the two of them they had hatched a plan to address both the free time and the wish for a summer respite. Lonnie much preferred to talk about fishing plans at this point.

His family had a cabin at Willow Creek, high in the mountains near the Gila Wilderness. There the streams ran icy cold even in the middle of summer, and mountain trout were plentiful and wily. Lonnie and Cody wanted to leave Las Cruces on Wednesday afternoon and drive up to the cabin to spend Thursday and Friday. Of course Tory was invited to go along, and of course Lonnie tried to disguise his relief when she declined. Fishing rated somewhere close to football on her list of favorite leisure time activities.

Tory did have one momentary urge to rain on their parade, to cry on Lonnie's shoulder about the problems with the stadium project, the uncooperative detective who had called her a suspect in a murder case, and the threatening letter. Not to mention her guilt at her relief that the murder victim was dead. But it wouldn't have taken much discussion about any of these subjects for Lonnie to decide not to leave town. And besides, she would have to back up all the way to her initial meeting with Hartman, and then she would have to explain why she hadn't told him about that when it happened. So she resisted the urge to spill her guts and agreed to the outing. After all, she would probably be putting in extra hours on the column study, she told herself, and it might be helpful to have the men in her life out from underfoot.

Her optimism about a bright new day evaporated as soon as she arrived at the office. As she drove up, she could see most of her employees clustered outside around the company fleet of vehicles, and she could hear Jazz cursing as she stepped out of her car. She walked up to the group to see what they were looking at. All four company trucks and the station wagon were sitting on flat tires. Tory knew before she even looked that the tires had been slashed. On top of that, she had an awareness of Sylvia shooting her an I-told-you-so look.

Everyone, even Jazz, was silent as Tory surveyed the damage. "Well," she said after a few moments. "I'm glad everyone here knows how to change tires." She tossed her keys to Jazz. "Take Bruce with you and rent a truck. Then come on back and take the wheels and flats off these vehicles to have new tires mounted on them. Everybody that has to be some-where this morning will have to use their own vehicles. Mean-while, unless you guys absolutely have to be somewhere this morning, I guess this will give everyone a chance to catch up on office work." And, wishing that she felt as nonchalant as she sounded, she walked into the office.

Sylvia was right on her heels and followed her into her office. Tory sat down and looked at her. "If it makes you feel better, go ahead and say 'I told you so.'"

"I would if I thought it would do any good. Don't tell me you're still not going to call the police about that letter."

"Sylvia, we don't know that one has anything to do with the other. The letter and the vehicles may be totally unrelated."

"And how likely do you think that is?"

Tory considered her question. She decided not to answer it, but to try a partial surrender instead, "Listen, we'll report the tires. Does that make you happy?"

"*Que no*, Tory. Don't act like you're giving in with that. You have to report the tires to get compensation from the insurance company."

Tory couldn't argue with that. "Sylvia. Calm down. I think I know who wrote the letter, and I can take care of it. I really think the tire-slashing was just a random act of vandalism."

"You think Emmett wrote the letter, fine. You think you can take care of him, it's not so fine. Whoever wrote that letter has problems you shouldn't be messing with, boss. I'm telling you, I'm picking up really bad vibrations about all of this, and they all seem to center around you."

At least Tory knew more than to take that personally. Sylvia was a great believer in her own mixture of New Age insights, psychics, folklore wisdom, Catholic mysticism, and horoscopes. How she managed to resolve the differences between all of them, Tory didn't know. Unfortunately, Sylvia had been right about amazing things more often than she or anyone else in the office liked to admit. Tory sighed. "I'm going to tell you something in complete confidence, Sylvia. Emmett got drunk Saturday night and threatened to involve this company in a fraudulent lawsuit. I don't think he has the guts to do it while I'm around and willing to call him on any move that he may make in that direction. But he may think that if he can get me out of the picture for a while, he can get things rolling to the point where I can't stop it."

"What about the part in the letter that says 'I've killed before'?"

"I think that's Emmett just trying to scare me."

"And I think that's you just trying to dismiss everything so you won't have to go around giving explanations to anybody. You figure that if you handle it yourself there won't be anything for people to talk about."

Tory looked at her in surprise. "Is that how you see it?"

"Boss, I like working for you. We all do. But sometimes you act like you have to handle everything yourself. Like maybe that will keep anyone from ever asking you questions. It doesn't matter if the police ask you questions, Tory. People around here already know that you came here out of high school, that your father was some kind of political big wheel out in Florida, and that you'd had an affair with some head honcho of your father's. Then you married someone who just happened to be one of your professors and twice your age. Everyone already knows all that, Tory. If they want to talk about it they can, and you can be sure that they already have. None of that matters. You're entitled to go to the police like anyone else."

Tory looked at Sylvia in speechless amazement. Sylvia made it all sound so simple. Tory wished it was.

Sylvia continued right on. "All that doesn't matter any more. You need to put the past behind you. Lonnie would marry you if you'd only have him. And Cody, you really think Cody hasn't heard it all before? He has, and it hasn't killed him. He's real proud of you. He wishes you wouldn't swear so much, but what kid is totally pleased with their parents? I don't want to see you make a dumb mistake and get hurt. What I'm trying to tell you is ..." Sylvia momentarily searched for words. "What I'm trying to tell you is that you don't have to live like a refugee."

Tory stared silently at Sylvia for a moment more before all the tensions from the last few days broke. Looking at her earnest secretary dressed in Cyndi Lauper style, concern radiating from every pore of her body, and Tom Petty words coming out of her mouth, Tory could almost hear the rhythmic guitar chords in the background. Pretty soon Sylvia might break into song. It wouldn't be any more surprising than everything else that had been happening lately. Helplessly, Tory began to laugh, and it was Sylvia's turn to stare in speechless amazement.

"I'm sorry," Tory sputtered. "The refugee bit, it's from a Tom Petty song." And she hummed a few bars. Understanding dawning on Sylvia's face, she began to smile. And then to giggle. And soon the two of them were laughing uproariously, tears rolling down their faces. Every time one of them would begin to stop, the other would start again.

This was how Jazz found them when he stepped into Tory's office to return her keys. "*Mujeres*," he muttered uncomfortably. "Women" was a single, all-encompassing term that Jazz used often to explain what he considered inexplicable behavior of the opposite sex.

Tory tried to pull herself together. "Sylvia and I were just sharing a joke," she explained weakly. "Give us a minute, okay?" Muttering something that distinctly sounded like "*loco de la cabeza*," Jazz wandered off and left them alone.

"Okay," said Tory, wiping her eyes, "I appreciate your concern. And you're right. I don't like to do anything to stir up the past if I don't have to. If I call the police, the first thing they'll want to know is who might have reason to threaten me, and the second thing they'll want to know is everything about me and about my business. But I'm not planning to do anything foolish. If anything else happens that I can't handle or put a stop to, I'll consider letting the police know about the letter. Deal? And you can call the police and report the tire-slashing."

"It doesn't sound like a deal to me. It sounds like you're going to do exactly what you want to do, as usual." But Sylvia sounded more resigned than argumentative, her naturally cheerful nature beginning to shine through her forebodings. "If something else happens, you tell the police *and* Lonnie *and* Jazz *and* Cody. Or I will."

"Okay, okay." Tory saw no reason to worry Sylvia further by telling her that Lonnie was planning to go out of town and that he was taking Cody with him. She was mildly interested to hear that her son had been added to the list of her potential male protectors. "Now get out of my office and let me get some work done. Go organize the troops out there and insult them all a little to make them feel like things are back to normal. I'm sure they've all noticed you moping around since yesterday. I have to make a phone call."

"Emmett Delgado?"

"Sometimes, Sylvia, you're too sharp for your own good."

Tory was relieved to see her exit with some of her old style. She could hear Sylvia asking Jazz if he'd shopped around or just paid the first price for tires that he'd come across. Tory shut the door and dialed the number for Webb Engineers and Architects in El Paso. The receptionist put her through to Emmett's private secretary, who informed her that Emmett had been out sick on Monday and was not expected in the office for the remainder of Tuesday. Tory didn't have to try very hard to visualize an "ailing" Emmett slashing the tires on her vehicles.

"Would you like to leave a message?" the well-modulated voice of Emmett's secretary asked.

"No, I'll call back." Tory hesitated. "On second thought, I will leave a message. Have you got something to write with?

Good. I'll need you to get this down exactly. This is Tory Travers. Tell Emmett that I called to say that if he doesn't stop screwing around with me and my company, I will personally cut off his shriveled little *cojones* and feed them to him for breakfast. I'll repeat that again so you can be sure you got it down exactly ... And ask me if you need to know how to spell anything."

If people were going to talk anyhow, like Sylvia said, she might as well give them something new and interesting to talk about.

Of course, all feelings of grandeur pass when the shoe is on the other foot. Tory remembered her grandmother saying something along the same lines to her, but she didn't expect to be on the receiving end of a threatening phone call so soon after telling Emmett's secretary exactly what she had in mind for him.

After getting the tires replaced on the vehicles, the day had more or less progressed normally. Sylvia had reported the damage to both the police and the insurance company. The police sent two officers out to investigate in the early afternoon. Sylvia handled most of the particulars, and Tory only had to talk to them briefly to confirm the facts that they had been told, and to tell them that she didn't have any idea about who might be responsible. Even in the short time that she spent talking to them, she couldn't help noticing that their manner seemed almost deferential compared to the arrogant detective she had talked to at the precast yard.

After that, the afternoon had been busy, and Sylvia had almost seemed her normal gregarious self. And then the phone call came.

Sylvia buzzed Tory in her office like she did whenever a call for Tory came through. Tory picked up her phone. "Yes?"

"There's a call for you on line two. Wouldn't say who it was. Said it was personal." Sylvia's reporting of the situation was full of skepticism. Vendors and sales representatives often tried to claim some personal relationship to try to get past Sylvia's screening. Sylvia's attitude was simple. If it was a personal call for Tory, Sylvia should know the caller.

"Okay, I'll handle it." She pushed the button for the second line. "Tory Travers here. Can I help you?"

"I hope so." The voice was muffled and unfamiliar. "I assume you got the letter?"

Tory hesitated. "I'm not sure what you're referring to."

"I told you to leave town for a while. I've called to give you the details of the arrangements."

"Who is this?"

"Get a pen and write this down. I won't be saying it twice, and I won't be calling back. You go to Denver. Stay in the Holiday Inn at the airport. Stay there two weeks. Communicate with no one. If you do everything that you are told, on the fourteenth day ten grand will be delivered to your room. You be there to personally receive it."

"Emmett, is that you, you son of a bitch? This is so melodramatic, it's stupid. Why in heaven's name would I go to Denver? For two weeks? You've got to be kidding."

"Don't ask questions, you stupid bitch. Just do what you're told, and don't tell anyone about this call or about the letter. Go this afternoon. If you don't follow directions, someone will get hurt. Soon. Go *today*."

"I'm not going anywhere—" But the line was disconnected. Tory hung up and watched the light on the line-two button shine on for a few more seconds before it went out. It took a couple minutes for the significance of that to completely sink in. Before she could decide on her next move, Syliva buzzed Tory again.

"Jazz on line two," she informed Tory, and disconnected before Tory could reply.

Feeling like she was in a bad movie, Tory picked up line two again. "Tory here. Uh, is this Jazz?"

"Yeah, it's Jazz. I told the Material Girl it was me. You okay? You sound out of breath."

"Yeah, I'm okay. We just had a little mix-up on incoming calls. What's up?"

"I'm running into all kinds of problems trying to calibrate this one column. I got preliminary calibrations on all the others, but this one has got me stuck."

"What do you mean you're stuck? The rebar is either there or it isn't. Just change the refraction until you compensate for the density of the specific column and shoot multiple shots around that range. When you find the setting that gives the clearest indication of what's inside, then optimize on that setting and shoot for detail. Then take those shots and analyze them against the design drawings."

There was a long pause on the other end. "Thank you for explaining all that to me, boss. I was wondering exactly what it was I've been doing all these years."

Tory counted to ten. "Give me a break, Jazz. Things aren't exactly a bed of roses around here. So what exactly is your problem?"

"The whole bit about whether the rebar is or isn't there. You know that's not as simple as it sounds if you can't limit your range. I've zeroed in on three of the four columns that we're looking at, and we should have shots good enough for analysis by tomorrow afternoon, if everything goes well. But the fourth one, it doesn't make any sense."

"Jazz, either the X-rays show you that something is there or they don't."

"Boss, you know that all the rebar in these columns is in cages, connected frames of bar. I get something distinct enough to work around at either end of the column. But when I use that setting for the middle section of the column, all I get is three little separate blips of metal. When I shoot on either side of that range, I get nothing. That's all I can get, either three blips or zip."

Tory and Jazz sat for a while and listened to each other breathing. "Boss, you still there?"

"I'm still here. I'm trying to think." Something that seemed to be getting harder and harder to do as the week went on, she thought to herself.

"It doesn't make sense that they would cast this one and put in three dinky little pieces of reinforcing bar in the middle, does it? I mean, I can see those assholes casting a column with part of the bar missing, with part of the bar going in the wrong direction, and maybe even without any bar at all."

"No, not without any bar at all. If they cast one of those columns without any reinforcement at all, it would never have made it up to the site in one piece. It would be in little chunks by now."

"I'm not sure I agree with that, completely. If there was still some residual curing strength, and if you were lucky in transporting the column, it might make it in one piece. But okay, so maybe they wouldn't cast a whole column without any bar. But it doesn't make sense that they would cast one with complete cages of bar on each end and then put three separate little pieces of bar in the middle section." There was a pause. "Does it?"

Tory refrained from telling him that less and less was making sense to her as the day went on. "Jazz, I don't have any answers for you. Want me to come out there?"

"*Creo que no.* I still have a few ideas. It sounds like you're up to your neck in alligators out there. We've had better days, *que sí*? I'm going to stay out here awhile and take some more shots. I have a few other things up my sleeve that I want to try. It looks like I'll be out here late tonight developing film to see if I can get anything to work, so I can get a jump on this thing tomorrow. I just don't want you on my ass about any overtime."

"Jazz, have I ever gotten on your case? I can tell just by talking to you over the phone that you have your hard hat on this very minute."

"*Por cierto*, boss. You think I'm going to let that *pendejo* Kemp write any more letters about me?"

"No, I didn't think so. How do the shots on the other columns look?"

"It's too early to tell for sure without comparing them to the design drawings, but I think everything looks all right."

"Good. Look, hang in there. I'm going to be working late tonight too, so I'll be here if you want to kick around any ideas. But hopefully by that time you'll have the whole thing solved."

"Don't hold your breath. This is one of the screwiest things I've come across, and I've come across some screwy things in my time. It would sure help if we could get our hands on the pour records, or even talk to any of the crew that poured this mother."

"I'm working on it. But I don't know if anyone will do anything in time to help us."

"Bureaucrats. They're all alike. Hang in there yourself." And Jazz hung up.

Tory sat for a moment, reflecting how it was easier to confront a bureaucrat than to do what had to be done now. Taking a deep breath, she buzzed Sylvia and asked her to come into her office.

Sylvia walked in and shut the door behind her without being asked. She sat down and looked at Tory defiantly, drumming her blood-red fingernails impatiently on the arms of her chair.

"Sylvia, did you listen in on my call?"

"With Jazz?" asked Sylvia innocently.

"No," said Tory patiently. "The call before that one."
They sat looking at each other in silence.

"Yes," said Sylvia finally. "I did. He said it was personal.
I know all the people who call you with personal calls, and
they never say the call is personal. And that's what was on
the letter—personal."

Tory sighed. "What are we going to do about this?" she
asked.

"Call the police," Sylvia answered immediately.

"I wasn't talking about the call. I was talking about you
feeling like you have to take care of me. Sylvia, I can handle
this. I'm not frightened, just concerned. And you're making
everything more difficult by getting involved."

"And you're making everything more difficult by not
calling the police," replied Sylvia doggedly.

"I'll think about it."

"And I'll continue to listen in on every call that doesn't
seem right. And keep on opening the mail. That way, when
something happens to you, there'll be someone around to
explain it all." And to Tory's astonishment, her secretary
broke into tears.

"Sylvia, I don't want you so upset about this. One of us
being upset is enough. Listen, if anything else happens, I'll
go to the police. I promise. And I know that you'll be breathing down my neck to make sure I keep my promise. Okay?"

"Okay," Sylvia sniffed.

"I wonder how many other people have their secretaries
dictate conditions to them." Tory was trying to inject a little
humor into the situation.

"More than you would think," answered Sylvia, and Tory had the distinct feeling that she was probably right.

Once Sylvia returned to her post, Tory dialed the El Paso Precast Concrete Company. She was told that Petey Lester was not in the office, so she asked for Jack Columbo. She had to wait for a few minutes while they paged him out in the yard. It sounded like they were hot and heavy into production.

"Columbo here."

"Tory Travers at Travers Testing in Las Cruces. Petey Lester has told you about our need for the records on the stadium column pours." She decided it was a good idea to start out making statements instead of asking questions.

"Yeah, but I hear you came down here and got our little problem about those records explained to you." Since she couldn't read his facial expressions over the phone, Tory couldn't tell if there was a slight sneer in his reply or if she was just imagining it.

"Yeah, well, we're running into problems down here with X-raying the columns, and it's in your best interest if we can do our evaluation quickly and easily."

"That's what I've been told by the boss. So what do you want? Nobody's turned up the missing records yet, and I sure as hell don't have them."

"Hartman may have kept notes in the lab. Are they letting anyone in there yet?"

"No way, José."

"Maybe we could document recollections that you or other crew members have of those pours."

"Lady, those pours are ancient history, now. You think we remember each individual pour? We're behind schedule and running overtime shifts seven days a week. You can forget about sending anyone down here to inspect the pour of that final column until sometime next week. I can't even get any clarification on the damn design drawings because the damn design engineer in charge has up and disappeared. And on top of all of that, there happens to be a little murder investigation going on here, in case you've forgotten."

For a moment Tory actually forgot the purpose of her call. "What do you mean the design engineer has disappeared? Do you mean Emmett Delgado?"

"One and the same. It's not like he was competent when he was around, but now I haven't even got anyone who's willing to take the responsibility to authorize field changes."

"I thought he was sick. Can't you get through to him if it's important enough?"

"Yeah, he's sick all right. I got hold of some temporary secretary who hadn't been briefed on professional confidentiality, and she told me that Delgado couldn't be reached for quite a while. She told me she'd heard that he'd checked into a treatment center for alcoholism. The prick."

Tory had little sympathy for Delgado's plight, either. Shit, she thought to herself, he couldn't be in a treatment center and up here slashing my tires. Not unless they take field trips wherever he's gone.

Tory couldn't decide what to do with this new information, so she went back to the columns. "Were you in charge of the pours for the stadium columns?"

"You already know damn well that I was in charge of the one your asshole foreman raised such a stink about. You guys sure know how to make a mountain out of a mole hill."

"But were you in charge of all the column pours?" Tory asked doggedly.

"Let me think. I did that one while your asshole guy was on site, and two, no, three others."

"Do you think the pours that we didn't observe were made according to design?"

"Hell, yes. What do you expect me to say? That I need you clowns babysitting me in order to get our job done right? Your guy was on site when we got busy and were short-handed. He would have never seen a mistake like that made around here, otherwise. And I would have caught it and corrected it eventually, anyhow."

That's not the story I heard, Tory thought, but she didn't interrupt Columbo.

"Everything came down on my head after that one, and I was encouraged to think carefully about the procedures for pouring the other columns." This time there was no mistaking the sarcasm. "Hell, yes. I'm sure that the others were poured according to design."

"You said that you supervised the pours on four of the columns. Who supervised the fifth?"

Columbo gave a short laugh. "Kent Colliney, lady. That column was poured on overtime and Kent was out here in charge that night. And if you want to talk to him, you can get in line. Right behind the police and his wife and his father-in-law."

"What about the crew? Can I talk to anyone who was on that pour?"

"Get real, lady. A night pour on overtime? How do you think we keep overhead down?"

"Are you saying the crew was illegals?"

"Not me. You're not going to hear me saying something like that. All I'm saying is that any of the crew that I can remember being assigned to that pour are long gone. It would have been a skeleton crew to begin with. Maybe two guys. You have a better chance of talking to Colliney himself at this point than to any of those guys."

And that was all that she was going to get out of Columbo. She had very little time to reflect further on the conversation before Sylvia put through a call from the Director. Tory updated him on the status of the column study, and the problems that she was encountering. Very politely Henderson conveyed to Tory his concern about the obstacles that she was facing, but that he still expected a recommendation from her regarding the acceptability of the stadium columns by Monday at the latest. She had no real choice but to reassure him that his requirements would be met. He hung up and she willed the phone to remain silent.

"I could give you a recommendation now," she said to silent phone, "but you wouldn't believe what I would be telling you. Three columns look okay and the fourth one is fine, except for the fact that it's missing its middle, so to speak. The problem is, I'm not sure that I believe it, either. Who knows, maybe Delgado designed it that way in a drunken stupor."

The damn phone buzzed again, and Sylvia informed her that Harold Kemp was on the line. "Tory here," she answered wearily.

"I've got a crew holding up a concrete pour over at the new Foodway because your inspector hasn't shown up, Ms. Travers. You better have someone get their ass over here, or I'll have to call the owner and ask who's gonna pay for the delay."

"We're running late today, Harold. I'm sorry. Someone slashed the tires on all the company vehicles. Can you give me a half hour? Besides, aren't you supposed to call up and give us warning before you assemble the crew?"

"Look at the contract, lady. On this job that's a voluntary notice, it wasn't written in as a contract requirement. Guess that one slipped by you, right? And I'm not giving you a minute more of time. The pour schedule was submitted with the construction schedule."

"Harold, that's not how we work, contract or no contract, and you know it. Those project schedules get changed all the time, and you're supposed to give us notification when there needs to be an inspector on site."

"Maybe on most jobs, but not on this one. And we're right on schedule."

"Why are you doing this? You're not going to gain anything from it. You know my people can make life miserable for you."

"And that works both ways, Ms. Travers. You like to play by the book, so we're playing by the book, too."

"What's going on, Harold?"

"I got stuck by Henderson with the entire cost for your column boondoggle, that's what."

"Pass it on to El Paso Precast."

"Lester said to take a flying jump. I'll never use him on another job, but that's not going to bail me out of having to pay for all the extra work you've caused on this one."

"I'm sorry, Harold, but I'm just doing my job. I don't think this is going to help the problem."

"Maybe not, but it's going to make me feel a lot better to see you in hot water with an owner. I got the short end of the stick on this mess, and all because of you. So now I've got you."

"Harold, if you've got me, and if we've missed an inspection, exactly why are you the one calling me?"

There was a short pause. "Because I just wanted to let you know, that's why." And he hung up.

Well, that seemed to rule Harold Kemp out of the picture for tire-slashing. He wouldn't have been able to wait for her to discover the damage. He would have had to call her up to make sure she knew about it. He probably just wasn't good criminal material.

There was no one else available in the office to cover the inspection, and Tory was expecting an irate owner on the site to boot, so she grabbed her hard hat and ran out to take care of the problem. She left her car phone in the office, because if she was out in the field, she couldn't get any more phone calls.

Tory wasn't really worried when Jazz hadn't shown up or called by eight-thirty that evening. She was beat. She thought about calling him at the site, but decided that either he would be outside the trailer and she wouldn't be able to reach him, or he would be deep in his work, and in a foul mood at being interrupted. In any case, she decided to call it a day, and go home and spend the remainder of the evening with Cody, before he left with Lonnie in the morning. It had not been the best of days.

The night didn't turn out to be an improvement: a call came at 1:00 AM; Tory was awake immediately. She answered it before Cody could.

"Is this Victoria Travers?"

"Yes, it is. Who's calling?" Even as she asked the question, she knew that the voice was totally different from the one earlier that afternoon.

"I'm calling from the University Police Department, ma'am. There has been an accident out at the stadium construction site, and it appears that one of your employees has been injured."

"Jazz." It wasn't even a question, but still she hoped that the officer on the phone would correct her, tell her a name that she didn't recognize.

"He has been identified as Jesus Rodriguez. Does he work for you?"

"Yes." At least the question hadn't been "*Did* he work for you?"

"And were you aware that he was out on the site tonight? Was he authorized to be there?"

"Yes, he was working late. But not this late. What happened? Is he hurt?"

"It appears to have been a freak accident, Ms. Travers. Your guy must have been out on the site without his hard hat when one of the beams overhead was dislodged. He was struck on the head and knocked unconscious. A student walking past on his way home just happened to find him. He's been taken to Las Cruces General Hospital, and you'll have to call there to find out anything more about his condition."

"But officer, he would have been wearing his hard hat on site. He had promised me he would." Even as the words came out of her mouth, Tory could imagine how ridiculous they would sound to anyone else.

"Ms. Travers, I can understand that you're upset. But these things happen. A worker is out on a deserted site all alone, he's going to slack up. It's not your fault. It was an accident. As long as we know that Mr. Rodriguez had a reason to be out on the site, there's no reason for us to suspect anything else."

"But officer …"

"Ms. Travers, call the hospital; find out about your employee. Maybe they'll have some good news for you."

"It won't matter if they have good news or bad news—not about this. There's no way it could have been an accident."

"Think about what I've said. Give yourself some time to get over the shock. And then if you still want to talk about it, come in and we'll talk."

"I want to come in and talk. I won't change my mind."

"Whatever you say." Tory couldn't help but notice the irony of the situation. Here she was, actually begging to talk to the police, and no one wanted to talk to her. She almost felt like calling up Sylvia to tell her about it. "Why don't you come in, say, around eleven on Thursday. Ask for Officer Snow."

"But tomorrow, I mean today, is Wednesday. I'm supposed to wait until Thursday?"

"That's the first time the officer who picked up your employee will be on a day shift. You wait and come in and talk to us then. Maybe it will make you feel better."

Tory was beginning to wonder if anything was ever going to make her feel better again.

CHAPTER SEVEN: BACKGROUND WORK

Alvarez's partner waylaid him at his desk early Wednesday morning before he left for Las Cruces. Faulkner was wearing the self-satisfied look that characterized a successful episode of fact-finding, and he was carrying a thick file folder. "Hey, man," said Alvarez before he could start. "Make it quick. I need to get out of here so I'll have time to rattle a few cages on the Hartman case before I go see Anna this afternoon."

"You'll want to t-take a few m-m-minutes to l-l-look at this," answered his partner. Alvarez sat down at his desk and gave his partner his full attention. He had seen that self-satisfied expression combined with an increased stutter too many times to ignore its portents. "You got this one solved, man?"

"No, not even close. I'm not even sure that what I've found has anything to do with the m-murder. But it's interesting. M-more than that, you'll like it." Faulkner pulled up a chair for himself, sat down, and tossed the file on Alvarez's desk. It was neatly labeled "Victoria Travers a.k.a Victoria Wheatley." Alvarez noted that the label was not in his partner's handwriting.

"Tell me the good stuff," he said, as he began to leaf through the file. "And remember that I'm in a hurry, so talk fast." One of the things that he liked best about his partner was that he could say things like that.

Faulkner paused a moment, obviously gathering his thoughts before embarking on the difficult task of discourse. "You know I can't t-t-talk fast. Victoria Travers was b-born in Ocala, Florida, and lived there until she was eighteen. They have a file on her in Ocala. Her own police f-f-file before she was eighteen. Do you want to know m-more, or are you still in such a hurry?"

"Suddenly I seem to have all the time in the world. Talk as slow as you want to."

Faulkner took another deep breath. "Victoria Wheatley, her m-maiden name, was b-born into a very influential and wealthy Floridian family thirty-five years ago. Her father is Tom Wheatley, who was in the state senate during m-most of the time she was growing up. A Democrat, like everyone is in Florida, but an ultra c-c-conservative Democrat. Pro-

Vietnam, anti the civil rights movement, that sort of thing. Her mother was LaBelle Wheatley, who was the only child of an Alabama governor. And there was a brother, s-s-seven years older, who was the apple of everyone's eye, the way I read it."

"What a cozy little WASP setup. Her mother's name was really LaBelle? You're not just making this up?"

His partner ignored Alvarez's questions, intent on continuing his story. "Until Victoria, then known as Vicky, became a teenager. Then the family started getting all kinds of p-press that they didn't want. Vicky d-definitely d-differed with the family politics. She marched for civil rights and participated in sit-ins to protest the war. And she was young when she st-started, fourteen or f-fifteen. She got hauled in for smoking pot and disturbing the peace several times, but nothing ever stuck, thanks to the t-timely intervention of the Senator."

"What an embarrassment to an upstanding family. So why didn't they ship recalcitrant little Vicky off to reform school?"

"That's just not the way it's done if you're the d-d-daughter of a senator."

"And that must be why I have you as my partner, so I can become educated about these things. You did notice my use of the word 'recalcitrant', didn't you? You know I'm always on the lookout to better myself. So what exactly is done in the genteel classes when the young female offspring frequents the police department involuntarily?"

"No one ever had to f-f-find out. Fate intervened and everything went to hell. As a show of s-support for the Senator, the older brother enlisted after he finished college and got shipped out to Vietnam. 'No special treatment for me' he said, and they took him at his word. He was one of the l-last casualties of Vietnam."

"Tough break."

"It was like the family went haywire after his d-d-death. The press got some pictures of a barely clad young thing at a motel with the Senator's top aide, and all of a sudden it was headlines that s-seventeen year old Vicky was sleeping with the top member of her father's s-s-staff, who happened to be married, by the way. A couple of years later the Senator's wife divorced him, and he lost the next election. S-soon after that he retired from public life."

"And was the errant daughter left out in the cold? How the hell did she end up in Las Cruces, New Mexico, working as an engineer?"

"It seems that her b-basic problem was a lack of judgment, not a lack of intelligence. And no, she didn't end up out in the cold. Her parents pretty much disowned her, but by the time the scandal broke, she had f-f-finished high school and turned eighteen. So then there was the t-trust fund."

"Trust fund?"

"You know how those w-w-work, right?" Faulkner was sweating now with the effort of all this conversation. This was harder for him than running the training obstacle course.

"Real vaguely. It's kind of like a foreign term to me. Mexicans don't have trust funds; it's against their genetic makeup or something. But don't slow down on my account. I'll try to keep up."

"Victoria's maternal grandfather had put a lot of m-money in a trust fund for each of his grandchildren to be used for college. What was left in her b-brother's trust fund came to her, t-t-too. So when Vicky was eighteen, she took the m-m-money and went New Mexico. P-p-probably a place as different from Florida as it gets."

"So that's how Victoria came to our part of the world."

"Yeah. She changed her name along the way. Vicky became Tory when she enrolled in college. No m-m-more protest or arrests. She enrolled in engineering, and one of her classes was taught by a professor named Carl Travers. The summer after her freshman year, Tory and the p-p-professor gave everyone something to talk about by starting to d-date openly. During Christmas break of her sophomore year, they got married."

"Was the guy married when she started going out with him?"

"No, he was a b-b-bachelor."

"Well, that's at least one step up from her Florida affair. And she tried to convince me that she was so morally superior. I guess there's more than one way to make the Dean's list."

"No, she m-m-made really g-good grades in everything, not just engineering. Anyhow, some of the rush to get married may have b-b-been due to the fact that the professor had a grim history of bone cancer. They h-had one kid the year after they got m-married, but Tory went on to finish school. Then she and her husband started an engineering consulting firm. Travers died five years later, and Tory has run the firm ever since. Successfully, it s-seems."

"Interesting story. Unfortunately for us, she turns out to be everything that she said she was."

"Except for one thing."

"The source of your information."

"Pretty g-g-good."

"I knew it was too complete and too quick to have come through the channels of our beloved department. Also, my heightened sense of observation tells me that this is not a department file. The handwriting is not familiar."

"Also, department files are legal-sized, and this is standard-sized."

"How come you never stutter when you point out something like that? Now, having ruled out that the information came from the department ..."

"The f-file came out of Hartman's briefcase."

"No shit?"

"No sh-sh-sh-sh-shit."

Alvarez winced and then looked sharply at his partner. "Why the hell did Hartman have a file on Victoria Travers?"

"There were several files in Hartman's b-briefcase. It l-l-looks like he did some freelance writing. M-mostly political reporting."

"That damn woman looked me straight in the eye and told me that she and Hartman discussed the stadium project when she met him Friday morning. I can't wait to hit her with this. Maybe we'll see some kind of real structural collapse."

"H-h-hold your h-h-horses. There were several articles in the f-f-file in addition to this one. There were articles on quality control at precast yards, and two of them were written by Ms. Travers."

"It's still too coincidental to let it go."

"There's still something else."

"I love it when you save the best for last."

"Do you want to know who she had the affair with b-back in Florida?"

"Hartman's father?" asked Alvarez, ever hopeful. This was getting better and better. He felt like a bloodhound on the scent of something good.

"Not even close. Mason Barkley."

Alvarez blinked. "Not even a knee jerk. So I don't win the cigar."

"Mason Barkley has been on the news lately. He's running for public office in Florida, and he's p-p-part of a lecture tour that's coming through here in a few weeks. Try Christians in Government and see if that rings a bell."

"CIG, of the famous slogan 'CIG, not CIA'? Tell me it isn't true." The two detectives had worked a particularly grisly case the year before involving the bombing of a health clinic that performed abortions. Unfortunately, this bombing had claimed the life of a two-year-old girl who had been at the clinic with her mother. Even more ironically, the mother had been there that evening seeking emergency help in trying to carry a high-risk pregnancy to term. The fetus had been an additional victim of the incident.

"I thought you'd like the connection," Faulkner said. Alvarez had been first on the scene that night, and both he and his partner had taken it hard that the case had never been solved. Christians in Government, or CIG, as they called themselves, had come as close to claiming credit as they could and still remain on the right side of the law.

Alvarez had seldom encountered a more unsavory group of religious fanatics. With money and powerful societal contacts, they had been able so far to justify many of their questionable actions as exercising their religious freedom. He remembered one bejeweled matron informing him that the death of the little girl mattered nothing compared to the many glorious deaths that had resulted from the Crusades. He mentally shuddered at the memory. He felt more comfortable dealing with a slimy drug pusher or a two-bit felon any day.

"So their leader is coming to El Paso," he said, trying unsuccessfully to tie the new information to Hartman's death. "But I can't see the connection."

"Neither can I. But Hartman m-may have had all this information on Travers' personal life because he was planning to do an article on her. It seems likely any article like that would have something to do with B-Barkley."

"So maybe he was blackmailing Tory Travers and she decided to ice him. She'd be physically capable of doing in Hartman, with a little luck. Maybe even without a little luck."

"You checked that out, did you? Her physique and general health?"

"Who says you don't have a sense of humor, Scott?

Of course I checked that out. How does my theory sound to you?"

"I don't know. It sure would t-t-tie up everything, except for two things." Alvarez groaned, but his partner continued. "I don't know how someone can be blackmailed with something that's already p-public record. And, that wouldn't explain why the precast yard records are missing." Faulkner sighed. "I'm worn out with all this t-talking." He leaned over to retrieve his file, but Alvarez intercepted him.

"Let me hang on to this. I will definitely drop in to see Ms. Travers while I'm checking out Lester's alibi."

"While you're at it, s-stop in at the University and look up Charles Henderson. He's the Director of Facilities Planning."

"That's one of the names that the infamous Ms. Travers threatened me with. What's up?"

"He called the Chief to request that Ms. Travers have access to the records at the scene of the crime."

"Gutsy broad. If her story about the stadium project is her alibi, it looks like she's prepared to run with it all the way. I wonder if she has any idea that this file exists. So what did the Chief say?"

"Why do you think he's the Chief? He p-passed Henderson on to me, of course, after telling me that there would be more than one dead body if any civilians had access to that area before it's cleared. So I started talking to Henderson about things in general. It t-turns out that Henderson was at the same functions Sunday that Lester claimed he was at. It also seems he has known Ms. Travers since she was a s-student."

"Viola."

"Viola? You mean maybe voilá?"

"Do you know how bad you make that sound? Charles Henderson has just made the top of my list of people that I want to see." Even though he was running late, Alvarez couldn't resist one last effort at storytelling. "It was like this: Travers met Hartman during some construction project, had an affair, and spilled her guts about her past to him. But Hartman loved politics more than Tory Travers. Turns out that Hartman was avidly pro-choice on the abortion issue, and he couldn't resist using the story about Tory's past to discredit Barkley when he rolls into town. The lady was pissed at having her past unearthed for a political cause, so she iced Hartman, and took the records to cover up the real motive."

"I kind of like the one about the accomplice in the wheelchair better."

"Every time you open your mouth today you prove my hypothesis about your stutter."

"S-s-so you think if I criticized you all the time I would be stutter-free?" Faulkner asked with interest.

"Let's not try it out," Alvarez said hurriedly. "So what do you plan to do while I'm gone?"

"I'm waiting for some information requests to come in, so I guess I'll sweat Lester a little m-more, take him through his story again. If the yard is into drug-running, or a racket involving illegal aliens, I figure that the b-bosses have to be in on it. And Lester's the only b-boss I'm able to put my hands on at the moment."

"Sweat Lester a little more? That's my territory, partner. I didn't think you used terms like that. Fact-finding is one thing, man, and the fine art of interrogation is another."

"I s-see. And I suppose you have a strategy for interrogating T-Tory Travers? Will it involve another complaint filed against us for officer rudeness?"

"Don't even bother asking. It's a trade secret. And what's your strategy for interrogating Lester? What are you going to do, sit around and compare country clubs?"

"No, I'm going to sit him in a l-l-little room and talk real slow and stutter at him until he c-c-cracks."

Alvarez gave his partner a look of genuine admiration. "And I keep underestimating you. You think maybe you can close the case without me, *que sí?*"

"*No comprende, señor. No hablo español.*"

"You ever notice you don't stutter when you pretend to speak Spanish?"

"You're n-n-not the only one trying to better yourself. I've been practicing the variations of 'your mother wears c-c-combat boots' that you taught me." And Faulkner uttered some Spanish profanities that even impressed Alvarez. And he didn't stutter, either.

Even while politely emphasizing his busy schedule, the New Mexico State University Director of Facilities Planning had no real choice but to gracefully agree to meet with Alvarez.

"It's a pleasure to meet you," the Director said with a firm handshake. "I'm at your disposal, and fully willing to cooperate in any way. I hope that this meeting will prove fruitful for both of us, and that the spirit of cooperation will prove to be a two-way street."

"I think I understand what you're talking about," said Alvarez easily, lowering his six-foot-two frame into one of the chairs in Henderson's office without being asked. "And I don't want to lead you into thinking you may get something in return for talking to me today. I assume you'll want us to grant Ms. Travers access to the El Paso Precast Concrete Company's lab and any remaining records."

"You assume correctly."

"There would be procedural problems in granting that request in any case. In this particular case, there is the added problem that Ms. Travers herself is under suspicion. Until we can establish that she had no connection with Bill Hartman's death, we have no way of knowing that she's not seeking access for the purpose of destroying incriminating evidence."

"Hogwash, Detective Alvarez. Plain and simply, that's hogwash."

Alvarez was surprised at both the form and the vehemence of the Director's reply. "Would you care to expand on that?" he asked.

"Why on earth would Tory Travers kill an engineering technician at a precast yard in El Paso?"

"She has a business association with them. Business means money, and money matters can mean murder."

"You're barking up the wrong tree, there. I don't know many people as straight as Victoria Travers. Some with more restraint, perhaps, but not with more ethical values."

"What do you know about her?"

"The same things I imagine you already know, Detective," answered Henderson shortly. "Let's not play games. I'm sure if you even mildly suspect she has some connection with this murder, you've already run a background investigation on her. And anything having to do with scandal turns up faster than anything having to do with a sterling reputation. Which is what we're talking about here, isn't it?"

"We may have some background information on her, but I still want to hear what you know about her. There may be some inconsistencies in our information."

Alvarez noted that Henderson tactfully glossed over Tory Travers' earlier history and emphasized her professional achievements. But the major points matched the information in Hartman's file.

"What did you mean when you mentioned a lack of restraint earlier?"

"Did I use those words? How can I explain this? Tory has a habit of rubbing people the wrong way if they don't happen to agree with her view of the world."

Alvarez wished that Faulkner were there to say "No sh-sh-sh-shit." He asked for an example, although he was pretty sure he already knew what the Director was talking about from personal experience.

"Well, when Tory and Carl were first married, they attended a faculty function that I was hosting. We had just hired our first black engineering professor, a guy named Howards, and he was talking to Tory and Carl. I was escorting a visiting alumni of some distinction around, who also happened to have some very archaic views about the proper place of black people in our society. If you get my meaning ..."

Alvarez nodded his understanding and Henderson continued. "Well, we had walked right into Tory and Carl talking to Howards, and there was really no way of getting around introductions. I decided to introduce Howards first. This guy actually told Howards 'I don't shake hands with your kind, boy', and then he turned to Tory and he almost leered. She was maybe all of twenty-two at the time. 'And who are you, honey?' the alum asked her. Tory never missed a beat or batted an eye. She told him 'Why, I'm Mrs. Howards, of course, and I'm just dying to shake your hand.' That was one of the few times that I thought my job duties might have to extend to dealing with a coronary victim."

Alvarez had to admit to himself that he also found the story amusing. "Has this trait of Ms. Travers made her any enemies?"

"No, no," the Director was in the middle of dismissing the question when he stopped and looked hard at Alvarez. "Why do you ask?"

"Because sometimes when people make enemies, they end up in situations where they feel threatened, or actually are threatened. And then sometimes they do things nobody would ever anticipate. And I could tell you thought of something just now. What is it?"

"Probably nothing. But I do have to admit that I, and about a hundred other people, heard Emmett Delgado threaten Tory last Saturday evening. But he was drunk."

"What happened?"

"It seems that he and Tory had some words. Mr. Delgado's company has been trying to buy hers for a long time. Anyhow, Tory lost her temper and slapped him. Knocked him over, in fact. So he was yelling something about making her regret the whole thing. Quite an unfortunate occurrence."

Alvarez was searching his memory of his conversations with various people about this case. Was it Petey Lester or Tory Travers who had mentioned Emmett Delgado? It didn't matter. "Emmett Delgado. Doesn't he have something to do with this stadium project?"

"Yes, he's the structural engineer of record."

"But he lives down in El Paso, right? Who could tell me more about the relationship between Delgado and Ms. Travers, and what happened that night?"

The Director sighed. "I was afraid of this. You're giving way too much importance to what was just an unfortunate turn of events."

"I'm afraid you'll have to let me be the judge of that. Who could I talk to?"

"Lonnie Harper. He's a rancher here in the valley."

"Ms. Travers' boyfriend?"

"You do like to jump to conclusions, don't you? I believe it would be more correct to call him Tory's friend, Detective Alvarez. They're close, but not close in that way. Mr. Harper lost his wife about the same time that Carl, Tory's husband, died. They've been a great deal of comfort to each other."

Alvarez could only imagine one effective form of adult

comfort, but he refrained from saying so. "And how do I get in touch with Mr. Harper?"

The Director gave him the phone number off the top of his head, a fact which Alvarez duly noted. That fact, coupled with what Alvarez already knew about Tory, led him to predict that Lonnie Harper would not turn out to be some poor shit-kicker. Those accustomed to privilege tended to attract the same type, he reflected to himself.

"I must tell you that I find this whole conversation very distasteful."

"I'm sure that you do. And I do appreciate your help. Let's get back to the original purpose of my visit. Can you document Mr. Lester's whereabouts between two and six p.m. last Sunday?"

Obviously relieved to change the subject, the Director confirmed that he had seen Petey Lester at the pool party at the Hilton on Sunday afternoon, and later at dinner. He had arrived for dinner at 7:30, and was certain that Petey had been there when he arrived. About the afternoon function, he was less certain. It had lasted from two until five, and although the Director had been there during the entire function, there had been people coming and going and he could not be sure if Petey had been there the whole time. However, his impression was that he had been.

"When you talk to Lonnie, you might ask him about that. He might be able to help you with placing Mr. Lester at the pool party."

"He was there?" Alvarez mentally awarded himself two points for his assumption about Lonnie Harper.

"Yes. Mr. Harper is from a ranching family in this area, and he's also a graduate of this university. He is invited to many of the university social functions. He was also at the dinner the Alumni Association gave that night. As a matter of fact, now that I think about it, Lonnie remarked to me that he had intended to bring Tory, but that she had changed her mind at the last minute."

The Director looked at Alvarez, horrified as the significance of what he had just said struck him. "I'm sure she didn't want to come because of the unpleasantness the night before. Emmett was also invited to both functions."

"And did he come to either?"

"No."

"And can you remember if Mr. Harper was at the pool party the entire afternoon?"

The Director regarded Alvarez like he would a rattlesnake. "No, I can't. I can remember seeing him there, but I can't tell you if he was there the whole time."

Alvarez thanked the Director for his help and asked permission to use his phone. Talking to Mr. Lonnie Harper had just become a big priority.

Alvarez requested to talk to Lonnie for the official reason of documenting Petey Lester's whereabouts on the Sunday that the murder had been committed. Harper agreed immediately, informing Alvarez that he had been lucky to catch him. He told Alvarez that he was usually out on his ranch during the daytime, but he had caught him packing for a fishing trip.

Harper suggested meeting Alvarez at a McDonald's near the University.

It was too early for lunch, and still a couple of hours before Alvarez was due at the home where his sister lived. He settled himself into a booth with some coffee and tried the old game of picking out the person he was waiting for. He was successful. The tall, weathered man who stepped out of a relatively beaten-up pickup truck looked a lot like he sounded on the phone, and was indeed Lonnie Harper.

Harper couldn't substantiate much more than the Director had been able to. So Alvarez moved right on to asking Harper why Victoria Travers had not attended the university functions that fateful afternoon and evening. But Lonnie Harper was not one of those helpful individuals who thought he had to answer questions just because the person asking them had a badge.

"Wait a minute," he said, narrowing his eyes and leaning back in the booth to consider. "Are you the guy who gave Tory such a hard time about getting the records she needs to study those stadium columns?"

"One and the same."

"So why are you switching subjects and asking questions about Tory?"

"Didn't she tell you that by virtue of showing up and insisting on seeing the very records that are missing, she's officially a suspect in this case?"

"No, she didn't. But then that's just like Tory."

"Look, I know you don't like these questions," said

Alvarez, starting to feel a little sleazy in spite of himself. "But I need to get the answers."

"No, I don't like these questions," said Harper evenly. "I don't much like you, either. But you have a job to do, I guess. At least, that's how it appears right now. And when it stops appearing like that, I won't be talking to you any more. Tory didn't go to the party or the dinner on Sunday because of what happened between her and Emmett Delgado on Saturday evening. And if you've just come from the Director's office, I'm sure you know all about that."

"What's between her and Delgado?"

"Emmett wants Tory's business, and he wants Tory herself. That's a potent combination. He got drunk, shot off his mouth, pushed her too far, and she knocked him down."

Harper must be one to call them like he saw them, Alvarez thought, noting that Lonnie didn't use Henderson's euphuism that she had only slapped Delgado. "What about him threatening her?"

"Wouldn't you try to save face if you were knocked down by a woman in front of a bunch of people? Or are you beyond those baser emotions, Detective?"

Alvarez made like he was his partner and let that one go over his head, although it did pose an interesting question. "One last question. Can you prove your whereabouts for the entire period between two and six p.m. on Sunday?"

Harper laughed a laugh totally devoid of any humor and shook his head no. "Don't tell me I'm a suspect now, too. You'll have to excuse me now, unless you have any more valid questions to ask me. I'm on my way up to the mountains. And you've just made me feel real sure that I'll appreciate the clean mountain air."

Alvarez let him go without a response, since there didn't seem to be an appropriate one. To take his mind off the potential validity of Harper's statement, he decided to study Hartman's file a little more before his next stop.

Cody insisted on accompanying his mother to see Jazz, after she woke him and told him where she was going. They learned no more during their vigil than they had in their first fifteen minutes at the hospital: Jazz was in intensive care, in a coma. The prognosis was wide open: he could open his eyes at any minute and not suffer much worse than a deep gash and a mammoth headache, or the coma could go on indefinitely. Or he could regain consciousness and there could be minor brain damage. Or major brain damage. That about narrowed it down.

Tory and Cody returned home around 3:00 AM to catch a few hours of sleep before facing Wednesday. Before Tory left for work in the morning, she was able to convince her son that there was no purpose in canceling his plans to leave later in the day to go fishing with Lonnie.

The staff at Travers Testing and Engineering Company had rallied and closed ranks to deal with the news of Jazz's injury. Schedules and assignments had been shifted, and there was unspoken acknowledgment that there would be a lot of extra hours required. Tory had arranged most of that.

What she hadn't arranged was her staff's decision to stagger their lunch hours so that someone would be with Jazz most of the day. Jazz had married briefly right out of high school. It had lasted less than a year, and even Tory didn't know the name or whereabouts of his ex-wife. In many ways, her employees were the only family that he had.

She had no heart for further fencing with Sylvia. She told her secretary that she had spoken with the police, and that she would be talking further with them tomorrow. Sylvia thought that was an inappropriate amount of time to wait, but took one look at Tory's drawn face and decided not to hassle her about it.

As for her part, Tory was trying not to think too much about the recent chain of events, other than to fervently hope that Jazz would recover, and soon. Maybe, just maybe, Jazz's injury had resulted from an accident. Maybe the letter and the phone call and the slashed tires were Emmett Delgado's last efforts to make her life miserable before he threw in the towel and admitted he was licked by his alcohol addiction. Or maybe the treatment facility was just a story fabricated by Emmett to allow him to engage in extracurricular activities without being hampered by his job duties. Or maybe Harold Kemp's ineffective attempt at being devious was just a cover up for a warped criminal mind.

All in all there were too many maybes, on a day when there were other pressing realities to deal with: number one, finish the stadium columns evaluation by the deadline. Without Jazz.

After looking at the film brought in from the trailer at the stadium construction site, Tory and her senior engineering technician decided to proceed with checking X-rays of the three columns that Jazz had finished against the design drawings. There were also multiple shots of the column that Jazz had been having problems with, and none of them showed that he had reached a resolution to the puzzling phenomena that he had described to Tory. "Leave it for now," she told her technician. "We're shorthanded as it is. These three columns look good. Let's finish up the analysis on them so we'll have something definitive to say about them. I'll go out on site later today and take a look at the last column myself and decide what we're going to do about it."

Having dispensed with that immediate problem, Tory barricaded herself in her office to deal with the multiple crises that seemed to arise whenever the office was shorthanded. There were inspections to reschedule, reports that Jazz had been working on to complete, and clients to contact to tell them that their work would be delayed. Sylvia guarded Tory's door zealously, and Alvarez would have found her a force to reckon with had he not spoken the magic words.

"Excuse me, I'm Detective Alvarez." Since he was technically out of his jurisdiction, he saw no point in going into details about just which police department he belonged to. "I'm here to talk to Victoria Travers. Is she in?" That was a rhetorical question, for he had seen the white RX that he remembered from the precast yard parked outside the office.

"Oh, I am so glad to see you," Sylvia said jubilantly, surprising Alvarez immensely. And her joy to see him didn't stop there. "I couldn't believe that they were going to make Tory wait until tomorrow until she could talk to you. Yes, she's in. Let me tell her that you're here. I know that once she tells you about everything that's happened, we'll have a chance to get things straightened out. You just don't know how awful this has been for everyone, especially Tory. You wait right there; I'll be right back."

After this effusive greeting, Alvarez had no intention of going anywhere. He didn't have long to wait.

Tory had followed a smiling and bubbling Sylvia to where Alvarez sat, but she herself radiated only icy civility. "Detective Alvarez. Lonnie Harper called and told me that you were in town. My secretary says that you are here to speak to me. She thinks you're with the University Police. Is trading on mistaken identities a habit of yours? Maybe a holdover from a previous profession?"

There was certainly no mistaking *her* identity. Alvarez smiled his slow, wide smile. "Ms. Travers," he said formally. "I appreciate you fitting me into your busy schedule."

Tory looked at him long and hard. "Let's just get it over with. My office is down the hall."

Alvarez stepped past Sylvia, who looked confused. She decided to stay with her sunny nature. "I just know you're going to be able to help us," she reassured him as he walked past.

He followed Tory into her office, noting his original judgment about her legs hadn't been wrong. The skirt today was black and straight, but with a nicely placed six-inch slit in the back. He sat down without being asked. No, he hadn't been mistaken in his conclusion that she was physically capable of killing Hartman. Those eyes were every bit as blue as he remembered them, even if they did have dark circles underneath them. She looked through those eyes now like she might be considering strangling him. He wondered if he could count on the secretary to come to his rescue, and if her nails were registered as lethal weapons.

"You look stressed out, and your secretary says things have been terrible. What the hell is going on here?"

Tory perched herself on the edge of her desk.

Body language for a short conversation, thought Alvarez. Think again, lady.

"My secretary thinks you're someone else. Whatever she was talking about is of no concern to you. There's only one reason why I'm talking to you right now: I want to hear if you've recovered the precast yard records, or if you've decided to give me access to whatever is remaining in the laboratory."

"Actually," said Alvarez easily, "I've come here to talk about some other records." He handed Tory the file labeled with her name, which she looked at quickly, and laid on the desk beside her without a second glance. She was still a cool one when she wasn't being hot-headed. "You've got a history of arrests, Ms. Travers."

"The latest of which is over eighteen years old, Detective. And I'm also sure that you're aware that I was never convicted on any of the charges."

"Money and position buy all kinds of things, don't they, Ms. Travers?" He wondered if she would rise to that bait, but he was disappointed.

"Exactly what are you here for?" she countered. "If you haven't come to give me what I've asked for, I don't see where there is anything for us to discuss."

Since the file didn't seem to shake her, Alvarez decided to use another prop. He pulled out a souvenir from the abortion clinic investigation. He handed her a large campaign button which read **WE NEED CIG, NOT CIA**. "What do you know about this?"

She also gave it a passing glance before placing it on top of the unopened file. "Absolutely nothing. Is this some sort of guessing game?"

"It may be some sort of game, all right, but if so, it's a lot more serious than a guessing game. CIG stands for Christians in Government. It's a powerful pro-life religious group, of which your old friend Jim Barkley is an important member. It seems like he's managed to put his past behind him and go on to bigger and better things since his little fling with you. There are sources in Florida which predict he'll be the next governor of that state."

"So I've heard," said Tory evenly.

"Did you know that he's due to speak in El Paso in two weeks for a CIG conference?"

"I don't exactly keep in contact with him." The tone was the same one she had used when she invited him into her office.

"You mean you haven't already run out and bought your

ticket for a front row seat for his appearance?" She regarded him in stony silence, refusing to answer, so he decided to try the more direct approach. "When was the last time that you heard from him?"

"More than eighteen years ago."

"Well, I don't profess to know what kind of guy Barkley was when you were keeping company with him, and I really don't have any idea about what kind of guy he is now. But some of these CIG people, they may call themselves Christians, but they're as radical as any group I've ever come across. I imagine that when they have this big conference in El Paso, we'll get some homosexuals and call girls beat up real good, at least a couple of bomb threats at the local abortion clinics, if not actual violence, and maybe a few good old incidents of defacing some synagogues."

"That doesn't have anything to do with me."

"I bet the El Paso press would be awfully interested in the fact that Saint Barkley has an ex-girlfriend just up the road in Las Cruces. And that she was his girlfriend when she was seventeen and Barkley was married."

"That's ancient history."

"Maybe so, Ms. Travers, but if that's the case, I find it all rather interesting ancient history. How do you suppose Barkley managed to square his past association with you with all his Christian constituents?"

"It was obviously a case of a wild and immoral girl lewdly tempting him beyond the endurance of human resistance to worldly pleasures," Tory snapped.

Alvarez studied her for a moment. "Maybe," he said non-committally. "I wouldn't know about that."

"Other than a perverse interest in my affairs, what possible connection does any of this have with your investigation of the murder of Bill Hartman?"

"The fact that this file was found in Hartman's briefcase," replied Alvarez, and had the satisfaction of seeing her blink in surprise. "Any revisions you want to make to your story about your meeting with Hartman last Friday?" he asked harshly. Come on, lady, he thought. Either lose your temper and start yelling things at me that I can use, or break down and confess. I can take it either way. But she didn't do either. Instead, she sighed. What a letdown.

"Everything I told you about our meeting was true."

"*Por cierto*, I never said it wasn't. But I get the feeling that you may have left out a few parts. People do that sometimes."

"Hartman did some political freelance writing."

"So tell me something that I don't know."

"He asked me for an interview."

"And you said?"

"No."

"I wonder how I knew that was going to be the answer. So did you kill Billy Hartman so he would never write that article, Ms. Travers? The one that he would have written even without the interview?"

"You appear to be extremely dense every time I talk with you. Hasn't it occurred to you that it would be senseless to kill someone to suppress a story that had already made the national wire services?"

"My partner's the smart one, Ms. Travers. And he did say something along those lines. But some of us that are dense make up for it in tenacity. And this file in Hartman's briefcase seems like a hell of a coincidence."

"So what does your tenacity tell you that the connection is?"

"That's just the problem," answered Alvarez plaintively. "I can't figure that out. But when I do, I'll be sure that I get to be the first one to let you know." He decided to switch tracks. "When I talked to your friend Lonnie Harper, he wasn't real sure why you didn't go to the pool party at the Hilton or to the Alumni Association dinner on Sunday. He thinks it had to do with some unpleasantness that occurred at a party on Saturday. But more to the point, Mr. Harper can't really say where you were on Sunday. Can anyone else?"

"I'd like you to leave my office now, Detective Alvarez. If you plan on talking with me again, expect to have my lawyer present."

There must be something wrong with his technique today, Alvarez reflected. He just couldn't seem to goad her into losing her temper. He could tell that she was angry, but somehow she almost seemed like she was too distracted by something else to give this conversation her whole attention. Well, he decided to give it one more shot.

He picked up the file and the campaign button. "For some reason, I get the feeling that there's something going on around here that you're not telling me about. The last time I saw you, you got to do the big dramatic threat scene. It's only reasonable that turnabout is fair play. If I find out that you're withholding information from me, I'll slap an obstruction of justice charge on you so fast it will make your head spin. As far as I can tell, there's no rich Daddy around these parts to keep your classy little ass out of trouble. *Comprende?*"

Her eyes narrowed and Alvarez could see that she was holding on to the edge of her desk where she was still perched. But still she didn't say anything, just sat tight and waited for him to leave.

He was barely into the hall on his way to bid Sylvia a fond farewell when he heard Tory's office door slam, and that made him feel a lot better.

It was a few minutes after nine when Alvarez pulled out of Horizon House. This had been Anna's home for the last ten years, and it had worked out better than Alvarez had ever dared hope. For a couple of years after their mother had died, Anna had lived with him. But as time went on, it became increasingly apparent that Anna was terribly lonely for more company than her brother was able to give her, consumed at the time with keeping his job commitments and completing his degree at the University in El Paso. And, if he were perfectly honest about the situation, Alvarez had to admit that having Anna live with him put a damper on his love life, which tended to be active for brief, but intense, periods.

So, between the two of them, they had set about finding Anna a place to live. Alvarez had initially resisted the idea of placing her in any type of institutional home, but there were really few alternatives. Anna functioned near a fourth grade level, and while there were many things that she could do, living alone was not one of them. Finally, they had settled on Horizon House. Run by a Catholic women's group, it was small, the residents were mainly of Mexican-American descent, and the house's charter encouraged the residents to seek outside work. This was a boon economically to the families of those who lived at the house, and to the self-esteem of the residents themselves. For eight of the ten years that she had lived there, Anna had worked part-time at the city library, first doing filing, and now doing some computer data entry.

At first, Alvarez had been worried that the distance would prevent him from seeing Anna as often as they were used to; there had been a period of adjustment. But Anna had settled in happily, and over the years he had come to realize that, just like anyone else, on the whole Anna preferred the company of those who were generally like her. He saw her routinely at least twice a month. Nothing would lessen the bond between them, but also nothing would refute the statement that over the years they had each developed their own, very separate lives. And that was as it should be, he reflected. It was certainly how it would have been had Anna not suffered from mild retardation.

Before making the turn onto the freeway, Alvarez spotted a lighted phone booth in the parking lot of the McDonald's where he had talked to Lonnie Harper earlier that morning. He glanced at his watch and pulled over. Though he would never have admitted it to Faulkner, he did attempt to adhere to certain rules in deference to Scott's status as a family man. One of these rules was never to call his partner after 10 PM unless it was an emergency. He had already established that it was an easy forty-five minutes from New Mexico State University to the precast yard in Anapra, but to get to his own house from where he was now would take at least an hour. So, if he was going to check up on Faulkner's progress with their case, he would have to do it now.

The baby was crying in the background when Scott answered, something that always slightly disconcerted Alvarez. "It's David. Can you talk now? I wanted to give you a call before I left Las Cruces, just to make sure you hadn't discovered any loose ends that I should check out while I'm here."

"Yeah, I can talk now. How was Anna? Did you wish her happy birthday for me?" Faulkner's stutter always underwent a marked decrease when he was at home, except when his in-laws were in close proximity. Maybe he'd put them to bed for the evening.

"Anna's fine, and I wished her happy birthday for you. So how have you been making out on your own, partner?"

"It's been rough, but somehow I made it through the d-day without you. I talked to Lester. He sticks to his original story. He was at the pool party from beginning to end; after the party was over at five he went up to his daughter's room to try to c-c-convince her to go to dinner with him at University. It was a no go. So he s-sat and talked to her and they had a drink together. He left her room about six-thirty and showed up at the University at seven."

"Pretty ironclad. Did you talk to the daughter?"

"She confirms everything Lester says, and then s-some. Says she was napping when he came up to her room and woke her up. He pointed out that it was only a little after five p.m. and she shouldn't be sleeping her life away. Then, when he left her room at six-thirty, he pointed out the time again to tell her that she still had plenty of time to get ready to go with him over to the University at seven."

"So she knows exactly when he got there and exactly when he left. Sounds too detailed to me for someone who's sleeping their life away. Let's keep in mind that the witness in question is this guy's daughter."

"I know. But I think she's telling the t-truth. I asked her if she would be willing to take a lie detector test, and she never even hesitated. She just agreed. She didn't even get pissed off, like most people would. I get the feeling that she's real concerned about her husband's absence, and being questioned by the p-police as to her father's whereabouts last Sunday is really secondary t-to that."

"Oh yes, the ever-absent Kent Colliney. What's the status on him?"

"The same as before. Zip. But this time around Lester did have some more candid things to say about his son-in-law. Like the fact that he never got along with Hartman."

"That's news to me. I thought the one he didn't get along with was his wife."

"Yeah. Kind of interesting, this story about animosity between Colliney and Hartman coming up now. Almost like

Lester is trying to f-finger the guy. Maybe he wants to get even with him for putting his daughter through such misery."

"Maybe. Then again, maybe it's true. Anyone at the plant have anything to say about it?"

"Not so far. Nobody agrees or disagrees. The problem is, except for Hartman, Colliney, and Lester, most everyone else is out in the yard all d-day, not in the office."

"What about the secretary?"

"She's new. She's only been working for the yard for a couple of weeks."

"So find the old secretary."

"Give me a break, David. You've been gone less than twelve hours, you know. The old secretary is not so old. She quit her job to get married, and from what I've been able to f-find out, she's currently on her honeymoon in Galveston. For some reason she didn't leave a phone number where she can be reached."

"That's civilians for you. Never around to help the police when we need it."

"T-tell me about it. The only other thing worth mentioning is that I'm almost positive the yard uses illegal alien labor when they can get by with it, but I haven't gotten anyone to outright admit to it, yet. And from what I can tell, that's standard operating procedure for that type of outfit, located where it is. And what have you been doing besides eating birthday cake?"

"I've been busy documenting Lester's alibi for him in case his daughter gets mad at him and refuses to cooperate.

I've met with the Director of Facilities and Planning up here and a guy named Lonnie Harper. I also talked on the phone with the stadium contractor, Harold Kemp. All three can vouch for Lester's presence at the pool party, although no one seems to be able to remember if he was there for the whole thing. He was definitely there when it kicked off, and Kemp seems to remember seeing him around four, when he himself had to leave. Kemp also verifies that Lester arrived at the University dinner on Sunday evening, around seven."

"All he needs is about an hour and a half, if you cut it to the bone."

"Yeah. That would be the tightest someone could make it from here. Say he leaves at four. You still have the daughter specifically saying he was in her room at five p.m. Maybe she could have been mistaken about how long he stayed."

"She's emphatic that he stayed for an hour and a half. Even if she's off some, he would have had to leave her room at five-thirty, not six-thirty like she said."

"I know. It's a long shot. But something about Lester and his absent son-in-law smells funny. Take her over it one more time tomorrow. I want everything they did during that period tied to a specific time. If she starts giving you too much detail, maybe it'll turn out to be a setup."

"Okay, but I don't think you'll get anything d-d-different. I get the feeling that Mrs. Colliney doesn't even really much c-care at this point whether we believe her or not. By the way, you haven't told me anything about Victoria Travers."

"She was real cool today. No fireworks or threats or anything like that, other than the standard 'next time I'll have my lawyer' line. She did admit that Hartman asked to interview her, but then she pulled your line about what would be the point in trying to cover up something that got newspaper coverage in the past. But I get the feeling that there's something real strange going on over at her office. The secretary was so happy to see me when I flashed my badge that I thought she was going to kiss my feet."

"So then what happened?"

"Did she kiss my feet? No, the boss lady was there, and I don't think it would have taken me having very many words with the secretary to have gotten my ass kicked out. I was firmly asked to leave as it was."

"I guess some of us have a way with women and some of us don't."

"And I'm such a great detective I can figure out which is which. I'm going to stop by the famous stadium site and take a look at these poles that are so damn important to our lady engineer."

"Columns. While you're at it, why don't you see how long it takes you to get from there to the precast yard if you really p-pull out all the stops?"

"Yeah, and will you pay my ticket when I get pulled over?"

"Depends on whether it's the New Mexico or Texas highway patrol that stops you. I don't like f-funding out-of-state police officers. In any case, you'll never know 'til you try it, will you?"

==========

It hadn't been necessary to ask for directions to the stadium construction site, because the cleared site with the standing columns was plainly visible from the freeway approaching Las Cruces. It was a little more difficult to actually get there, with having to negotiate the many one-way and closed-off streets that were becoming common to all campuses trying to control their motor vehicle traffic. By the time Alvarez pulled up to the edge of the site, it was dark, and he was disappointed not to be able to see the construction as well as he would have wished. This was one of the few overcast evenings of the summer, and that made as much as an hour's difference between dusk and dark.

Alvarez was ready to hop out of his car and take a closer look, when he noticed the white RX parked in front of the site trailer labeled Travers Testing and Engineering Company. Light shown from the windows, and a strong outside light illuminated the front door.

Alvarez began having an argument with himself. One part arrogantly informed him that it was a free country, and that he was entitled to have a look at a construction site if he was so inclined. The other part soberly informed him that he was really out of his jurisdiction, and that his presence could be construed as harassment. He never had to resolve the argument, because at the point of decision, Tory came out of the trailer. Alvarez noticed that she didn't turn off either the inside or outside lights, a fact he put down to routine security procedure: a lighted trailer was much less likely to be vandalized than an unlighted one.

She had obviously been home to change since his conversation with her that morning. Now she was wearing jeans, a T-shirt, and tennis shoes. She was plainly illuminated where she stood in front of the door, juggling a bunch of papers and apparently having some trouble with the lock. Alvarez watched her unobserved, sitting in the darkness in his car. He professionally noted for the third time that she was a damn good-looking woman.

He heard the shot a split second before he saw Tory drop the papers she was carrying and duck to the ground in front of the trailer door. He was wondering if she was hit even while his hand was automatically retrieving his gun from the glove compartment. There was one second required to release the safety and another second required to disconnect the dome light in his car, and during this time he heard two more shots. Then he was outside, gun in hand, searching for the source of the shots.

Out of the corner of his eye he saw Tory move, reaching her arm up to the door knob and flinging it open. Then she was inside, and almost immediately the trailer lights went off. Smart lady, he thought, in spite of the current distractions. And then he heard the sound of a car in the distance, and he sensed, he knew, that the danger was over as suddenly as it had begun.

Nothing like a little gunfire to get an adrenaline rush, he thought as he put the safety back on his gun and stuck it in the back waistband of his pants. It was too dark to hope to catch sight of the retreating vehicle, which Alvarez assumed had been parked some distance away. The shots had sounded like a rifle, and considering the lighting on the front door where Tory had been standing, it wouldn't have even been necessary to use a night scope to get a good shot.

He was pretty sure from the way Tory had moved that she hadn't been hit. He wondered if the assailant had been a nervous shot, or if the bullets had missed their mark intentionally.

Now to rescue the damsel in distress, he thought, walking to the trailer door. Maybe gratitude will finally result in some straight answers.

"Ms. Travers? Are you okay? It's David Alvarez." No answer. She's probably shaking under a table somewhere, he thought to himself. He opened the trailer door and and stepped inside, groping for the light switch. "Ms. Travers? Tory? You can come out now. Everything is okay."

And then he switched on the light and stopped trying to reassure her. It didn't seem to be really appropriate. Tory Travers was standing across the room from him, so pale that her eyes looked bluer than ever. But she was holding a .38 caliber snub-nosed Smith and Wesson in a no-nonsense two-handed grip.

And it was pointed approximately two inches above his belt buckle.

CHAPTER EIGHT: TEMPORARY TRUCE

There were things that one got used to in police work, and things that one never got used to. Alvarez had never gotten used to having a gun pointed at him at close range. It had happened about ten times in his career, and at each incident it was as if time stood still and his stomach tried to exit his body and crawl away. To avoid freezing up with fear in the situation, he had always said the first thing that came into his head, and this time was no exception.

"I hope you have a license for that gun, or you're going to be in big trouble."

Her very blue, very wide eyes got even wider. "I can't believe this," she said. "You're supposed to be an officer of the law, and you're telling me that I have to have a license for this gun. As long as it's not carried concealed, I don't have to have any license for this gun. And it's not concealed, in case you've been too busy to notice."

He noted with disappointment that even though her voice shook slightly, her hands, grasping the gun in a regulation two-handed grip, did not. "In any case, you can get in a lot of trouble pulling a gun on a police officer, whether it's licensed or not."

"Not if the police officer has been caught shooting at innocent people."

In a flash he understood what had happened. Dropping to the ground after the first shot, she had been facing in his direction and his motion in getting out of the car must have attracted her attention. Either before or after she got back in the trailer, she must have seen him with his gun drawn. He cursed his stupidity in stepping inside the dark trailer, even while he relaxed slightly. It didn't seem quite so likely that she was going to shoot him in cold blood. Although he wasn't prepared to completely rule out the possibility.

"Listen, lady. I had just pulled up here in my car to take a look at these cement—I mean concrete—columns you go around making such a big deal about. I saw you come out of the trailer and heard someone take a shot at you. It was a rifle shot, and it came from up on the bluff. So I got my gun and got out of the car to help. I'm a police officer. What the hell do you expect me to do in a situation like that?"

"I don't believe you," she said flatly. "Ever since I first met you, you've been standing in the way of everything I need to do. Then I find out you've been digging into my past. You talk to my friends about me, you show up at my office, and then you show up on my construction site. I think you're some kind of psychotic or something. Maybe you're not really a detective after all. Maybe you're just impersonating a police officer. And not doing such a good job. Police officers are supposed to be more cooperative than you are."

In spite of being held at gunpoint, he couldn't resist entering the debate. "Give me a break. Talk about being uncooperative. There's something going on around here and everywhere I look I see indications that you're in the damn middle of it. You have a past that should be written up in a drug store novel. You're jumpy, and everyone in your office looks jumpy. Your secretary damn near kissed my feet when she found out I was a detective. And what do you have to say about all this? 'No comment.' So I show up out here and someone is taking potshots at you. And I'm willing to bet

your response is still 'No comment.' For uncooperative individual of the year, you take the prize."

The gun had never wavered during this speech, and neither did her gaze. Some detached part of his mind noted
that the front of her T-shirt said I'M AN ENGINEER ... WHAT'S
YOUR PROBLEM? Where was he supposed to start?

"You're trying to confuse me," she said.

"From what I can see, you're confused already. Normal
people don't stand around pointing a gun at a police officer—
have you thought of that? Just what do you plan to do now?"

"Call the University Police."

At that point he forgot to be afraid. "Oh, God," he said.
"Not those turkeys. Look, why don't you just go ahead and
shoot me? I think I'd prefer it to having to explain to some
campus cop how you managed to hold me at gunpoint."

The undisguised exasperation in his voice took her aback,
and he thought he saw her lower the gun a few millimeters.
He decided to press his advantage. "Listen, this is so depress-
ing that I'm going to have to sit down." He pointed to a
chair beside him. "If you have to shoot me because of that,
go ahead." He took a deep breath and sat down. No shot. So
far, so good.

"Look," he continued conversationally. "Before you call
the campus boys in blue, you might want to consider what
I've said. Regardless of what you may think, I am a damn
good detective. If we sit down and talk about this together,
we may be able to figure a few things out. Whereas if you
call the University Police, you're going to be asked a lot of

questions, and from what I know of you during our short but intense acquaintance, you're not too fond of questions."

It wasn't his imagination—she was actually starting to look a little undecided. "Come on, Tory," he said, using her first name impulsively, "give it a shot. Wait, I don't mean that literally. At least I already know all about your dirty laundry, so you won't have to go through it twice. I know it's pretty confusing to be shot at, but if you think it through you'll realize that I don't have any reason to be the one shooting at you."

There wasn't any more progress in the lowering of the gun, so he decided to try a little flattery. "If you think I'm stalking you or something farfetched like that, let me assure you my efforts are all just part of my job. You are a damn attractive woman, which could put another light on me showing up here tonight, but I think it's only fair to tell you that I prefer women of *La Raza*. So fair skin and blue eyes rule you out. Not to mention that your personality isn't the most appealing one that I've come across ..."

This informal line of reasoning didn't have the desired effect, either. If anything, it had made her look even more determined and grim. And the gun had definitely not dropped any lower. "Everything you're saying may be true," replied Tory evenly. "You've only made one small miscalculation: I have you exactly where I've wanted you since the first time I met you and had to listen to your bullshit."

Alvarez couldn't think of an appropriate reply. Before he could come up with one she continued. "But I can't argue that what you say makes sense, and as much as I'm tempted to go ahead and shoot you, at least in the foot or something, I doubt it would improve my situation. Facts are facts," she said. She lowered the gun and slumped dejectedly against the wall.

There were a few more moments of silence while they eyed each other warily. Then she said flatly, "I feel like I'm going to throw up." Alvarez took that as a positive sign that he was out of danger.

"That's probably because you're about to faint," he said helpfully. "It hits you like that sometimes—the nausea first, then the dizziness, then you faint."

The word faint had brought her head up defiantly. "Are you so arrogant that you're really going to tell me how I feel?"

"That's how I feel every time someone shoots at me or holds a gun on me," he replied, matter of factly. "Why do you think I had to sit down just now?"

She was really looking pale now. It took her a moment to digest this. "Oh," she finally said, looking like she was about to keel over any moment.

"I would suggest that you sit down, to begin with," he said, carefully. "I'll be glad to try to help you. But I would appreciate it if you would put your gun down first. All the way down."

"Oh," she said again, looking at the gun in her hand like she had never seen it before. Obviously deciding not to stand on ceremony, she kind of slid down the wall to the floor, sitting in a crumpled pile before him. She put the gun deliberately down on the floor beside her and looked at him. "How's that?" Her pale face had taken on a distinct green tinge.

"Pretty good." First things first, he thought, standing up and stepping over to her. He gingerly picked up her gun and put it on safety and stuck it in his waistband along with his. When he lowered the hammer he noted that it was not a hair-trigger action, the worst of all policemen's fantasies.

"Now put your head between your knees." She half-heartedly complied. "All the way between your knees," he directed. He bent over to press her neck farther down, and he could see the pale sheen of perspiration where her hair parted on either side at the nape of her neck, falling like a dark curtain on each side of her face. It wasn't his imagination—he could smell her, and she smelled good, a combination of fresh-out-of-the-shower smell and some light perfume. Maybe he should pat her down to make sure she didn't have another weapon on her ... Stop it, he commanded himself. To be turned on by someone who had just been holding him at gunpoint was not a fetish he wanted to develop. If this kept up, he might as well transfer to Vice. All the lines for those guys had blurred a long time ago.

"Where's a bathroom?" he asked. Without even trying to reply or lift her head, Tory gestured vaguely to the right, and following her direction he found the bathroom. He wet a paper towel with cool water, and returned to place it on the back of her neck. And then he sat back down in the chair to wait.

"So how come you don't feel like this?" she asked in a muffled voice, still not raising her head.

"Because I got over it watching you," he answered. "Feel any better?"

Instead of answering, she lifted her head to look at him with those big blue eyes and ask her own question. "Did you really mean what you said about talking this over without calling the University Police?"

"Not really," he said frankly. "I was willing to say anything to get you to put down that damned gun. You scared the hell out of me."

She continued to sit motionless, looking exceedingly dismal. After a few minutes, he began to feel distinctly uncomfortable. "Oh, all right. I'll really be going out on a limb, but I guess this could go unreported for a little while. The fact that you didn't shoot me is definitely in your favor." She looked up at him hopefully. "But don't get any ideas," he said quickly. "I'm only willing to go along with this on one condition—that you answer all my questions, and you answer them truthfully." She nodded her head too quickly. "And you tell me anything you know about that might have a bearing on all of this, whether I ask the right question or not," he added, just to be safe. "You got that?"

After a longer pause, she nodded again. "We have to think of somewhere to go," she said. "I don't want to be seen with you."

"You don't mince words, do you?"

She looked at him as if that were a senseless question, and simply said, "No."

"Are we concerned about word of this meeting getting back to Big Lonnie Harper?" he asked. Either he couldn't break the habit of baiting her, or he wanted to see what her reaction would be. He didn't stop to analyze which prompted his question.

That seemed to shake her out of her temporary mental stupor. "No, 'we' aren't concerned about that," she answered contemptuously. "Lonnie's taken my son out of town on a fishing trip. If you've been talking to people around here, they know you're a detective. If we're going to try to figure this out, it's not going to help if someone involved sees us together. *Comprende*, Detective Alvarez? Think your ego can handle it?"

"Yeah, I *comprende*. How about your place?" Even as he said the words, he regretted them, especially in light of what she had said about her son being out of town. Come on, Alvarez, he told himself, pull yourself together. Your sense of style is rapidly going down the toilet.

"No." She dismissed his suggestion out of hand, and this time he didn't question her reasoning. She looked at him contemplatively for a moment, and then said, obviously pleased with her decision, "I know just the place." She stood up, taking him by surprise. It was hard to believe that just a few minutes ago she had been crumpled like a rag doll on the floor, for now she was impatient to be off. "You can follow me in your car," she said. "But first I have to make a phone call."

She didn't move toward the phone, though, and it took him a few moments to realize that she was actually waiting for him to offer her some privacy. "No way, lady. This is the end of secrets between us. You want to make a phone call, you do it here and now." And he leaned back in his chair as if he meant to remain planted there all night.

She didn't like it, but she didn't argue, which he considered substantial progress. It was always amazing how an episode with gunshots could bond two individuals together, he reflected, whether they had anything else in common or not. She walked over to the desk beside his chair and dialed a number. He noted that it wasn't one she had to look up. "Intensive care, please. I'm calling to ask about the condition of Jesus Rodriguez." There was a long wait, and then she simply said thank you and hung up. Whatever the information was that she had gotten over the phone, she certainly didn't look happy about it.

"The only reason I'm not asking you about that interesting little phone call is because I'm assuming it will be covered in the little heart-to-heart conversation that we're about to have," he said, still not moving from his chair.

Ignoring his statements still seemed to be an ingrained habit of hers. She held out her hand. "I want my gun back."

He stood up. "Not so fast. We go. We talk. And then, maybe, you get your gun back." She wasn't happy about it, but after a moment she nodded acquiescence, and turned to go. "And one more thing." She turned back to look at him. "I go out the door first," he said.

She was not impressed. She sketched a little bow. "After you, Mr. Machismo."

If he caught a bullet meant for this lady, he was going to be damned pissed about it.

==========

He followed her little white RX to Mesilla, through the lighted plaza, and down the couple of blocks of dark narrow street that brought them to El Palacio Bar. He pulled up behind her and checked out their destination. Either the place was deserted, or most of the clientele came on foot. After a moment of consideration, he put Tory's gun in his glove compartment, but stuck his back in his waistband. He grabbed a light windbreaker from the back seat and shrugged it on to cover the gun.

She had stepped up to his car impatiently while he was doing this. She tapped on his windshield. "Let's go," she said. "Don't tell me you're struck with 'carjones'?"

He stepped out of his car. "'Carjones'? What's that?"

"Having balls only when you're in a car."

He couldn't really think of a reply, although it was a good enough line that he filed it away for future use. He followed her through the door into the adobe structure.

The air was so thick with smoke that the whole room appeared to be encompassed in a hazy cloud. Mexican music played in the background. There were no booths, and no bar with swivel bar stools. Instead, there was a decrepit-looking chest-high counter running the width of one side of the room. Its function appeared to be merely to separate the liquor from the patrons, for there were no stools in front of it. The rest of the room was crowded with a variety of makeshift tables, many of them card tables, and mismatched chairs.

The clientele were as assorted as the furniture. A group of young-looking kids, dressed in the latest street attire, were gathered around the three pinball machines which stood in one corner. Apparently Space Invaders had not yet invaded El Palacio. Several middle-aged, Mexican-American men, dressed in the jeans and T-shirts of the laboring trades, were scattered in small groups. There was a group of old people in the middle of the room, both men and women, who had been talking earnestly in Spanish when Alvarez and Tory walked in. All conversation ceased as they entered the room, and Alvarez felt all the eyes in the place focused on them. He instinctively wondered how many of them made him when he walked in the door.

Tory never hesitated, making her way up to the bar as if the sudden silence had nothing to do with their entry. As she waited there, Alvarez stood at her elbow and murmured, "I wish you wouldn't go out of your way to impress me like this."

She didn't deign to answer him, but focused her attention on the old woman behind the bar who, apparently for lack of another possible candidate, was the bartender. "*Yo quiero dos cervezas, por favor,*" said Tory in flawless Spanish. She turned to Alvarez. "I guess I was supposed to ask if you're on duty. If you are, don't worry, I can drink them both." Alvarez had had court dates that had been a better time than this.

The old woman behind the bar slowly and deliberately picked up two glasses and filled them with beer from a tap somewhere below the line of vision. Alvarez doubted that this setting would ever make it into a beer commercial, for the generic request for beer seemed to be all that was required. He wondered if there was anything like a brand name associated with the beverage going in the glasses. The two drinks were placed on the counter, and he had his money clip out, faster than Tory could dig any money out of her jeans. He noticed she didn't carry a purse, but maybe makeup and breath freshener were not high up on her list of priorities right now.

She fidgeted like she didn't know quite what to do when he paid for the drinks. "Tough, huh?" he asked her while the old woman was getting change.

"What?" She didn't turn to look at him.

"The protocol for this meeting isn't exactly described in Miss Manners. Why this place?"

"Why not?"

"Is it because you think I'll fit in here better than some other place? Boy, do I feel at ease, or what? It's too bad I left my switchblade at home tonight."

Now she turned to look at him. "Do you have a chip on your shoulder or something? Let me make this clear. The fact that I can't stand you has nothing to do with some racial bias you seem to keep implying. It has everything to do with you specifically. I picked this place because I can't think of anyone involved in this whole business who would be here tonight. And I thought you'd have a chance to meet some nice women of *La Raza*," she added as a sarcastic afterthought, and picked up her beer.

Alvarez collected his change and gave the old woman tending bar his most dazzling smile. After a moment, she returned it in kind, but without the benefit of any teeth. He picked up his beer and followed Tory, who was threading her way through the room toward the most deserted corner area. He didn't like the heavy silence that still lingered in the room, and he wondered if push came to shove if he could count on the old woman to cheer for him in a bar fight. He'd already risked taking a bullet for this broad, and he wasn't too enthused about getting into a barroom brawl just because she had a penchant for going where she didn't belong.

But then one of the laborers who was watching them called out, "*Qué pasa, Señora Travers?*" and she answered "*No mucho, Ricardo. Como está Rosa? Y usted?*" They exchanged a few more casual pleasantries, and suddenly everyone else was engaged in their previous conversations. The ominous silence was over as quickly as it had begun.

In spite of himself, Alvarez was impressed, not to mention relieved. He sat down in a folding chair at the table Tory had selected, and looked at her. "How do you do it?" he asked.

"What?"

"Come from the beaches of Florida, privileged and pampered, and manage to fit in here?"

She drank deeply from her beer before answering. "It wasn't really so hard," she said. "Contrary to popular opinion, Florida is not all beaches. A lot of it is ranching country, just like here, only green instead of desert. There are cowboys and horses and cattle, and a lot of Spanish-speaking people, many of them from Cuba. The dialect and the slang are different, but the language is the same. I grew up around Ocala. That's where Secretariat is from."

He shook his head. "The famous racehorse," she explained. "Anyhow, my parents owned a horse ranch there. My father still does, and that's where I grew up. So it wasn't exactly like I hopped off a sailboat and arrived here carrying a surf board."

"No, that's certainly not how you arrived, from how I hear it."

"If you're referring to the fact that I left an unpleasant situation behind me when I came to New Mexico, it's really not necessary to go over all of that again. It's not my past that's the problem, it's my present." She drank some more beer.

"I'll decide what's necessary to discuss and what isn't. I always tend to think it's rather important when somebody does a whole identity change, name and everything."

"Don't most women you know change their name when they get married?"

"Not most women like you. And it wasn't just your last name. You also changed the name you went by when you got here. Don't tell me that wasn't part of your plan?"

Tory sighed and shook her head. "It's just incredible how the people who think they've researched everything about me never get their stories right. Otherwise my life would have turned out a lot different." Alvarez thought that was a strange thing to say, but if she was actually going to talk to him, he didn't want to interrupt the flow. "If your facts are really all that complete," she continued, "they'll show that my freshman year my roommate was Vicky Costa and one of my suitemates was Vicky Alonzo. We drew straws, and one of us stayed Vicky, one of us became Victoria, and one of us became Tory. Think you can figure out which was which?"

"Everything you tell me turns out to be so damned farfetched. Three out of four girls assigned to a dormitory suite were named Victoria?"

"Do you really think I made this up?"

Alvarez couldn't help himself. "So what was the fourth one named?"

"Vivian." She didn't give any further explanations and looked him straight in the face as she uttered her answer without flinching. Alvarez had to squelch an inappropriate urge to laugh.

"You may be working on some split identity plan for your life, but I need to know about both Vicky and Tory, and any other aliases you might have had in between." She gave a snort of disgust. "Well, that was ladylike. Don't look at me like that. If you'd started giving me complete answers in the beginning, I wouldn't have to worry about asking all the right questions."

"Okay, let me save you some time, so that maybe we can get on to some more important things. I did a lot of wild things as a teenager, things that my parents didn't approve of. I wasn't a very happy kid, and I didn't fit in too well where my family was concerned. Then, when I was a senior in high school, the press discovered I was at a resort with my father's top aide, and that we were spending the weekend together. They had a heyday with it, and the pictures made every newspaper in the state. I was absolutely disgraced. I left home to come here to college, and met my future husband, who happened to be a professor. And he was not a pervert or a child molester, in case that's what you've heard. He happened to be a decent guy who introduced me to engineering, who didn't care about my past, and who believed that I could make something happen in my life besides headlines. Unfortunately, he also happened to have terminal cancer. End of story. Can we go on to more important things now?"

Alvarez was silent for a moment to let her wind down. She had been playing with her empty beer glass during the whole recital, and looked like she would be pleased to throw it at him with the slightest provocation. "Okay, let's go on," he agreed.

She looked nonplussed, having nothing to argue with, and hesitated. "Where should I start?"

"How about with another beer?"

She looked down at the empty glass in surprise. "I don't drink very often," she said.

If you were more experienced in the subject of interrogation techniques, you would never have told me that, Alvarez thought to himself. "Why don't you make an exception for tonight? You're pretty wound up. Getting shot at can do that to you."

"How about you?" She looked at his untouched beer.

"I don't drink on duty."

Tory looked at him in surprise. "You're really on duty? Even now?"

"Oh, lighten up, Tory. Can't you take a joke, lady? I just couldn't resist saying that. One of the fringe benefits of this job is that you get to use so many clichés."

"And I bet you never miss an opportunity."

"I try not to. Listen, bottoms up. We both have something to celebrate tonight." She looked at him quizzically. "We both managed to avoid getting shot." She thought a moment and nodded her head in agreement. He tapped his glass against hers and drained it.

Not wishing to rely on the establishment's table service, he walked back to the bar to order another round. This time the old woman flashed him a toothless smile with no encouragement, and waved away his proffered money clip after she had drawn two more beers. Finally, he thought to himself, I'm on a roll, and with a woman of *La Raza*, at that. He wondered if she was more than twice his age. He winked at his new patroness and walked back to the table to see just how good it was going to be.

Tory decided to start with last Saturday night, when, from her viewpoint, everything had begun to go wrong. Alvarez just sat and listened, letting her words, the story as she saw it, come out naturally and flow over him with its store of new information. Once she got started, she had a lot to say, and in the intensity of the telling, she drank the beer he put in front of her. He matched her drink for drink, and twice more got up to refill their glasses before the storytelling was done. And in the storytelling, she told him a lot about herself and the life that she had built around being an engineer.

She told him about Emmett, and his threats before she slapped him, and his threats after she slapped him. She told him about what a malicious lawsuit could mean to a firm like hers. She told him about Sunday, and how she had spent the day alone in her office, going over her records of the project which Emmett had named in his threat to involve her company in a lawsuit.

She told him her version of the meeting with him at the precast yard on Monday, still warming to the subject of the unfairness of his actions. She told him about her efforts to meet the original schedule for completing the study even without the precast yard records, and about the problems with evaluating one of the four columns under study. She told him about the anonymous threatening letter, pulling it from her pocket to show him. She told him about the slashed tires, the threatening phone call, her conversation with Jack Columbo, and her confusion when she had been told that Emmett had entered a treatment center for alcoholism. She told him about the contractor named Kemp trying in a heavy-handed way to put pressure on her. And last, her face clouded with concern and guilt, she told him about her foreman's injury and why she didn't believe it was an accident.

And then she stopped. It took Alvarez a moment to realize that she was so obsessed with trying to figure out what had happened to her foreman, that for the time being she had forgotten the incident that had resulted in them sitting together in El Palacio bar. She didn't even include being shot at in her list of worries.

"So what do you think?" she asked. He wished that the blue eyes that were focused on him weren't so intently expectant, but he didn't say that.

"I think you didn't kill Bill Hartman," he said instead.

That was worth nothing to her. She shrugged impatiently. "I already knew that. What good is all of this, if you can't tell me anything that I don't already know? I might as well not have talked to you at all."

"It wasn't really your choice," he reminded her. "There was the small matter of bribing me not to notify the campus police about a shooting. Not to mention holding an officer of the law at gunpoint," he added.

She glared at him. "By the way," he said mildly. "I'd like to ask you a few questions about that. Is that gun yours?" She nodded. "And you know how to use it, don't you?"

"Both Carl and Jazz thought it would be a good idea. It's not like I carry it around with me. If there's a site where I'm often working alone at night, I keep it there. That's why it was in the trailer tonight."

He asked the question he had been leading up to. "Why didn't you lock the trailer door behind you when you ran in there?"

"Because," she said evenly, "I figured that if whoever was shooting at me was going to come after me, I'd rather they came in the door where I'd have an even chance to be ready for them, instead of breaking in one of the windows to find me on the floor trying to call the police, who are notoriously slow about showing up at the scene of a crime sometimes."

She was really amazing, he thought to himself. That light skin and the blue eyes were looking more and more attractive to him. He must be getting slightly drunk, he thought. Getting involved with someone who knocked people down at parties, got threatening letters and phone calls, and pulled a gun on you was not his sober idea of fun.

"I didn't mean to insult you."

"What?" He hadn't realized that he had been silent for that long.

"I mean about the police being late to the scene of the crime sometimes."

"Oh, don't worry about it. I've heard lots worse in my time, believe me. Besides, I'm a Texas cop."

"Then why did you ask?"

"Ask about what?"

"Ask about the door to the trailer not being locked when you came in."

Tory looked infuriating sober. Probably the anxiety involved in her discussion of the events of the past few days had accelerated her metabolism of the alcohol, he told himself. "It was just one of many questions that I have for you, Ms. Travers. That was our deal, remember? Not only would we talk, but you would also answer any and all of my questions."

"Okay. You're right, that was our deal. But what's going on? I was Tory until just a few moments ago. Almost everyone calls me Tory unless they call me 'boss' or 'mom.' Or *Señora* Travers, if you want to opt for that. *Señorita* is definitely out. I keep wondering about that, and maybe you can help me with it. Is there a Spanish term for Ms.?"

"I'll opt for Tory," he said hastily, before things could get more complicated than they were already. "Let me get you another beer."

"I don't need another beer."

"Who's in charge of this interview? You may not need another beer, but I need for you to have another one." So he got her another beer and sat down to have her tell the stories that he needed to hear, instead of the stories that she chose to tell.

"Do you sleep with Lonnie Harper?"

"Do I what?"

"You heard the question. Do you sleep with Lonnie Harper?"

"No."

"Why not?"

"What do you mean, why not?"

"I mean, why not? Is he impotent? Is he gay? Or is it that he hasn't asked you?"

"No, no, and no. I don't sleep with him because I choose not to."

"So do you, or did you, sleep with Emmett Delgado before your little falling out?"

"No, I never slept with Emmett Delgado. And before you ask, I never slept with Harold Kemp or Charles

Henderson or Petey Lester or Jazz or my son's Transylvanian Hound, either."

"Transylvanian Hound?"

"It's a rare Hungarian breed."

"Yeah, sure. Is this another privileged background thing? Like the breed of the week?"

"No, it's not the breed of the week. Carl knew someone who raises Hungarian breeds and the guy gave Cody a Transylvanian Hound puppy after Carl died. They're real protective. They're also known as Koppos, and the word cop came from that type of dog."

"You've got to be kidding. Can you take pictures of it?"

"What do you mean, can you take pictures of it? Oh, I get it. That's really cute, Detective. Exactly what business is it of yours who I sleep with and who I don't sleep with?"

"It's my business because with the exception of Bill Hartman's death, all the events that you have described seem to center around you, and you only, Tory," he replied evenly. "If what you've told me is true, even your foreman's accident was just a means of getting at you. And regardless of what they show on TV, good old thwarted love affairs are still one of the biggest motives around for threats and violence."

She just glared at him, silent. "Relax, Tory. I'll take your word for it that you lead a celibate life. I've heard of stranger things, although one doesn't come to mind at the moment. Just as long as we don't get to the point where you blow your credibility by telling me that you never slept with Jim Barkley, either." He was surprised to see the blood drain from her face for the second time that evening. "What is it?"

"Nothing. It's just ... just that this is difficult."

He looked at her for a long moment before deciding not to pursue it. After all, he had a lot of territory he wanted to cover, and the night wasn't getting any younger. "Okay, we'll leave past and present personal relationships alone for the moment. Let's talk about this business of yours. Who might stand to profit from you disappearing temporarily, or, after tonight, permanently?"

"No one."

"Come off it, Tory. When you wanted to get into that lab at the precast yard, you were trying to convince me that your work was more important than a murder investigation. And I know the stadium can't be the only project that you have going. Tell me what you're working on, project by project, and let's see where that leads us."

She started out grudgingly, still angry about the questions that he had asked about her personal life. But it wasn't long before she was talking animatedly, and through her enthusiastic descriptions, he began to see, plainer than she could, a world where reputations, vast sums of money, and even lives could be influenced by the work conducted at Travers Testing and Engineering Company.

First there was the greyhound race track. The track conditions were so important to the outcome of a race that tampering with the consistency of track maintenance could easily determine a winner. Even more detrimental, someone desiring to permanently damage a competitor's dog could theoretically plant clumps of hardened material in the track subsurface, near the starting box where a dog would be running in a relatively predictable portion of the track. The odds were better than even that such an action would result in a greyhound with a shattered leg.

Then there were the materials testing activities. One of the contracts that Tory's company held involved random testing of building materials being used by contractors who were building elementary schools. The test results could be used to justify the rejection of large amounts of materials, which would already have been bought by the contractor. Needless to say, there was not much of a resale market for faulty building materials, and a contractor failing the quality tests stood to lose large sums of money.

There were the construction inspection jobs, of which the University Stadium was one. Tory's inspectors had the authority to recommend shutting down multi-million dollar projects, and if this authority was invoked, the projects would stay shut down until the identified problem was rectified. During this time, the contractor could incur penalties of several hundred dollars per day for not meeting construction schedules. Taken to its extreme, continued inability to meet inspection requirements could result in a contractor being thrown off a job. And at the end of a project, the contractor could not make final pay requests for the money due him until all the inspection criteria had been satisfactorily met.

There were projects involving expert testimony. Tory's company was involved in one of these, concerning the collapse of a parking garage under construction in Albuquerque. Although the collapse had occurred in the early evening hours, when no work crews were present, damage awards of millions of dollars were being contested by the owner, the architect, the structural engineer, the soils engineer, the contractor, their lawyers, and of course, their insurance companies.

And then there was something called professional ethical responsibility, which applied to all the engineering projects that Tory's company worked on. As she explained it, this was a moral responsibility to inform the appropriate officials whenever she or any of her employees became aware of a situation which could constitute an endangerment to the public. This included discovering design deficiencies, determining that a facility did not meet current building codes, or discovering an existing materials problem, such as using asbestos-containing materials. Reporting any of these could result in the virtual destruction of a professional reputation, and the requirement for significant sums to be spent to rectify the problem.

"So if Emmett Delgado is the structural engineer for the stadium project, there's always the chance that you might uncover some mistake of his while you're performing your routine inspection services?" Alvarez asked. She nodded, obviously pleased that he was catching on to the relationships and intertwined responsibilities that she was describing. But nothing unacceptable had been discovered from that end, she assured him, and it was really an unusual occurrence for a significant design error to come to light during inspection. Usually, if there was a problem of any great magnitude, the contractor would become the first to be aware of it. Reputable contractors wanted no part of building something that had not been designed correctly.

When she finished her explanation, he told her that he thought there were quite a few individuals who could have a vested interest in removing her from running her company for a period of time. She doggedly disagreed, stating that her project load was normal for a company the type and size of Travers Testing and Engineering, and that all the problems had started when she began to investigate the stadium columns.

"Are you sure that you're not confusing a technical problem with what's been going on for the last few days?"

"What do you mean?"

"You keep talking about figuring out the reason for these threats and figuring out what the X-rays of that column mean, as if they're connected. That's like assuming that Hartman's death and everything that's happened to you are connected."

"But it must be. Everything that's happened has had to do with that stadium project."

"No, it just looks that way to you because you're in the middle of it. If Delgado is involved, like you suspect he might be, that has nothing directly to do with the stadium. The threats might be related to another project you're working on. Or they might be related to getting you out of the area while Barkley is here. If CIG is behind this in some way, I can guarantee you that they don't give a damn about the stadium and those columns that you're obsessed with. Tell me more about you and Jim Barkley."

She looked at him a long moment in distaste, but she didn't protest again about addressing the subject. She told him in the barest possible detail about her affair with Barkley. What was missing was any emotion in the recitation of the tale, and any explanation about why she was attracted to Barkley in the first place. It was the first time he could remember her talking about something without any strong feelings. But the affair with Barkley had happened a long time ago and had been extremely unpleasant for her, he told himself. Maybe she had managed to purge all the related emotions, and all that was left was a textbook-like version of that episode in her life.

He noticed that she took pains to make a couple of things perfectly clear. One was that she had had no further contact with Barkley since she'd left Florida eighteen years ago. The other was that she had had no further contact with her parents since that time, either. When Alvarez looked at her in surprise, she added that her husband had called her father when their son was born.

"Carl said he was happy to get the news, and wanted to know how I was doing. I think Carl wrote to him from time to time. I don't know; I never asked. By that time there just didn't seem much point trying to talk to him, after everything that had happened and all ..." Her voice trailed away. They sat in silence for a while.

"Is that all?" she finally asked.

"All what?"

"All your questions?"

"Yeah, for now. I'm afraid to ask anything else for fear that we'll uncover some other complication in your life."

She decided to let that go, for she had something more pressing on her mind. "So are you going to report the shooting?"

"Not tonight. Maybe not tomorrow. There're some things I want to look into first. See if I can find out where Delgado is, for one thing. Although, if he's in any kind of authentic treatment center, they may pull patient confidentiality bullshit on me. To protect the patients' anonymity, it's become trendy these days not to release the identity of anyone at these places."

"Can't you get around that?"

"Yeah, but it might take a couple of days."

"I wonder if they have anything on file in the personnel records at Webb ..."

"You let me worry about things like that. The way you request information, you might as well take a sledge hammer with you." He grinned at her. "There's something else, too."

"What?"

Why should he hesitate about announcing a professional decision? "I'm going home with you tonight. If your son and Lonnie are out of town, you're a sitting duck. And I don't want you on my conscience if I don't report this shooting tonight and someone finds you dead in the morning."

She looked at him, considering. "Whether or not Lonnie is in town has nothing to do with me being a sitting duck.

He's not my keeper. But I'll agree to your charming proposition on one condition."

"Lady, you're really not in any position to bargain, but just for grins, what is your one condition?"

"That you give me back my gun before you come home with me so I'll be able to defend my honor if I have to. Or what's left of it."

He looked at her in surprise. And then, for the very first time since he had met her, he saw her really smile. It was an illuminating experience. "Lighten up, detective. Can't you take a joke?" And he saw that in spite of everything, she was beginning to enjoy herself. That in itself would be a good sign, if he weren't the convenient target of her sudden good humor.

He slid a five-dollar bill under his empty beer glass and stood up to go. She looked at him brightly and said, "I really do have one last question."

"What's that?"

"Are you sober enough to drive?"

Shaking his head, he abandoned all thoughts of politely escorting her out of El Palacio, and let her trail behind him as he walked out, giving the old woman behind the bar a two-fingered salute. He didn't try to help her into her car, either, but climbed into his Corvette determined not to lose her little white RX as he followed her home. Some things were just too humiliating to consider living through.

They were greeted by the exuberant Transylvanian Hound, Tango, with which Tory had disavowed having an intimate relationship. Tory pointed out Tango's outstanding watch-dog characteristics, which Alvarez frankly found to be less than impressive, as Tango had taken one look at him and decided that they would be lifelong friends. So Alvarez declined to be convinced that the dog would suffice for protection for the night.

He also declined the offer of the guest room. "I'd rather sleep there," he said, indicating the couch in the den that also appeared to serve as Tory's home office. "It's more central to the house, and besides, I'd just as soon not be too comfortable." He did accept the offer of a shower in the guest bathroom, though.

"Do you need to call someone?"

"You mean, like ask permission for a sleepover or something?" he replied, her recent sallies at his expense fresh in his mind.

"No, I mean, like a wife or something." He looked at her intently, refusing to help out. "I just mean maybe there's someone who will be worried if you don't return home tonight." He watched her with the slightest hint of a smile on his face.

"I'm just trying to be courteous," she said in exasperation.

"Are you trying to ask me if I'm married?"

"No. I'm not," she said shortly. "Every time I try to be nice to you, you turn obnoxious again. There's the phone if you want to use it. Or don't use it. I'm going to take a shower."

"I'm not," he called after her retreating figure, "married, that is." And, grinning to himself in satisfaction, he waited until he heard the water stop running in the back of the

house before taking a shower in the bathroom she'd indicated. He hadn't taken on his self-appointed task of guard
duty to have them both caught in the shower like sitting
ducks.

He returned to the den to find Tory sitting on top of her
desk, talking quietly on the phone. Her hair was damp from
her shower, and she was wearing an oversized tank top and
sweat pants, the latter donned for his benefit, he was sure. She
chewed on a fingernail while she waited for a response, and
when it came, it was obviously not one that pleased her. She
hung up and turned to look at him. In spite of all the pressure
she was under, and drinking more beer than she had a right
to, she still looked amazingly fresh and clean and desirable, he
noted. It made him acutely aware of how long he had been in
the same clothes, regardless of taking a shower.

"No change with Jazz. They say to call back tomorrow
morning." She looked at him. "What are you looking at?"

Work was always the best distraction, and Alvarez's work
was asking questions. "I'm wondering why you turned into
such a hell-raiser as a kid. Why didn't you just sit back and
enjoy being young, and rich, and beautiful?"

She gave serious thought to his question. "Well, for one
thing, I never considered myself to be beautiful. My mother
was a real honest-to-goodness southern belle. Her name was
even LaBelle, if you can imagine that. I guess I'm lucky that
she didn't name me Scarlett. Anyhow, we look just alike,
except she's five foot two and I'm five foot ten. I spent my
whole life being a larger, grotesque version of my petite, per-

fect mother. The only one more appalled by my tasteless height than me was LaBelle."

Alvarez shrugged. There wasn't much response that he could make to that. He certainly didn't intend to tell her that he found petite women disconcertingly fragile. You'd never find Scott's wife playing tackle football at the police picnic.

"But it was more than that," she continued reflectively. "I just never felt like I fit in." She shook herself slightly, as if shaking off some distant memories. "But you wouldn't understand about that," she added briskly.

"Don't bet on it," Alvarez was amazed to hear himself say. "Someday I'll tell you what it was like to grow up in a border town 'barrio' with a blond, Kansas farm girl for a mother, a nonexistent father, and a mentally retarded sister." Where had that come from? He didn't know which of them was more surprised at this little speech. "Forget it," he said, flashing his famous smile. "It's been a long day."

It was lucky he hadn't been expecting any sympathy because that's certainly not what he got. "So that's why you're so arrogant."

This was getting out of hand. "Listen, before we share any more true confessions and say our sweet goodnights, we need to get one last thing straight. You better be damn sure that you've been telling me the truth about everything that we've talked about. I'm going way out on a limb on this thing, especially considering that you're still theoretically a suspect in Hartman's murder. If I find out that you've been stringing me along, you won't need to worry about your mystery adversary."

"So now you're reverting to the heavy-handed detective, concerned about whether or not you've been 'strung along.' Are you really starting to have doubts about my answers to your questions? Maybe I killed Hartman after all, is that it? Well, just in case you're feeling insecure about staying here with me tonight, I'll let you hold onto my gun until tomorrow. I plan to get up at six. I hope that will be agreeable with you." He nodded his agreement. "Goodnight, then, Detective. If anything happens, call me. I'm not the type that plans to go lock myself in the bathroom while you battle the bad guys all alone. And remember, one of the questions that you didn't ask me was whether I owned more than one gun. And if I do, where I keep it." She smiled at him sweetly and disappeared down the hall.

He shook his head in resignation and settled in on the couch. He had barely gotten comfortable and closed his eyes when he was joined by Tango. Since he estimated Tango at close to eighty pounds, it made for close quarters. But hey, who was he to argue with an eighty-pound Transylvanian Hound in the throes of first love? By morning, Tory would be the only one of the two of them who could still claim not to have slept with the dog.

Right before he drifted off to sleep, he was able to put his finger on what was bothering him. Tory Travers sure sounded good while he was talking to her, but he had that deep-seated uneasy feeling that he always got whenever a witness was holding out on him. He tried to remember at what points in their conversation things had rung less than true, but it was no use. He was too tired and had had too much beer to drink. It would wait until morning. Soon he and Tango were snoring lightly together.

CHAPTER NINE:
TRYING TO READ THE DATA

The morning after is notorious for being awkward between two individuals of relatively short acquaintance. The fact that one of them had slept in the bedroom and the other on the couch didn't do much to alter that truism, Alvarez reflected to himself. It also didn't help that the two individuals involved were both hard-headed people, each intent on disclaiming any implied truces or commitments of the night before.

When Alvarez heard Tory up and about, he shoved Tango off the couch and retreated to the bathroom to give the lady of the house a period of solitude in which to make herself ready to face the day. For himself, he both looked and felt like he had slept in his clothes. He took a half-hearted swipe at his hair and brushed his teeth with his finger and some toothpaste. Then he killed some time sitting on the bathroom counter and reviewing the incidents of the past few days.

He still felt good about his basic conclusion that Tory had not killed Hartman. Two things bothered him now: the first was the lack of an established connection between Hartman's murder and the threats and attack directed at Tory. The facts, as they had been presented to him, indicated no relationship. On the other hand, for all these things to be happening at the same time seemed terribly coincidental.

The second thing that bothered him was Tory herself. On the one hand, she seemed to be everything that she represented herself to be—a woman caught up in a frightening chain of events, intent on figuring out the reason for the violence that was disrupting her life. On the other hand, something just didn't ring true, and he couldn't put his finger on what that something was. For all her intensity and all her sincerity about her desire to solve the puzzle, something about her struck him as being characteristic of a woman with a secret. And women were infamous for keeping secrets to protect others. But who could she be protecting? Finding no apparent answers, he decamped from the bathroom.

He found Tory in the kitchen, looking disconcertingly fresh and ready to face the day. He could have sworn that she had even been humming when he walked into the room. He had hoped to find her less attractive in the bright light of morning than she had appeared to him the previous evening. He was disappointed. She had on dark mahogany pants which were the same color as her hair, and a loose, filmy gold blouse which clung nicely to the lines of her body as she moved around the kitchen. Any meager hope that she might have dressed that morning with thoughts of impressing her house guest were dismissed as she got down to the business at hand in typical fashion.

She placed a mug of coffee on the breakfast bar for him. "So where do we go from here?" she asked.

The coffee was black; no sugar or cream were offered. Typical, he thought to himself. Cover the basics and forget the frills. "We don't go anywhere," he said, emphasizing "we." "I'll sit on reporting last night's shooting for today, and I'll see what I can turn up about Delgado. But if one other thing out of the ordinary happens, I want you on the phone to the police *ahora mismo, muy pronto*, or real quick, in Anglo talk. Call the police first. Then call me."

He handed her a card. "I wrote my home phone number on the back." He smiled pleasantly at her. "I want you to realize that I don't give my phone number out to just anyone, so don't go passing it around among your girl friends." He was rewarded by the clenching of her jaw. "Uh, you do have some friends, don't you? Well, never mind. Between the department switchboard and my home phone number, you should be able to reach me any time," he informed her.

"Won't you get into hot water if I do end up reporting last night?" she asked.

"Lady, you have enough trouble going on without worrying about me. Let me repeat myself. If anything else happens, you call the police here. Then you call me. I may be going out on a limb on this, but not so far I can't talk my way out of it if I have to."

She looked at his card and placed it on the kitchen counter. Then she bent over to fish something out of a bottom cabinet. Alvarez leaned over the breakfast counter to admire the view. "Personally, I prefer the jeans myself," he said conversationally.

She straightened up and placed some breakfast rolls on the counter in front of him with a bang. "That is a totally out of place remark. You make them habitually, you know."

"It's an important job skill."

"What, being obnoxious?"

"No, keeping people off balance. It helps to see which way they're going to jump."

"You make obnoxious remarks because you think it helps you do your job, not just because it's an inherent personality trait of yours?"

"It's not like that. It's more like ... like not interacting in the way a person is used to being treated. You get a hooker, or someone real good looking who trades on her sexuality, and you ignore it. Even treat the person like she's kind of unattractive—it makes her crazy. But then you take your normal middle-class respectable married woman. You make some remark acknowledging her sexuality and she goes crazy trying to figure out how to handle it, because she spends most of her life pretending that part of her doesn't exist."

"Fascinating," said Tory drily. "I guess I should be relieved that doesn't apply to me, because we've repeatedly ruled out respectability in my case. Those kinds of comments don't throw me off balance, they just make me angry. I've been dealing with them all my life."

"Oh, I've got lots more tricks where that came from," replied Alvarez helpfully.

"You're very sure of yourself, aren't you?"

"It's a requirement in my job."

"Well, it's a requirement in my job, too," replied Tory evenly. The stood and eyed each other in silence as they sipped their coffee. Then she asked challengingly, "Do you want me to call you if I find out anything else?"

"See, you catch on faster than you'd like to let on. That's a good example of the old bait and switch tactic. But I'll go for it. What do you mean, if you find out anything else? What the hell do you plan to do now, Tory? Some Lone Ranger tactics? I think you better let the cavalry do their job."

"I'm not going to go around looking for trouble. But I'm not going to sit on my hands and wait for you or somebody else to bail me out, either."

"I should have known this was coming. All right, Tory, exactly what do you plan to do today? Tell me now, and tell me everything, just to save us time later on down the line."

She looked at him in exasperation. "I plan to do what I would normally do. I'll go into the office. I'll continue to work on the column study. And I'll visit Jazz in the hospital."

"You're not to be out at the stadium site alone. Got it, Tory? Not at night, and not in broad daylight, either. You give me your word on that right now, or last night's little incident gets reported to the police before I leave town."

She conceded the point because she had no choice. "All right. I'll take a technician out to baby-sit me."

"That's that, then. I need to get out of here."

Tory switched from looking irritated to looking uncomfortable. She was unconsciously reducing her uneaten breakfast roll to crumbs.

"Okay, what is it?" he asked her. "I've been around you just long enough to know when you're trying to figure out the best way to phrase something. Please don't tell me that you're going to ask to get into the precast plant again."

"I hadn't thought of that," she said, looking surprised. "That would be really helpful ..." Her words faded away as she looked at his expression. She cleared her throat. "What I wanted to say was ... thank you."

She never ceased to surprise him. "Could you say that a little louder, please?"

"You heard what I said. I ... I appreciate you trying to help me. When someone was shooting at me and then later, trying to help me figure out who is doing all of this. It occurred to me last night that you didn't have to do any of the things you did."

"So say 'thank you, David.'"

"Thank you ... David."

He drained the dregs of his coffee. "That's a nice touch." He grinned at her. "It almost makes up for sleeping on the couch. Don't let that get around, okay? It could ruin my reputation. Now say 'I promise I won't go out on the stadium construction site unless someone is with me, David.'"

"It just doesn't pay to be nice to you."

"No, it probably doesn't. When is Lonnie Harper coming back, by the way?"

"Why?"

"Because I'd feel a lot better if someone with some common sense was around to put the brakes on you."

"He's not coming back until Friday afternoon. So somehow I'll have to make it through a little more than twenty-four hours without one of you around to guide me."

He refused to rise to the bait, and instead, stood to look at her intently, wishing that he could see right into her head and know what she was thinking. He walked around the breakfast bar to stand in front of her. He placed his hands on the bar on either side of her, effectively trapping her where she stood. Damn, she smelled good. He looked down at her intently, his face only a few inches from hers. This was his preferred position for intimidating witnesses, so he didn't know why his pulse should be the one to quicken.

"You don't have to do everything by yourself, Tory. It's not a requirement in life," he told her quietly. Now for the big moment. "Before I go, is there anything else you need to tell me? Maybe something that you forgot to tell me last night?" he asked her.

She calmly leaned back against the breakfast bar and met his gaze unflinching. "Yes." He waited in anticipation. "Before you go, I want you to give me my gun back." He shrugged. Sometimes you win, sometimes you lose, and sometimes you end up coaching your opponent in how to play the game.

Sometimes you're just so clever you outwit yourself, Tory berated herself in irritation. Anyone who counted on El Palacio for a private meeting had obviously not counted on the extensive community connections of Sylvia Maestes.

Tory had wondered why Sylvia had beamed at her so approvingly when she arrived at the office. She didn't have long to wonder. Sylvia was brimming with so much approval she couldn't contain herself, and she followed Tory into her office. "Oh boss, I'm so glad you changed your mind!" And Tory actually found herself being hugged by her secretary.

Tory disentangled herself and asked warily, "Changed my mind about what?"

"About Detective Alvarez. I thought you were giving him your usual brushoff. But you were just playing it cool, in case anyone was watching, huh?" Sylvia looked down the hall to make sure that none of Tory's employees were lurking in the shadows, listening to this conversation. When they had become suspect individuals, Tory didn't know. "That was so smart, to go meet him later at El Palacio when no one was around. My cousin told me all about it."

Tory looked at her secretary with something akin to horror. Sylvia gushed on, unaware. "Isn't he handsome, boss? He's so tall, and that smile, it just makes my heart skip a beat. Trust you to meet a cop that's good looking. All the ones that my family have dealt with have been uglier than sin," she said, frowning momentarily at memories that Tory hoped would remain unshared.

"Oh, really?" Tory said, her mind spinning with possible renditions of the tale told by Sylvia's cousin. "Yes, I suppose he looks okay ..."

"Oh, you suppose?" Sylvia grinned at Tory knowingly. "My cousin drove by your house later, you know. I spread the word, asked my family to keep an eye on you. I told them that I thought Emmett Delgado might be planning to hassle you a little."

Tory closed her eyes for a moment. I have got to get control of this situation, she told herself. My whole life is getting totally out of hand. She was saved by a phone call.

"Travers Testing and Engineering Company." Sylvia automatically reverted to her professional persona, answering the phone on Tory's desk. Her eyes got really wide. "Really?" she asked. "Really?" she repeated even more incredulously after listening for a few more minutes.

This is all I need, Tory thought. Now Sylvia is having an extended phone conversation with our anonymous caller. I wonder if he's good looking. Maybe we can all arrange to get together at El Palacio tonight, if Sylvia's cousin is free ...

"Well, that's just wonderful," proclaimed Sylvia emphatically. "Yes, I'll let her know." She hung up, jumped out of her seat, ran around the desk and gave the seated Tory another impulsive hug.

"What now?" asked Tory cautiously, speaking into Sylvia's ample breasts, not sure she really wanted the answer to her question.

"That was the police. Jazz woke up early this morning, so the hospital called them first. Typical, huh? He doesn't remember anything except being grabbed from behind by someone, so it looks like it wasn't an accident, after all. He's resting now, but it looks like he'll be fine in a few days. The police want you to be sure and come by this afternoon and talk to them. They say you should ask for Officer Snow. Why don't they want you to talk to Detective Alvarez? I think we should stick with him, if you ask me."

"Yes, well," Tory said noncommittally, grabbing her brief-case and purse. She could recognize an avenue of escape when she saw it. "That's wonderful news about Jazz. I'm going over to see him at the hospital. Then I'm going out to the stadium site." She was almost out the door when she realized guiltily that she was already reneging on a promise that she had made. "Send Bruce out there to give me a hand in about an hour," she directed her beaming secretary.

She felt a surge of relief at the news of Jazz's imminent recovery. After all of this dissembling, tackling the technical problem of the puzzling stadium column was going to be a piece of cake.

Alvarez didn't have to contend with an extensive Maestes family network, but he did work with an outstanding detective who noticed even the smallest details with dismaying frequency. It was a choice of making it into the office bright and early looking the way he did, or stopping by his house for a change of clothes and going in late. Alvarez opted for the latter, for all the good it did him.

"Big night?" asked Faulkner without looking up when Alvarez walked in. True to form, he didn't stutter when he said it, either.

"Yeah, when we're hot we're hot," Alvarez replied, arranging himself comfortably in his chair.

"You d-don't show up late to work in the middle of a hot case. So don't try to impress me with some t-t-tall tale. What have you found out?"

"Do you know what 'carjones' are? Have you ever heard of a Transylvanian Hound? Do you want to know the real reason that Vicky Wheatley changed her name to Tory?" Faulkner nodded yes to all three questions, so Alvarez regaled him with the details of the latest developments in the case. When he finished, Faulkner looked less than happy. "So what is it? Are you unhappy with my investigative techniques? And here I worked into the small hours of the night. Don't tell me you're going to question my intentions."

"It's n-not your intentions that I'm worried about. I have some more information about Victoria Travers. It's something that doesn't f-f-fit with everything else that we've been told about her."

Alvarez tried to ignore the knot of disappointment in his gut. "So let me have it," he said evenly.

"In doing a background, I requested her health records from the University infirmary for the p-period when she was a student. Institutional records are a lot easier to access than the records of a p-private physician."

Alvarez nodded his understanding, still waiting. For the first time in his life, he wished his partner wasn't quite so painstaking in his research efforts. "When Victoria Travers was a freshman, she went to the infirmary to request b-birth control measures." Faulkner cleared his throat. Whatever this was, it obviously wasn't easy for him, and that had nothing to do with his stutter.

"I thought that was a standard part of freshman orientation back in the good old pre-AIDS days," said Alvarez, trying to help him out. "College infirmaries were handing out birth control pills like they were candy back then. No one was concerned with the potential liability of side effects."

"Well, our subject didn't want birth control pills. N-not wanting the Pill was unusual enough that the doctor wrote down p-p-parts of their conversation." Faulkner opened a file in front of him and began to read from it. "She told the doctor that she didn't have sex every day, so she didn't want to subject her body d-daily to some artificial medication concocted by male doctors."

"Sounds just like her."

"He also recorded her opinions because it t-turned out that he couldn't give her what she wanted. He wouldn't pre-scribe an IUD, and he couldn't f-f-fit a diaphragm for her."

"Why, was she a transsexual or something? What are you trying to tell me?"

"She was a virgin, David. The doctor told her to use c-c-condoms and to come back after she'd had intercourse."

Alvarez sat motionless for a moment while the full impact of his partner's words sank in. Then he hit his desk in explo-sive anger. "Damn it, she lied to me. I knew something didn't fit, and here the whole thing about her affair with Barkley is a lie. Either that, or they had some platonic relationship in that motel room, which I don't believe for a moment. Maybe she has an identical twin? And if so, are we dealing with the evil Vicky or the good Tory? What the hell is going on?"

His partner looked at him without a single story for an answer.

Alvarez picked up Hartman's file on Tory and leafed through it until he unearthed what he was looking for—newspaper clippings of pictures taken with a long-range lens looking into a motel window, fuzzy to begin with, and definitely not improved with age. Alvarez studied a picture of an obviously naked Tory reaching up to put her arms around the neck of an obviously naked Jim Barkley. "Scott," he said slowly. "You got any idea how tall Barkley is?"

"No," answered his partner. "But I b-bet I can find out. What are you onto?"

Before Alvarez could reply, a uniformed officer was at his desk. "I've got a message here for Alvarez and Faulkner."

"Yo."

"The Chief wants to let you know that a couple of officers answered a call on a suicide attempt last night. Subject by the name of Tiffany Colliney. Taken to Southwestern General Hospital. Also, he wants to let you know that if it's not in your own backyard, you probably never missed it to begin with. Uh, do you know what that's supposed to mean, sir?"

"Skip it," said Alvarez. Faulkner was already on his phone.

"But isn't it from the Wizard of Oz?"

"Skip it," Alvarez repeated. Then seeing the officer's reaction to his tone, he relented. "It has more to do with Las Vegas than the Land of Oz. Go see if you can work it out." The officer shrugged and gave it up.

Alvarez waited for Faulkner to get off the phone. "Well?"

"Attempted overdose on Valium. She's going to b-be all right, but she won't be c-c-coherent for another c-couple of hours. Sounds c-clean. There was a suicide n-note which has been identified as being in her handwriting. It said that she knew her husband didn't l-love her any more and she couldn't go on living without him."

"Who found her?"

"A neighbor who wanted her to baby-sit. Saw the c-c-car there and figured Mrs. Colliney was there, so she finally walked in an unlocked b-back door."

"Is her father with her?"

"Yes. They couldn't reach him 'til this m-morning. But he's there with her now."

"Where'd she get the Valium?" He had complete unshakable faith that Faulkner would continue to have the answers to all his questions.

"She's been seeing a psychiatrist for d-depression for a couple of years now. Sounds like she's had a standing p-prescription, and just decided to take them all at once instead of one at a t-time."

Alvarez considered. "I think I know how he could have done it," he said finally.

"Who?"

"Petey Lester. Only I don't know why he did it, or if he did it."

"T-two unknowns out of three isn't too great. At least that's what they t-teach you in the Police Academy."

"I know. Find out about Barkley for me."

"What's the connection between Barkley, Petey Lester, and T-T-Tory Travers?"

"I'm not sure there is one."

"So why do you care?"

"Professional honor. I made Ms. Travers a promise based on the truthfulness of her answers. I plan to keep it."

"Okay, I'll get Barkley's height for you. Then I'm g-g-going to try to get in to see Tiffany Colliney's psychiatrist."

"You know what we need in this case?"

"A m-murder conviction?"

"Besides the obvious, *pendejo*. We need another player."

"Like Kent Colliney?"

"You read my mind. Somehow I have the feeling that he's going to show up today."

It was 3:00 PM before Alvarez got all the information that he was seeking. The minute he had the last piece, he was on the phone to Travers Testing and Engineering Company.

He searched his memory for the friendly secretary's name and got it right the first time when she answered the phone. "Your name's Sylvia, right? How are you doing? This is Detective Alvarez, remember? I met you yesterday. I'd like to talk to your boss."

"She isn't in right now," answered Sylvia. Could these subdued tones belong to the same person that had greeted him so jubilantly yesterday?

"Where can I reach her?"

"I'm sorry, but she can't be reached right now. I can have her call you when she gets back to the office if you'll leave your phone number."

Alvarez grit his teeth and kept his tone pleasant. "Sylvia,

Tory told me all about what a valuable secretary you are. About how you can always get in touch with her if it's something important. This is important, Sylvia. Tell me where I can reach Tory."

"I don't know. I don't know where she's gone. Nobody does." And an unmistakable sniffle traveled along the phone lines into Alvarez's receiver.

"What's going on, Sylvia? Why doesn't anyone know where she's gone?"

Now there was unmistakable crying on the other end. "It's so awful. And she'll be so angry if I tell anyone, but I don't know what to do anymore."

"You can tell me, Sylvia. You know that I'm trying to help her."

"I'm not really sure about anything, not after everything she said," Sylvia wailed into the phone.

Alvarez held the phone a couple of inches away from his ear until the worst had subsided. "She was just upset, Sylvia. You know how people get when a bunch of unpleasant things are going on. And I know all about everything that's been going on with Tory. So tell me what's happened. Maybe I can help."

The sniffling decreased a little. "Well, she was working out at the stadium site."

Alvarez held his breath. "Did she have anyone from your office with her?" he croaked out.

"Yes, she took a technician out there with her, which was really weird, see, because most of the work on the columns has already been done. It's not like they're out there shooting their entire lengths or anything. There's just this one little area that they're trying to figure out, and Tory always likes to be left alone when she's trying to figure something out ..."

He could breathe again. "Sylvia, what happened?"

"What? Oh, yeah. Well, I got the mail. And there was another one of those awful letters in the mail; I could recognize it, because it looked just like the other one." There was a pause. "She did tell you about the other one, didn't she?"

"Yes, of course," Alvarez reassured her.

"Well, I got in one of the trucks and drove out to the construction site because I didn't want to open it, and then Tory stormed out of there—"

"Sylvia," said Alvarez patiently. "Did you see what the letter said?"

"Of course I did. After she read it she threw it down on her desk, and anyone could read it. You know how big the letters are that they cut out—"

"So what did it say?"

There was crying anew. "It said 'Leave town or your son will be next.'"

Alvarez sat and listened to Sylvia cry for a moment while he considered this new development. "So where did Tory go after that?" he asked gently.

"I don't know, I already told you that. And I'm so worried about her. She has such a temper, and she always thinks that she can do everything by herself."

"Yeah, I know all about that. Listen, she must have said something to you before she left."

"Yeah, she said something all right."

"I want you to tell me what she said, word for word as accurately as you can remember it."

"Word for word?"

"Yes, word for word."

Sylvia took a deep breath and complied dutifully. "She said the damn police could go fuck themselves. She was going to figure this out and put an end to it for once and for all."

It was about what he had expected.

Tory's white RX was pushing 85 MPH on the freeway to El Paso when she caught herself and slowed down. The last thing she wanted now was to be stopped by the police for speeding.

"Think, Tory, think," she admonished herself. Tempting as it was, now was not the time to let her anger run on automatic pilot. She felt some of the adrenaline rush leave her body as she spent the next ten miles working out the details of her loosely formulated plans.

She pulled off at a rest area to find a telephone. She always ended up leaving her car phone in the office when she needed it. Looking around her, and seeing nothing out of the ordinary, she walked over to a pay phone and gave the operator her credit card number in order to place a long distance phone call. Summoning up the phone number from the distant reaches of her mind, she breathed a prayer that phone numbers were more permanent than most other things in life.

"Wheatley Acres," answered a male southern drawl. Tory breathed a sigh of relief that her hunch had been correct.

"I'd like to speak to the Senator, please."

"I'm sorry, he's not available at this time. If you'd like to leave your name and phone number, perhaps he could get back to you ..."

Even under this duress, she couldn't quite bring herself to say "It's his daughter calling." "It's extremely important that I talk with Senator Wheatley," she said, resisting the urge to scream. "Tell him it's Vicky. Tell him it's Cody's mother."

"I'm afraid I don't understand."

"Just do it, damn it. Tell him I need to talk to him, and that it's vital to his grandson's well-being."

Then there was a long pause on the other end, and Tory was beginning to despair that the Senator was in truth unavailable, and not just having his calls screened. She was about to cut the connection because this call was eating up precious time. Then someone came on the line. "Is this really Vicky, or is this some kind of joke?"

How could that dictatorial voice that had held crowds captive, that had governed every aspect of Tory's childhood, how could that arrogantly self-assured voice have become so frail? "It's really Vicky, sir," Tory said automatically.

"Vicky? Well ... how are you doing?"

Manners will out, thought Tory. I have to grant him that. "I'm fine. No, I don't mean that. I'm not fine at all. I've never asked you for anything, sir, not since I left home. But I need to ask you for something now. Cody's life may be in danger."

"Tell me what you want, Vicky. What can I do for you?"

Could it really be as simple as that, after all these years?

Tory didn't have time to reflect upon it. Briefly she explained what had been happening, and Alvarez's suspicions that the events of the past few days were connected with Jim Barkley and the Christians in Government organization.

Her father listened in silence, giving her recitation his full attention. "Well," he said finally. "I still see Jim now and then, but of course, we aren't really close any more." My Father, thought Tory, the King of Understatement. "The thing between you and him hasn't gotten any press down here, but then maybe that's because it was, well, overexposed when it happened."

Tory grit her teeth. You could call the national wire services overexposure, she supposed. "You know, after that sort of thing, people tend to forgive and forget," the senator continued. "Kind of like that Chappaquidick thing. Besides," he continued after a pause, "opinion always ran kind of strong around here that the whole affair, so to speak, was your fault."

Tory was gripping the phone so hard her knuckles were white. "So you don't think that Jim's campaign people have any interest in threatening me or Cody?"

There was another silence while her father considered the question. "No, I can't see it," he said finally.

"Thank you. That's all I wanted to know."

"Glad I could be of some help. Anything else I can do?"

"No. I don't think so, sir." The habits of a lifetime were hard to break.

"Vicky?"

"Yes?"

"It was real good to hear from you. You take care, you

hear? And let me know how everything works out. I'll ... I'll be real worried 'til I hear from you, you understand?"

"Yes, I hear. Goodbye, sir," she said, and hung up the phone.

Returning to the office, Faulkner almost collided with Alvarez on his way out. "Where are you going? Don't you want hear what I've f-found out?"

"All you can tell me are things to confirm what I already know."

"T-try this. Tiffany Colliney contracted syphilis from her husband. The clincher is that he didn't t-t-tell her about it. She discovered it symptomatically, and by then s-some significant damage had already been done. She'll n-never be able to have children."

"How about that?" said Alvarez, momentarily distracted from his exit.

"Well, at l-least I got your attention."

"Yeah, it fits. There had to be some kind of rancid emotion underlying all these nice little family relationships that we've been dealing with. It was either that or money, and we haven't been able to dig up anything out of the ordinary about the precast yard or the finances of the major players here."

"So now what? You're ahead of me on this."

"If only Hartman were Kent Colliney, the whole thing would fit."

"Kent Colliney may be dead, anyhow."

"You're not so far behind me; the thought has occurred to me. If he is, you can bet his wife doesn't know it."

"Maybe Hartman knew that Lester k-killed Colliney and so Lester had to kill Hartman."

"I can't see Hartman sitting on that kind of knowledge, considering the kind of true-blue guy he was. And it's damn improbable that Lester killed Colliney in front of Hartman that Sunday afternoon, cleaned up the mess, concealed the body, and then proceeded to knock off Hartman. Not to mention that Lester was supposedly partying or holding his daughter's hand up in Las Cruces the whole afternoon. And I don't think Mrs. Colliney would supply her father with an alibi for killing her husband."

"Okay. So s-s-someone else killed Hartman, and Lester is getting his revenge by trying to implicate his son-in-law in the m-murder. The problem is, there's just no motive for killing Hartman. Every path we take d-dead ends with that fact."

"The records."

"Which may be a red herring."

"Or they may not."

"Okay, if they're not, why did somebody k-k-kill to get them? What can be in the records of a p-precast yard that's important enough to kill for? This is where we started, in c-case you haven't noticed." Then Faulkner brightened. "But I do know how tall Jim Barkley is."

"Save it," said Alvarez. "Unless he's over six-foot-eight, you won't tell me anything that'll change the conclusions I've already come to."

"He's six foot t-tall, just so you know," Faulkner informed him dutifully. "So where are you going? Does this have anything t-to do with Tory Travers?"

"I can't decide whether to try to make some sense out of the mess she's gotten herself into, whether to let her get in further over her head and maybe get shot, or whether to shoot her myself."

"I don't think you should sh-sh-shoot her. It took me long enough to get used to you; I'd hate to have to start all over again."

"I'll take that as a compliment."

"Of course, maybe a n-new partner would keep me m-more informed about what he's doing," said Faulkner thoughtfully.

"Okay, you don't need to make me feel guilty. Try this. It's a long shot, I'm telling you that to start with. When Tiffany Colliney comes to, ask her what her father was wearing when he came up to her room."

It only took a few moments for understanding to dawn on Faulkner's face. "I get it," he said. "It would be a start toward b-breaking his alibi."

"Right. And since I've addressed a possible how, I'll leave it to you to find out if there was a why."

"What a d-deal. I g-guess you still aren't going to tell me where you're going."

Alvarez saluted his partner and headed out. "That's because I haven't narrowed down my choices yet."

===========

It was 4:50 PM when Tory finally got to meet with Horace
Webb, Senior, and it took less than ten minutes to find out
that he either couldn't, or wouldn't, give her the information that she was looking for.

"I'm sorry, Mrs. Trappers," said the old man, looking at
her disdainfully. In light of his impeccable three-piece suit,
and the luxurious shag carpeting in his office, Tory felt every
implication of the disadvantage that she was at, dressed in
slacks and an almost frivolous gold silk blouse. It had seemed
like a good choice in apparel that morning. But then she
hadn't realized that she was going to be storming the Webb
corporate fortress. She thought about correcting his impression of her name, and then decided that it would be just as
well if he thought she was someone else. Not to mention that
every communication had to be practically yelled at him, for
apparently he was too vain to wear a hearing aid.

"What you ask is impossible," the old man continued
deliberately, pronouncing every word slowly and distinctly,
as if talking to a wayward child. "Not only is it in violation
of our policy concerning impaired employees, it is also information that is only available to the personnel department. I can officially tell you that our records of employee
location indicate that Mr. Delgado is on sick leave. That is
all I can tell you. I cannot comment upon his projected
whereabouts or date of return."

"One of your secretaries told the foreman at the El
Paso Precast Concrete Company that Emmett had entered
a treatment center for alcoholism. How do you explain
that, Mr. Webb?"

"How does one explain the incompetence of help these days, Mrs. Trappers? Good, reliable employees like Mr. Delgado are hard to find."

"Mr. Delgado is an asshole, sir. I can understand that you may not care if he's endangering me, but he may also be endangering the viability of the University stadium project."

"I beg your pardon, young lady? What project are you referring to?"

Tory looked at him in defeat. "You really don't know which project I'm talking about, do you?"

"We have so many projects these days, young lady. It's impossible to keep track of them all. Not like when my partner and I first started ..."

"Have you heard of a firm that your company is trying to acquire, Travers Testing and Engineering Company?"

"Is that the testing lab down in Marfa?"

"Do you know who Emmett Delgado is?"

"Well, of course I know the name. I just can't put a face with it ..."

Deliver me from a fantasy of growing into a Fortune 500 company, thought Tory to herself. She thanked Webb and left him still deep in thought, remembering the days when he had known every project and every employee by name.

Tory made her way back to the front lobby and signed out, smiling a friendly smile at the receptionist as she turned her visitor's badge back in. Then she threw up her hands in exasperation. "I left my briefcase in Mr. Webb's office," she said apologetically. "I need to dash back there to get it before they lock up, or I'll really be up the creek." And Tory walked briskly back the way she had come. No one called out after her. So far, so good.

She found an elevator and checked the directory. Then she headed for the women's restroom on the fourth floor, the same floor as the personnel office, and shut herself in one of the toilet stalls. She made herself wait a full hour after the last female employee had come in to freshen up before heading home. Then she cautiously stuck her head out of the restroom door to size up the situation. The hall was still lit, but empty. Thankful for her rubber-soled flats, she made her way silently to the personnel office.

It was a disappointment. Even the entrance to the waiting area of the personnel office was locked up tighter than a drum. At this point Tory had no qualms about what constituted breaking and entering, and she would have cheerfully chucked one of the potted plants through the glass portion of the door in order to gain entry; only her uncertainty about whether the door might be wired to an alarm stopped her. She decided to check out Emmett's office before forcing the personnel office door.

Walking around in the deserted hallway was pretty creepy. With no exterior windows visible, it was impossible to tell whether it was light or dark outside. All the offices that she passed were dark, or lit dimly with security-type lights. On her way to the stairs, not wanting to risk using the elevator, she did pass one hall that had a lighted office at the end of it. Whether someone was actually in there working late or not, she would never know.

Emmett's office was located on the second floor, according to the directory. Her heart beating in her temples, she skulked down seemingly endless corridors until she found Delgado's office. For the first time that day, luck was with her: his door was unlocked.

She entered the office, decided to risk turning on the light, and shut the door behind her. She took a moment to assess the surroundings that Emmett Delgado worked in daily. It was nice, she had to admit to herself. Even though the office had no windows, it was large, tastefully furnished, and carpeted. There was a door on one side that Tory assumed connected with an adjacent office, but opening it, she found her assumption was wrong: the door led into a small, private washroom. Tory whistled softly under her breath in appreciation of benefits that were unheard of at Travers Testing and Engineering Company.

Closing the door to the washroom, she turned her attention to Emmett's desk, which had the appearance of belonging to an executive who had been out of the office for several days. The IN box was piled high, and there were a stack of phone messages tacked on the small bulletin board next to the telephone. Out of curiosity, Tory looked for her phone message. The tactful secretary had not taken down her full communication to Emmett verbatim, but had instead simply directed him to call her.

The problem was, she wasn't really quite sure what she was looking for. Tory opened the top drawer of Emmett's desk. Nothing interesting in there beyond the usual personal stuff—

architects' and engineers' scales, note pads, conversion tables, pens, pencils, vitamins, and aspirin. Tory had a sinking feeling that she was going to need to assault the personnel office. But before giving up, she turned her attention to Emmett's file drawers. Both were locked, but both were standard office equipment, and soon yielded to Tory's trusty Swiss Army knife, which resided permanently in her purse.

Scanning the files, she was diverted from her original purpose when she discovered Emmett's project file for the El Paso Savings and Loan Office Project. She pulled it out of the drawer and weighed it in her hand, undecided. To take it would be unadulterated theft. She could perhaps find a copy machine and copy the contents, but how could she ever prove the origin of the material without incriminating herself? Still, maybe it would simply be helpful to have access to the information. And maybe there were other files which would be of interest to her—

She heard footsteps coming down the hall. A custodian, she tried to tell herself above the pounding pulse in her temples. Then why isn't he stopping in every office? Maybe it's simply a late worker on his way out of the office. She silently replaced the file and closed the desk drawer, dropping her knife into the pocket of her slacks. It was too late to turn the light out without attracting the attention of the person walking down the hall, and it was also possible for that someone to see through the glass portion of Emmett's door into his office. She had to make a quick decision between being discovered by the passerby walking down the hall, or being trapped in the washroom if this someone entered the office.

She tried to tell herself that, logically, if the person coming down the hall was specifically looking for her, it really wouldn't make much difference if she was trapped in the office or in the washroom. Her chances wouldn't be too good either way. "Emmett, you asshole, why couldn't you have rated an office with an outside window?" she asked herself to keep her courage up as she quietly picked up her purse and crossed the office to shut herself in the washroom.

Tory hated closed-in spaces, and, as soon as she shut the door, waiting in the small dark washroom seemed infinitely worse than waiting in the office. She thought longingly of the .38 Smith and Wesson which Alvarez had not seen fit to return. Damn him. The door to the washroom opened out, so there wasn't even a chance to stand behind it if someone opened the door to peer in. For lack of any better ideas, she picked up the ceramic top to the back of the toilet, and, thus armed, stood and waited.

The footsteps drew nearer and stopped. Tory held her breath. Then, with a sinking heart, she heard the door to Emmett's office being opened. "Why didn't you lock the door behind you?" she whispered to herself, and then immediately added: "Although that wouldn't have done a whole hell of a lot of good if that's Emmett out there."

And then there wasn't any more time to carry on further conversations with herself, because the door to the washroom was flung open and Tory was temporarily blinded by the light shining in through the door.

CHAPTER TEN:
TRADING INFORMATION

"**A**nd you told me that you weren't the kind to hide in the bathroom when the going got tough," Alvarez said conversationally. Tory was speechless with fright. "You know, you look kind of silly standing there holding that. Put it down real slow, and then put your hands behind your head and step out here."

In shock, Tory complied. She could see that Alvarez had his gun in hand, although it was currently pointed up, not at her.

He kept up a running chatter as he guided her out of the washroom to face the office wall, and professionally patted her down. It wasn't nearly as much fun as imagining it had been, but he tried not to let that bother him.

"You know, a lot of women always ask me the next day if I still respect them. So I want you to know that I still respect you. Otherwise I wouldn't be going to all these precautions, but I try not to let anyone pull a gun on me twice. I need to look after my health, you know. And if I don't do it, nobody will ... Now, what do we have here?" He finished his efforts, pocketed her Swiss Army knife, holstered his gun, and moved away from her. "Okay, you can sit down now." Done with the banter, his voice was icy cold.

Tory wordlessly sank into Emmett's office chair. Alvarez sat on Emmett's desk and looked down at her. "Kind of shakes you up, doesn't it, all this cloak and dagger stuff?

That's okay, I can wait as long as it takes for you to regain your power of speech. I've got some questions, and we're not leaving here until I get some answers. Real answers, this time."

"What are you doing here?" Tory finally pulled herself together enough to ask.

"You still don't get it, do you?" The anger in his voice sounded ugly even to him. "I'm the one with the gun now, so I get to make up the rules. Remember that game, Tory? Here's the big rule—listen carefully: I'm asking the questions, you're supplying the answers. What do you know about Hartman's death that you haven't told me?"

"I don't know anything about Hartman's death. I'm here because someone is threatening my son."

"I know. We'll get to that later. After I get my answers. Let's spin the wheel and ask another question. Who was it that was shooting at you last night?"

"I don't know. If I knew, do you think I'd be here looking for clues?"

"Sound the buzzer. You broke a rule again—no questions, remember? Don't screw up again, Tory, because we're going for the grand prize question. Who the hell was it that had an affair with Jim Barkley?"

She looked at him in horror. "What do you mean?"

"Who had the affair with Jim Barkley?"

"Why are you asking me that? It has nothing to do with anything."

He stood up to resist the overpowering urge to strike her. "Damn it, this isn't a game. I'm up to my ears in criminal activity, and almost all of it seems to center around you. Don't fuck with me anymore. Who had the affair with Jim Barkley?"

All the fight seemed to suddenly go out of her. She looked down at her lap. "My mother had the affair with Jim Barkley," she said quietly.

He had thought that he would be pleased with her admission, but he wasn't. "Well, we're making progress," he said, with no change in his tone. "Finally an honest answer."

"That's the only thing I lied to you about," she said defensively, looking up at him. He was taken aback to find that there were tears forming in her eyes. He felt an urgent need to continue before he lost his momentum.

"Do you sleep with Lonnie Harper?"

"No, I don't sleep with him."

There had been the slightest emphasis on the word *don't*. "Have you ever slept with him?" he badgered her.

"Why do you want to know?"

"I want to know because I want to know, damn it. Those are the rules. Have you ever slept with Lonnie Harper?" he almost yelled at her.

"Yes, once." Instead of looking down, as she had with the previous admission, she continued to look steadily at him.

"Why only once?"

"Because it meant something different to him than it meant to me. So it didn't seem quite ... ethical to do it again." The tears spilled over and rolled down her cheeks, but she ignored them. She looked right at him. "What's the next question, Detective?"

She just kept getting away with turning the tables on him. He shook his head in resignation and sat down on the desk again, all his anger suddenly gone. "You see, Tory," he said quietly, "the problem with lying to a police officer in an investigation is that it makes every other answer and action on your part suspect. Trust is like cold, hard cash. Once you discover a counterfeit bill you start worrying about the rest of it."

"Everyone has secrets that they're entitled to keep to themselves."

"Honey, that's a luxury that only exists in civilian life. If your secrets blow up in our face, we're not worrying about emotional fallout. We're worrying about falling body parts."

"I only lied to you once, about one single thing that has nothing to do with any of your investigations." She distractedly rubbed the tears off her cheeks.

"You lied to me about your affair with Barkley, you lied about your relationship with Lonnie Harper, and you keep lying every time you say that you only lied to me once."

"Do you have any idea how juvenile that statement sounds?" she retorted. He did have an idea how juvenile it sounded, and it didn't make him any happier to have her point it out. "I didn't lie about my relationship with Lonnie Harper," she continued. "As you so delicately put it, the question was 'Do you sleep with Lonnie Harper?' and the answer was no."

"Don't pull that semantic bullshit with me. Do you remember agreeing to tell me everything that might have to do with Hartman's murder and the little incident out at the construction site, whether I asked the right question or not?"

"Yes, I remember. And the fact that I slept with Lonnie Harper one time four years ago has nothing to do with either of those things." They sat and glared at each other. "I guess you could call this a Mexican standoff," she said finally.

"So now you're going to start with the racial slurs," he replied automatically, although his heart wasn't in it.

"Yeah, sure. I figure if you dish it out you should be able to take it."

A lot of tension had left the room, and try as he might, Alvarez just couldn't quite get back his feeling of righteous indignation. But he gave it a try. "Damn, you get me off the track every time I talk to you. I want to know why you lied to me, what you're doing here, and what the hell is going on."

"I don't think I can answer your last question, Detective Alvarez. If I could, I wouldn't be here."

"Just start with the first one, Tory, and we'll take it from there."

"I don't think I could explain it to you."

"Give it a try."

"I lied to you about my affair with Jim Barkley because so few people know the truth about it that by now even I almost believe the lie. And I couldn't see where it had anything to do with what's been happening or with the questions you were asking, or with your investigation of Bill Hartman's death."

"Keep going," he commanded her.

"My mother, LaBelle, and Jim Barkley were approached by the photographer who took the pictures of them that weekend. I think that's the first time they realized someone was on to them, although I'd thought they'd been having an affair for some time. It wasn't the first time I'd thought LaBelle had something going on. Obviously, the guy wanted money for the pictures. It gave LaBelle and Jim some time to think while they looked at those photographs and figured out what to do. I don't know which of them decided that the pictures were blurry enough that they could get away with telling the guy that the woman in the photographs was me." Two new tears had taken the place of the recently vanquished ones. Tory wiped those away, too.

"Go on."

"Well, LaBelle and Jim figured that the story would come out sooner or later, and this way only one of them had to sacrifice their reputation. Jim Barkley was so totally obsessed with my mother that he would have walked on burning coals for her. I don't know if they ever completely convinced the photographer, but that didn't turn out to matter much. The year after he sold the pictures to the newspapers, he was killed in a plane crash. So I'll never know if he totally bought their story, or was just going along for the time being and planned to approach them again later."

"So why did you go along with it?"

"Well, for one thing, I didn't have a lot of choice. LaBelle had already told the photographer her version of the story before she told me what was going down. She got to express her moral determination not to be blackmailed, even if it meant sacrificing her own daughter. Then she told me that if I said anything, it would always be her word against mine. And Barkley's, too. And she told me that if my father ever found out the truth, it would kill him."

"That sounds rough."

"I don't need your sympathy."

"Listen, settle for what you can get. After I found out that you lied to me, I was pissed enough to shoot you myself."

"I thought you weren't supposed to get emotionally involved with your cases."

"I always get emotionally involved with my cases. That's how they get solved. Just go on with your story."

"There isn't any more. If my brother, Tommy, had still been alive, it might have been different. But as it was, there just didn't seem to be any point in trying to stay and fight my mother. My father had been disgusted with me since I was thirteen, so I didn't figure my leaving would be any big loss to him. So I took it on the chin and split. In a way, it was even kind of a relief."

She sat a moment in reflective silence before she continued, "You know, it's funny. All the things that I thought I was saving ended up getting lost anyhow. My father lost his senate seat in the next election, and then my mother divorced him."

He waited a moment to make sure that she was finished, because his next question was vital and he wanted her to be able to focus all her attention on it. "Tory, who knows the truth about this, besides you?" he asked quietly.

She looked surprised at the question. "Me, my mother, and Barkley, obviously. I would have thought you could figure that out."

"Cut the cute remarks. You aren't off the hook yet, not by a long shot. Does anybody else know? Think about it carefully, Tory, it's important."

"No, no one else knows. Unless my mother or Barkley told someone, which I find highly improbable. Carl knew, but Carl's dead," she added simply.

"Does Lonnie know?"

"No, he doesn't know. There's no reason for him to know."

"How about Cody?"

"He doesn't know, either. I plan to tell him some day when he's older. Maybe when his grandparents are dead. He's had to shoulder a lot in his life without having to know something like that."

"If that's the case, then why did Carl have to know?"

"There are things you just have to tell some people sometimes," she hedged.

He thought about that a moment before the meaning of her statement dawned on him. "Was Carl as surprised as I was to discover that this *femme fatale* of Florida politicians was actually an innocent, virginal thing when she came to college?"

"Contrary to what you may think, sex doesn't have a lot to do with innocence. And what was between me and Carl is none of your business," she said levelly.

"For once you're right. It's not," he replied mildly. "Well, I guess it just goes to show that you can't tell a book by its cover, and all that."

"I really hate to distract you from your continuing interest in my sex life, but what does all of this have to do with anything?"

"Anytime you're one of a few people who share some secret knowledge, it puts you in danger. You can become a potential target if someone either wants your secret or wants to make sure you never divulge it."

"But who would care?"

"Barkley's publicity people, for a start."

"Enough to shoot me? Enough to threaten my son?"

"Maybe." Alvarez shut his eyes and thought for a moment. He still couldn't make it all fit. "Where's your mother now?"

"I don't know. I think she was done with Barkley before she left my father. I know she went to Miami after the divorce, but I have no idea where she went from there, or where she is now. What are you getting at?"

"How do you think she's set for money?"

"I don't know anything about the divorce settlement. I've told you, I haven't spoken to those people since I left Florida." Tory paused. "Well, actually, that's not true. I called my father today to ask if he knew what was going on."

And Alvarez thought his childhood had been rough. He didn't know anyone else who referred to their parents as "those people." "And what did he say?"

"The same thing that I keep saying, that the whole affair

is ancient history. Nobody seems to care about any of it, except maybe you."

"So how do you think your mother's set for money?" he asked again.

"I don't know. Pretty good, I guess. She was independently wealthy before she married my father, and I'm sure she got something out of the divorce settlement. Although ..."

"Although what?"

"Although, to my mother, there wasn't any such thing as enough money."

"Do you think your mother would be capable of blackmail?"

Tory closed her eyes and thought for a moment. "I think," she said finally, "that LaBelle would be capable of anything that she put her mind to. But I can't figure out ..."

"That's not your job," said Alvarez. "It's mine. All you need to do right now is answer my questions. Where is your son, by the way?"

"He's with Lonnie, fishing in the Gila wilderness. I've thought and thought about it, and I don't think anyone would be able to find them. I've been up there with Lonnie once or twice, and if I hadn't been with him I would never have been able to find the cabin where they are."

"Well, that's a break in our favor, for a change. Assuming that Lonnie's the true blue guy you seem to think he is. And that brings us to the subject of what you're doing here."

"I'm trying to find out whether Emmett Delgado is behind all of this."

"And have you been successful?" he asked.

"No," she admitted.

"Too bad. If you'd left that up to me like I told you to, I wouldn't have to be sitting here trying to decide whether or not to charge you with breaking and entering."

"I didn't break and enter. I just kind of stayed after closing time. And the door to Emmett's office was unlocked," she replied.

"And I suppose the lock to his file drawers had already been forced when you arrived on the scene?" Alvarez inquired pointedly. Tory didn't seem to have an answer to that, so he continued. "I think it would be a good idea if we continued our conversation out in the parking lot in my car. If someone happens to ask why we're here, I can always flash my badge, but it might kind of put you on the spot. Now, since you've been busy teaching me not to make any assumptions where it concerns you, let me ask you another simple question. Are all of Delgado's files back in his drawers?"

"Yes," she answered glumly. "There was one on the El Paso Savings and Loan project that I wanted to look at, but you came down the hall before I had a chance to see what was in it."

"Those are the breaks. Now," he proffered a handkerchief dug out of the depths of his slacks, "I suggest you take a few minutes to wipe off everywhere you may have left your fingerprints. I realize this little exercise may take a while, but I'll wait."

"I see you came prepared," she said, noting the thin leather gloves he wore.

"Yes, I did. And if you decide to pursue a life of crime in the future, I would suggest that you do the same. I told the security officer I'd been asked to take a look around to comment on the general security of the building. It's not my fingerprints that they'll find in here if the whole thing comes crashing down around my ears. I always try to plan ahead so I won't compromise any evidence I might need later. You might try that sometime. Thinking things through ahead of time." She glared at him before taking the offered handkerchief, and then systematically began to wipe down the office, starting with the outside knob of the office door and working through the room. "Don't forget to put the top of the toilet tank back where it was," he called after her helpfully when she disappeared into the washroom.

When she was done, they left the office. Alvarez turned off the light and pulled the door shut behind them before shedding his gloves. They traveled in silence in the elevator down to the first floor, and he took her arm to escort her past the front desk, through the lobby, and out the front door. Alvarez bid the security guard at the desk a good night, but the man was so engrossed in the newspaper he was reading that he didn't even look up.

It was beginning to get dark when they reached the parking lot. Alvarez's Corvette and Tory's white RX were the only cars there. "I'll give you another hint while we're at it," said Alvarez. "The next time that you're going someplace that you shouldn't be, don't park your car in the parking lot. It's the sign of a real amateur."

"I'll keep that in mind, next time," said Tory evenly.

Alvarez opened the door of his car for her, settled Tory in the passenger seat, and then went around and climbed in the driver's seat. She waited for a moment to see if he would speak, and when he didn't, she asked, "What are we supposed to be doing out here?"

"I'm trying to figure out what to do next," he answered truthfully.

"Oh," she said, sounding quite subdued. And then, "Are you done being angry with me?"

He turned to look at her in the fading light. "Not totally. Why?" he answered cautiously.

"Because I'd like to talk some things over with you. Tell you some of my opinions about what's happening. But I need to be able to ask you some questions, too."

"Okay, shoot," he said simply.

"You really mean it?"

"Yeah, I really mean it. What's your problem?"

"I thought maybe you were being sarcastic."

"I think maybe you're being a little too humble, and it makes me nervous. So don't keep me in suspense. Ask your questions."

"How did you know where to find me? I mean, I know my car is out in the parking lot, but you must have had a reason to be looking in this particular parking lot."

"I called Sylvia. She told me what had happened, what you'd said about figuring out things yourself, and that you'd taken off and nobody knew where you'd gone. Which, by, the way, isn't real bright when you've recently been used for target practice. Anyhow, I figured you must be here or at the precast yard. Or going to get your son. The truth of the matter is, this was the closest place to check, so I came here first. And I thought maybe even you would hesitate about trying to break into a crime scene."

She didn't reply to that, and he groaned in exasperation. "Were you really planning to hit the precast yard after you finished here?" he asked.

"I wouldn't exactly call it 'hitting the precast yard,' but, yes, I was planning to head there next." After taking in his expression, she quickly said, "It figures that Sylvia would tell you anything you asked. As far as she's concerned, you rate up there right next to God. She knows that you spent the night at my place."

"My god, what about my reputation? And you went to so much effort to assure me we were being discreet. Doesn't make El Palacio's look like such a great choice for a secret meeting, does it?"

She shook her head. "It doesn't matter now. So why did you come looking for me in the first place?"

"Three reasons." He counted them off on his fingers. "One, I made you a promise that you'd have me to answer to if I found out that you were lying to me. Two, I kind of felt responsible for whatever might happen to you since I didn't report the shooting last night."

"And the third reason?"

"The third reason is that I actually kind of like you, although God knows why, and I'd just as soon you don't get yourself killed while you're out playing Lone Ranger in this whole mess. I figured that if I could predict how you would react, someone else might be able to predict it, too. Didn't it ever occur to you that someone could have followed you here and that you would have been a sitting duck in that office up there, with no one knowing where you were? Your body wouldn't have been discovered until opening time tomorrow morning."

In spite of the warm summer evening air, Tory shivered. "Yes, it occurred to me," she admitted.

"When?"

"About the time I heard you walking down the hall."

"But that was just a little late for the realization to have done you any good."

"I know. That was one of the worst experiences in my life, waiting in that office to see what would happen. Lots worse than being shot at. That happened so fast that I just reacted automatically, without thinking about it. I think this is the first time that I've seriously started to believe that I might really be in danger."

"Well, then maybe we're finally making progress. You better believe it. If he recovers, your foreman will believe it."

"So Sylvia didn't tell you everything. No wonder. This morning seems like a week ago. Anyhow, Jazz regained consciousness this morning and he's going to be okay. All he remembers is someone grabbing him from behind, knocking his hard hat off and then knocking him unconscious. I always thought that Emmett was a real asshole, but not actually dangerous. It's hard to believe that I could so badly misjudge someone that I've known for so long."

"Oh, I believe that Emmett Delgado can be dangerous all right. Any active alcoholic or drug addict has a great capacity for violence, usually even greater than they realize themselves. But theorizing about Emmett Delgado doesn't have anything to do with your current situation."

"What do you mean?"

"Emmett Delgado has been in a treatment center since he returned home after the party you all went to Saturday night. Seems like his wife had given him several ultimatums, and when he plowed down the tree in their front yard upon returning home from the party, she had all the mechanisms in place. He may not have gone willingly, but he went, all right. Your mouth is hanging open in a very uncouth way, Tory."

"Why didn't you tell me this before?"

"When I caught up with you I didn't exactly feel like being a nice guy."

She let that pass. "How did you find out? And how are you sure that Emmett is really in this treatment center? I thought you told me that there was all this patient confidentiality stuff about saying who was actually in a treatment center and who wasn't."

"I found out from Delgado's wife, Tory," Alvarez answered mildly, "which is a little bit easier than the illegal-entry method, and also a little more productive. And I know he's in there because his wife is one pissed-off person. She assured me that she had been to visit each day just to make sure herself that he was there. Sounds like a marriage made in heaven to me. She was so anxious to prove that he hadn't been out causing any more mischief that she invited me to go with her to see him this afternoon. And that's what I did before I came here. I figured you wouldn't do anything really stupid at either Webb or the precast yard until after closing time, and I was right."

"How is he?" asked Tory automatically.

"Detox isn't beautiful," Alvarez answered flatly, "whether you do it in a city jail cell or in a plush treatment center. But from what I could get out of him, he went through that Saturday-night party in a blackout. I really don't think he has any recollection of threatening you."

"So if Emmett is in a treatment center, who's behind all this?"

"Ah, I was wondering when you were going to get around to that question. I'm putting my bets on Barkley or someone associated with CIG. His presence here next week and your past coming to Hartman's attention were awfully coincidental to begin with. Now I find out that you know something about him that maybe only one other person in the world knows. Bingo—a reason to hassle, threaten, and possibly kill Tory Travers."

"You're crazy."

"I wish you'd stop telling me that. Have you got any better answers?"

"Yes. It all has to do with this stadium construction

project. There's something going on with those columns that someone doesn't want me to find out."

"Who cares, Tory? I've given a lot of thought to everything you told me about how a construction project works. If there's something really wrong with that last column that you're so obsessed with, so what? If the precast yard screwed up, Harold Kemp goes after them to pay for any liquidated damages that he may get stuck with if the project is delayed. And Petey Lester is so busy watching his world fall to pieces around him that I doubt he's given you or that project any thought in days. He has a missing partner and a suicidal daughter. His yard may go down the tubes whether he's screwed up that project or not."

"What about Emmett? He's the structural engineer for this project."

"What about Delgado, Tory? First of all, from what you tell me, it's highly unlikely that there was a design mistake resulting in a screwed-up cement column that you or someone else didn't catch by now. Secondly, even if something so unlikely had occurred, who but Delgado himself would be crazy enough to try to cover it up? From everything you've told me, it's likely that Webb's professional liability underwriters require early disclosure of any hint of a claim or the insurance policy is void. So that rules out any of his co-workers on the project."

Tory was looking at him in admiration. "You really listened to what I told you. And you even understand it."

"Your astonishment at my capabilities never ceases to flatter me."

"Well, I really am impressed. But it's a concrete column, not a cement column. You see, cement is like the glue that you mix up with—"

"I've already had the lecture," Alvarez cut her short. "Before you get us off on one of your famous digressions, the point is that there is no reason to associate the things that have been happening to you with the stadium project, or with Bill Hartman's murder, for that matter."

"I still think you're wrong. If you're so sure that there's no connection, then why don't you take me out to the precast yard and let me look around?"

Alvarez just looked at her for a moment before answering. "God, you've got *cojones*, lady, and they don't come from sitting in a car. I go out on a limb by not reporting a shooting, and then I catch you illegally riffling through someone's files. I still haven't decided whether or not to charge you with breaking and entering."

"Trespassing, at most. And I don't believe you; I think you have already decided."

Alvarez had to agree. "Okay, but giving you two breaks doesn't mean I have to give you a third. Besides, the precast yard is off limits to you."

"Why?"

"Because I told you that it was. You're still officially a suspect in Hartman's murder."

"But if I went with you it wouldn't be off limits."

Alvarez shook his head in exasperation and thought for a moment. "Okay. I must be crazy for doing this, but maybe it'll get the notion out of your head that all this has something to do with your damn construction project."

Tory reached for the door handle. "Great. I'll meet you there."

Alvarez reached over and grabbed her arm. "Don't get carried away, Tory. You're going with me, get it? That means you shut up and let me do any talking that needs to be done. And you do what I tell you when I tell you. Got it?"

"Got it." She looked at him, considering, and then obviously decided to go ahead and ask the question that was on the tip of her tongue. "Can I have my Swiss Army knife back?"

Tory's white RX pulled into the precast yard behind Alvarez's Corvette, which was encouraging, Alvarez reflected wryly to himself. At least she hadn't tried to beat him there. Although it was almost dark, the yard was lit like a Christmas tree lot and there was a flurry of activity as workers moved from form to form. He recalled that Tory had told him the yard was running overtime to make up for lost production, but even so, this amount of activity surprised him.

They made their way through numerous small forms toward the office. "Can you tell what's going on?" Alvarez asked.

"Yes, they're pouring the concrete seats for the stadium," she answered him. "It's a relatively simple element that they can mass produce if they have the available crew and forms, and it looks like that's what they're trying to do."

Going up the steps to the office they met Columbo coming out. Alvarez informed him that they were going into the lab, and introduced him to Tory when he remembered that the two of them had never actually met in person. Columbo grunted his acknowledgment of the introduction, but didn't offer to shake hands. He told them to look around all they wanted, but just not to get in the way. Production, he informed them, was scheduled to go on until midnight.

Tory waited for Alvarez to open the door to the lab for her, which he considered restraint on her part. "I agreed to do this on your terms," she said, "and I intend to. What can I look at? Are there things that I shouldn't touch?"

"I'm impressed that you asked," he answered. "Maybe there's hope for you after all. Go ahead and look to your heart's content. We'll probably open this up on Monday in any case. The only thing I need to impress on you is that nothing, absolutely nothing, is to leave this room with you. Understood?" She nodded her agreement, obviously itching to get inside the door. "I'm going to make a phone call in Lester's office. Then I'll check back with you," he informed her. He opened the door and let her into the lab.

Faulkner answered Alvarez's call on the first ring. He got right to the point without Alvarez even asking. Somehow he had managed to get in to talk to Tiffany Colliney, as Alvarez had suspected he would.

"Your hunch p-paid off. From what Tiffany Colliney remembers, which is p-pretty scattered at this point, when her father came to her room last Sunday afternoon, he wasn't in his swimming clothes. He was dressed for the d-d-dinner party."

"Oh ho."

"Oh ho is right. That m-means that the half hour that he supposedly spent getting ready for the dinner party after visiting his d-d-d-daughter was not necessarily spent getting ready."

"But even with some margin of error concerning when he entered and left her room, the most we can come up with now would be another half hour. That gives us a total of an hour unaccounted for, and at least an hour and a half would be required to drive to the precast yard from Las Cruces, murder Hartman, and drive back."

"Besides the t-time factor, we're also missing a motive," pointed out Faulkner helpfully.

"I know, I know. Maybe Lester did spend that half hour after he left his daughter's room polishing his shoes, and truthfully called it getting ready. And then again, maybe this is a start on cracking his alibi. What did he say when you asked him about it?"

"He hasn't b-been back here to visit his daughter since this morning, and I haven't been able to reach him at home or at his office." Something about that statement set off a bell in Alvarez's mind, but he couldn't quite put a finger on why it did. "That's it from this end," Faulkner continued. " Where are you, anyway?"

"Out at the precast yard."

"Oh. Do I want to know what you're d-doing out there?"

"I've let Tory Travers have access to the lab. She still thinks there's a connection between what's happening to her and the stadium construction project."

There was a pause while his partner digested this. "Oh,"

he said again. It was sure nice that Faulkner wasn't one to get all excited over minor deviations from protocol. The one syllable reply was so full of well-intentioned restraint that Alvarez had to laugh.

"Don't worry. I know what I'm doing. I'm giving her just enough room to let her figure out that I'm on the right track, and then she won't have any choice but to do what I want her to do."

"I just hope that you know what it is that you want her t-t-to do, because I don't. From what I can t-tell, all she's been is trouble from the moment that she set f-foot out there."

"Well, that's got some truth to it. But I think I'm onto something else entirely unrelated to this case. It may eventually give us a chance to nail somebody at CIG. Listen, I'll explain it all to you in the morning."

"I hope so. Take care, buddy. Don't do anything I wouldn't d-d-do."

"Never."

Tory didn't look up when he walked back into the lab. She was intently studying a variety of sheets of paper which she had spread out on top of one of the lab desks. He sat down on a stool next to her and asked, "So what great discoveries have you made in my absence?"

She looked up at him and bit her lip. "Not any," she admitted. "There are some rough notes here about some of the other pours, but nothing on that particular column. Of course, that's not entirely unusual, since that pour was scheduled during overtime and run by Colliney. I get the impression that he didn't supervise many pours, so maybe he wasn't in the habit of keeping very accurate notes. Or then again, maybe he entered his records directly into the binder that's missing, bypassing Hartman. In any case, there's nothing here to help me," she concluded dismally.

"I'm sorry," he said sincerely. "But I think you're finally going to have to accept the fact that there's no connection between what's been happening to you and what happened here. Which means that you're going to have to look elsewhere, even if that means dredging up some things that you'd rather not deal with."

He watched her face as she considered and yet again rejected his conclusions. "Okay," she said finally, "if you think there's no connection, then you tell me why you think Hartman got killed."

"If there's not a crazy involved, murders usually boil down to one of two motives: personal reasons, usually having to do with family relationships or sex, or murder for financial gain."

"I'm listening."

"We haven't been able come up with a personal reason for someone wanting to kill Hartman. But we've started to unearth some significant problems between members of the owner's family."

"Like the fact that Kent Colliney gave his wife syphilis, and she'll never be able to have children?"

Alvarez looked at her in astonishment. "How did you know that?"

"I have my connections," she answered archly.

"Why didn't you tell me that?" he asked, his voice beginning to rise in volume.

"Don't get angry at me again. To tell you the truth, I never even thought about it until just this moment. I still don't see what it could have to do with Hartman's murder."

"Neither do we," admitted Alvarez glumly.

"So what about murder for financial gain?"

"We haven't made a lot of progress with that, either. Some of the things that we're looking at include illegal alien labor, covering up evidence for a potential lawsuit, or even somehow distributing drugs through this outfit."

"Lonnie did tell me that he thought Kent Colliney had connections with drug suppliers across the border."

"So Lonnie Harper is your source of information. Figures. What else did he tell you?" Alvarez asked with avid interest.

"That's about it. I really don't know if he knew any more. It wasn't important to me beyond passing interest, so I didn't pursue it."

"If only it had had to do with a construction project. Then you would have been interested."

"Probably," she said. "But remember, you're the one who told me you get emotionally involved in all your cases. It's just a matter of individual taste."

"Do you think Lonnie Harper would tell me what else he knows about Kent Colliney?"

"Probably. If he knows anything else. If I asked him."

"Will you ask him?"

She considered the question a moment. "Yes," she said.

He decided to go for it while he was on a roll. "Will you let me put you into protective custody until we can locate your mother and check into Barkley's people?"

The atmosphere of cooperation that had prevailed in the room disappeared instantaneously. "No way," answered Tory flatly.

"Listen, you run the danger of getting hurt, or getting killed dead, even, as they say in the department. There's no way that you're going to solve this thing running around by yourself like a loose cannon."

"Why not? You may think you're a damn good detective, but I happen to be a damn good engineer. And that's what engineers do—solve things."

"You won't solve anything because you don't have the right training, you don't have the right support system, and you're emotionally involved with the whole thing."

"And you're not?"

"It's part of my job." Surely she couldn't realize how much he wanted to protect her, because it came as a surprise even to him.

"You're so enamored with your own professional opinions that you don't want to risk the fact that someone might prove you wrong."

"And you're so pig-headed and tunnel-visioned that you can't see what's the best for you when it's staring you right in the face."

"Well, good night then, Detective," Tory said with an

icy formality that would have been humorous if the situation wasn't so serious. "Thank you for letting me into the laboratory."

Alvarez had to move fast to catch up with her before she was out of the lab. "Is this your version of love them and leave them? Remember how nice you were while you still needed me to get you in here? Let me walk you to your car, at least. Then maybe something won't happen to you until you're out of sight and I won't have to feel so damned responsible."

They walked across the lit yard, Alvarez cursing steadily under his breath in Spanish.

"You do remember that I understand perfectly everything you're saying, don't you?" Tory asked.

"*Sin duda*," Alvarez answered flatly, with no small amount of vindictive satisfaction. "Here," he said, reaching into his pocket. "I might as well give you these back. I really don't know which is worse at this point, you having them or not having them." He handed Tory her gun and her knife.

Tory took them without comment. Then her look changed to one of intense interest. "What's that over there?" she asked, looking beyond him, and took off on a detour among the numerous forms and workers. Alvarez had to hurry to keep up, and he almost overshot her when she came to a sudden stop in front of a jumble of metal bars. "It's a column cage," she said excitedly.

"It's a what?" Alvarez asked, wondering glumly if this little digression was going to involve another lesson in engineering semantics.

"A cage of rebar, like what goes inside the columns. See,

those are individual rebars, tied together with steel ties. I've studied those damn column design drawings so many times that I can see them in my sleep. That's exactly the configuration that was supposed to go inside the columns."

"Isn't it a little, uh, short?"

"Yes, that's the point," she answered him as if his observation were obvious. She took off across the yard again, not stopping this time until she caught up with Columbo, who was busy directing a pour. Alvarez stood and watched. It was obvious that Columbo didn't want to stop and talk to Tory, but she stood her ground. Finally he turned to her in resignation, and Alvarez watched the gesturing that followed with the ensuing conversation. There was a lot of pointing in his direction, which Alvarez assumed had to do with the jumble of metal in front of him. He didn't think he could compete with the rebar for the interest of the two individuals involved.

Tory returned more slowly than she had gone, obviously not as elated as she had been at first. "He says he doesn't know anything about this," she said, joining Alvarez in his contemplation of the cage of rebar. "Of course, I'm not sure he would tell me if he did. It looks exactly like part of the stadium cage—the part that appears to be missing in that one column where all we pick up is three separate pieces of metal."

"Even if it is, I can't see where this changes anything. You're grasping at straws."

She didn't answer for a moment, she was concentrating so hard on the object in front of them. "Maybe," she said slowly, "maybe they hid something in the column that they don't want anyone to find. David—" she turned to him, speaking animatedly now, "maybe they hid drugs in it!"

So, they were back on a first name basis again since he wasn't arguing with her or trying to get her to do something. It wasn't bound to last long. "Tory," he said gently, "are you always this naive? The only reason to hide drugs is so you keep them safe until you can sell them. How the hell could anyone get drugs out of the middle of a cement, I mean concrete, column? Especially when that column is in the middle of a university football stadium?"

She looked at him, undismayed. "Okay, so it's something else, then. This is finally something that I can get my teeth into. Depending on what the material inside that column is, if I change the refraction of the X-rays enough, I should be able to pick it up. Maybe I can even get the results in time to make the deadline for the report," she concluded.

Alvarez didn't even try to dissuade her. He was tired. Her problems weren't even his case. Keeping an eye on her was turning into a full-time job that he hadn't bargained for. He could call the Las Cruces police and ask them to put a tail on her, he reasoned.

Then she gave him her dazzling smile, the second real one of their acquaintance, and proceeded to give him an enthusiastic hug, much to his amazement. "Thank you, David. Thank you for everything. You don't know how much it helped for you to let me come here tonight. When I figure it out, you'll be the first person I call." He watched her walk quickly to her car, give him a wave, and drive away.

Maybe he'd rethink his decision. Maybe he could baby-sit her one more night, and still get into work and come up with something on the Hartman case. Maybe tomorrow he'd be able to talk some sense into her ...

But first he needed to shut down the lab and secure it, for it was still a No Admittance area. And with the amount of activity going on around the yard, he couldn't afford to walk off and leave it unsecured. The chief might put up with bending procedures on occasion if it yielded results, but sloppiness was an unforgivable sin. It could only be so long before it resulted in serious, sometimes fatal consequences.

He took his time to get back to the building, picking some workers at random and talking to them briefly about their impressions of Hartman, ignoring Columbo's disapproving glares. Then he continued to take his time in the lab, replacing the notes that Tory had perused, reflecting back on each event that had occurred since he had first entered this room last Sunday evening. It was as he was turning out the light, locking up, and resecuring the restriction tape that the pieces fell together, and he could see the whole picture.

He knew what had been hidden in the column, and who had hidden it. The problem was, by now Tory had a good forty-five minute lead on him.

CHAPTER ELEVEN:
DESTRUCTIVE TESTING

Tory pulled onto the interstate at Anapra, leaving the precast yard behind. From here it was a straight shot to the New Mexico State University exit forty-five minutes north.

She drove past the rest area where she'd pulled off hours earlier to call her father. She resisted the temptation to examine that conversation in detail. There would be plenty of time to think about that later. Right now, she told herself, there were more pressing matters.

She hadn't told David Alvarez about the real deadline she was working under. He kept accusing her of being tunnel-visioned, so it might have surprised him to find that her deadline had nothing to do with the stadium project schedule or meeting her commitments to Henderson.

Tory's driving concern was Cody's return sometime in the next twenty-four hours, sometime Friday evening. Once Cody was in town, she would be hostage to his presence, acquiescing to whatever measures were purported to keep him safe.

I wonder if I could send him to my father, she mused to herself. Certainly anyone who knew anything about me would never suspect that I would send him to Florida ... But that conjecture had too many ramifications to consider, and she resolutely turned her thoughts again to her more immediate concerns.

She glanced at her watch. She should be able to be at the

construction site by about 11:15 PM. That should give her at least a couple of hours to work on the column problem before overwhelming fatigue set in. It had, after all, been a really long day. Preceded by a really long night. Preceded by another really long day.

No more pouring over the X-rays and trying to decide the meaning of what was shown in the shots that had already been taken. The new plan was to start figuring out X-ray settings which might show something inside the column besides metal rebar. The first thing to do would be to tabulate all the settings that Jazz had used in calibrating his shots, because those settings could be ruled out. Except, Tory thought, if the calibrations had been done on one of the other columns, and not on the one she was investigating. This was not going to be as simple as she had hoped at first. It never was.

Then there was always the chance that whatever was inside the column couldn't be picked up by the X-rays. The energy particles that were strong enough to penetrate the concrete to look inside the column might go through any other material like it was paper. There were other geophysical tests that might work, she thought, but any of those would have to be jury-rigged for this unusual application. If nothing else worked, maybe she could drill out a core from the middle of the column. She tried not to think what Kemp's reaction would be to that.

Going over her plans, she was at the first interchange for Las Cruces before she knew it. Taking this familiar turn-off, only five minutes from the stadium site, she forced herself to face another possibility: If Alvarez was right, the only thing inside the middle of that concrete column was more concrete, and she might even now be a sitting duck for the unknown person behind all her troubles. As a concession to his cautions, and to prove to herself that she was teachable, she decided to park her car elsewhere on campus and walk to the construction site. As Alvarez had pointed out, there was no point in making it easy for someone to trace her whereabouts twice in one day.

She parked her car at Garcia Hall, an undergraduate dormitory that she had lived in once herself. She wryly noted the warning sign stating that all unauthorized cars would be towed. She just hoped the diligent parking patrols weren't out after 11:00 PM—a towed vehicle would be about the last straw.

Tory had been concerned that she would be edgy during the walk between the dormitory and the construction site, but that wasn't the case. After being trapped in Emmett's office, anything that was out in the open seemed easy to handle. The evening was beautiful, the daytime summer heat had dissipated, and she appreciated the solitude of the late hour after the events of the day. She reached the Travers Company trailer feeling calm and collected, with a plan for determining if something was inside the middle of that one column besides three small pieces of metal.

The five columns on site stood straight and tall, like sentinels in place to watch through the night, abandoned bulldozers and a crane scattered amongst them. Tory walked over to the column that was the focus of her attention, and touched it searchingly, as if her fingers could reveal the secrets its interior held. But the column certainly wasn't sending out any vibes to her tonight. Those things only seemed to work for Sylvia. Sighing, she let herself into the lighted trailer and got to work.

"I wonder if this has something to do with that guy we picked up here two nights ago," the campus police officer remarked to his partner as they approached the stadium construction site.

"I don't know," answered the older officer. "The guy's big concern was that we keep an eye on Tory Travers. He said that she'd either be here, at her house, or at her office. Said she'd be driving a white RX."

"And that's all he said?"

"Well, he gave me his ID number with the El Paso police force and a number to call to confirm it. He said he'd get back to us with more details after we located her."

"That's nerve. Wait 'til we find out he's working on some big collar outside his jurisdiction and he was too concerned about having someone horn in on it to let us know what was going on."

"Maybe," said the older officer mildly. Unlike his younger companion, he was no longer so concerned with who got the collar. His priorities currently focused on making sure the good guys did in fact win one once in a while, and getting through one more night safely.

"Looks okay to me," said the younger man as they drove slowly through the deserted construction site. "There's no one out here, and the trailer lights are on. That's just the way it's supposed to be, according to campus safety regulations concerning construction sites." The younger man had a fondness for quoting applicable regulations whenever a chance arose, which was a little too often for his partner's liking.

"Looks like you're right," agreed the older man. "No sign of her car. Let's swing by Mrs. Travers' office, and then by her house, if she's not there."

"But that's off our routine beat," protested his partner.

"There's nothing more routine than honoring the request of another officer," said the older man quietly. "I have a pretty good hunch that this is important, or the guy would never have asked for a favor. Let's keep that in mind." And the trailer lights gradually faded from the patrol car's rearview mirror as the officers diligently drove off into the night to check on the safety of one Victoria Travers.

Tory was making some progress, mainly due to the systematic records that Jazz had kept, describing all the procedures he had used to find settings that worked. "When you come back to work again, I promise not to hassle you so much. Just some of the time," Tory vowed to an absent Jazz.

The sound of a car interrupted her train of thought. She walked to the window to look out, taking care that her movement wouldn't be visible from the outside. She saw the University Police patrol car making its slow reconnaissance of the construction site, and she waited to see if the officers would stop and approach the trailer. But after making one long, slow circle of the site, the car sped up and drove off.

"A routine patrol," she told herself. Or maybe a non-routine patrol. After all, it would make sense that the police would check out the site where Jazz had been attacked just two nights previously. Pleased that Alvarez's tip had kept her presence in the trailer undetected, she went back to work.

She didn't know how long she'd been perusing Jazz's records when she realized that there was another noise out on the site. Unlike the sound of the patrol car, this one gradually snuck up on her consciousness, because it was a noise that she had been conditioned to expect. But she sat up in sudden realization of the inappropriateness of the sound—there was no reason on earth why a crane should be moving around a deserted construction site at midnight.

She darted to the window to confirm her suspicions, and sure enough, there was a crane operating out there. And more than that, whoever was in the crane was attempting to load the mysterious column onto a flatbed truck!

The metal loop that had been set into the column for transport had not been removed yet, and the crane had hooked that loop and was gradually hoisting the column off its foundation. Tory watched in disbelief as the column swung free of the ground, suspended in the air by the crane. In pure outrage she threw caution to the winds, and rushed out the door to dance up and down on the steps in front of the trailer, trying to get the attention of whoever was operating the crane.

"Hey, what are you doing? Are you crazy? No one is supposed to be out here," she yelled.

The crane stopped, as if in answer. But then, the machine started slowly and deliberately toward Tory and the trailer, still bearing the column, swinging suspended from the arm of the crane.

Realizing almost too late the implication of the change in events, Tory darted inside the trailer. She was not a moment too soon, for the crane gathered speed in its approach, and was at the trailer by the time Tory closed the door behind her. For one moment, Tory thought the crane was actually going to drive into the trailer after her, but the operator obviously had a better idea.

Mesmerized with horror, Tory watched as the crane's arm drew back and then swung forward, swinging the concrete column into the trailer much like a wrecking ball. An instant before the column hit, she realized that whoever was in the crane intended to beat her to death inside the trailer. She was knocked hard into the side of the wooden desk, which knocked them both almost directly in front of the trailer window facing the marauding crane. A jolt of nauseating pain shot through her left arm where she hit the desk. Struggling to regain her balance, she realized that she couldn't control the movement of that arm, and her left side hurt with each breath.

She watched almost with detachment as the crane arm withdrew to prepare for the next blow. Tory didn't do a lot of work with aluminum structures, but she knew for sure that the trailer had never been designed to withstand conditions like these. She figured it would take one, maybe two more blows to shear the trailer in half. She might have had a better chance outside on foot, but it was too late to think about that now. The only way out was the door that faced the crane; she didn't think she could get through one of the small trailer windows with her injured arm.

Never taking her eyes off the crane arm and its dangling load, she groped with her right hand in the top drawer of the desk. She felt her hand close upon her gun at last, and she managed to take off the safety before she had it free of the drawer. Leaning against the desk to steady herself, trying to ignore the incapacitating pain in her left arm, she raised the gun with her right hand and smashed the barrel through the window. Then she lined her gun up with the crane cab as best she could while the column started to descend on the trailer again.

"I bet Alvarez would tell me to keep my eyes opened," she thought with deadly calm, "but then, he'll likely never know about it." And she closed her eyes as she emptied her gun into the crane cab and waited for the impact of the column hitting the trailer again.

Her mind at first refused to believe it when the impact didn't come, but after several more seconds, she could no longer come up with an excuse for keeping her eyes closed. She opened them, and through the shattered window, saw several things happen in quick succession.

The crane, careening wildly, had turned from the trailer and was weaving off crazily in the other direction. Then the crane hit another one of the columns, knocking it down.

The crane arm continued to swing wildly around with its remaining momentum, striking still another standing column with the column that it held. The column that the crane held cracked in two, and the bottom part fell to the ground. A human hand stuck out from the sheared edge of the portion of the column that the crane still held.

Tory leaned against her desk and studied the hand protruding from the column through the shattered glass with detached interest. It gave her a reason to avoid looking at the motionless crane and the cab with shattered windows. Then, just like watching a movie, she saw a familiar Corvette skid onto the site and pull to a screeching halt beside the crane. She saw David Alvarez, gun in hand, jump out of his car and cautiously approach the cab. "Just like a man," she said to herself. "Never around when you need him." And then she didn't see anything else, because everything went black.

She regained consciousness choking on the acrid smell of ammonia. She was propped up against the wall, surrounded by broken glass, and Alvarez was squatting next to her, his face close to hers. He had broken a capsule of smelling salts under her nose, and now that she had come around, he was busy taking off his windbreaker and wrapping it around her.

"Tory, it's me, David. Can you hear me?"

"Of course I can hear you," Tory answered irritably, trying to move her head to get away from the ammonia.

"Just hold still. I don't want to lose you again, but I also can't have you put your head between your knees. The less we move you, the better. I'm pretty sure your arm is broken."

"I don't know what I would do if I didn't have you around to keep me informed about things," Tory said with her eyes closed. "I already know that my arm is broken." In spite of his jacket around her shoulders, and the warmth of the dry summer night air, she was beginning to shiver violently.

"Well, if you're able to make bitchy remarks like that, you must be okay," he replied. He sat down next to her and carefully put his arm around her, holding her good shoulder and cradling her injured arm next to him. He wanted to get some of his body heat next to her, because he didn't have anything else to wrap her in, and that gold filmy blouse was damn thin stuff. "I've radioed for help, so there should be someone here in a matter of minutes."

"Did I kill Petey Lester?" Tory asked, still keeping her eyes closed.

"No, you didn't kill him. When did you figure out it was him?"

"When I saw the hand fall out of the column. When did you figure it out?"

Alvarez looked at his watch. "About thirty-five minutes, twenty-seven seconds ago."

"I think it must be Kent Colliney who's in the column," Tory said. "I think Petey Lester killed Kent Colliney." Her tone was blandly conversational, but she started shaking harder. Alvarez tried to tighten his grip on her without jolting her injured arm.

"Yes, I think you're right," he said, being careful to match her tone. "But Petey Lester isn't dead, Tory, so you haven't killed anyone, although it would clearly have been self-defense if you had." He continued reassuringly, trying to take her mind off the body in the column. "I don't even think he's very seriously injured, although he's out cold. I think he ducked to the floor of the cab when you started shooting at him, but then he lost control of the crane and when it crashed into the column it knocked him out. He's pretty bloody right now, but I'm pretty sure that he's going to be all right. I hand-cuffed him to the seat, so he's not going anywhere."

That seemed to satisfy her for the moment, and they sat in silence while he wondered where the hell the Las Cruces police were. He remembered her comment about their tardy arrivals. Was it only last night that they had sat talking in El Palacio?

"David?"

"Yes?"

"I feel like I'm going to throw up."

Alvarez thought this over for a moment. It sounded familiar. He reached out with the arm that wasn't around Tory and grabbed a wastebasket from under the desk. "Well, if you have to, you have to," he said philosophically, standing the wastebasket in readiness in front of her.

A few moments went by in silence, and then Tory opened her eyes. "I feel better now that I told you that," she said simply.

"Good."

"David? I have a lot of questions that I want answers to."

"I know, Tory. You'll get all your answers, but not right now. There are still some things about all of this that even I haven't figured out, if you can believe that," he said lightly.

"Will you come and tell me as soon as you have all the answers?"

"Tory, as soon as someone gets here I'm sending you to the hospital with a police officer. You need to have that arm set and make sure that there aren't any internal injuries. They'll probably want to keep you overnight in the hospital. And then they'll want to take a statement."

"I'm not staying overnight in any hospital. I know that I have to go have my arm set and make a statement, and I know that you'll have to go book Lester and make a statement and do whatever procedural things you need to do. But I want you to promise to come and talk to me after that. I like to know the answers to things."

Alvarez looked at her wryly. "I know you do. Tory, it's not going to be tonight." He looked at his watch. "Or this morning, I mean. Look, they're going to shoot you full of dope and have you get some rest. I'll come as soon as I can, I promise. So you have to promise to do whatever the doctors tell you to do."

She relaxed and closed her eyes again. "Good. You know how to get there."

"The hospital?"

She opened her eyes to look at him in exasperation. "No, not the hospital. My house."

"Listen, I have an idea. Why don't we just arrange to meet at El Palacio? I had such a good time the last time we were there."

She smiled a little at that. "David?"

"What now?"

"There's one thing you can tell me now."

"What's that?"

"How did you figure out that it wasn't me with Jim Barkley?"

"My partner figured out that it wasn't you. He got hold of your health center records and they showed that you came to the university as a freshman, uh, sexually inexperienced. After I got that information, I figured out that the woman in the pictures had to be your mother."

"How did you know that?"

"From what you'd told me about the two of you looking alike, and the difference in your heights. You see," he said lightly, "I was always real aware of how tall you are."

"Why?"

"Because I'm six foot two, and I kept noticing how the top of your head came to the level of my eyes every time you tried to look down your nose at me."

"You never quit, do you?"

"No," he said.

"Aren't you glad that you decided to give me my gun back?"

"Yes," he said simply and sincerely.

They sat in companionable silence until they heard the patrol car pull up, siren going. "Come on," Alvarez said. "I'll help you up. Let's take it slow, but let's get you out of here."

Tory got to her feet with no small amount of help, and Alvarez waited patiently until he was sure she wasn't going to faint again and she was ready to walk. They made their way slowly out into the night air, Alvarez with his arm securely around her. "I want to go look," she said when they made it down the trailer steps to the ground.

"There's no point in it, Tory. I told you he would be all right. But there's a lot of blood, and he looks pretty gruesome right now."

Tory looked at him blankly. "It's not Petey Lester that I want to look at," she said. "I want to look at the column."

Alvarez conceded and helped her walk over to the column. She swayed slightly as she intently studied the hand hanging overhead, protruding from the broken end of the column.

"See the watch," she said finally. "That was one of the pieces of metal that we kept picking up with our X-rays. The other two will be his belt buckle and a pocket knife, I bet."

Shaking his head, Alvarez handed her over to one of the campus police officers for safekeeping. Faulkner was really going to want to hear about this one.

CHAPTER TWELVE: 100% COMPLETION

Alvarez spent the early hours of Friday morning debriefing the Las Cruces police and making the necessary phone calls to coordinate with his department. About 2:00 AM they let him in to talk to Lester, and he was able to get answers to his remaining questions concerning the case. Soon after talking to Lester, he drove home, showered, and got a few hours of sleep before heading into the office. He spent the morning doing the required work in his office, which started with giving his partner a blow-by-blow description of the prior evening's events. He was on the road back to Las Cruces by 11:00 AM.

He didn't even bother stopping at the hospital. There was only one car at Tory's house besides Tory's white RX, Alvarez was glad to see. He had no desire to deal with the press, which he figured would be insatiable once they got wind of the Body-in-the-Column story. The University Police were being successful in keeping a lid on the more sensational details of the case for the time being. probably due to the timing of Lester's arrest in the early morning hours.

He knocked on the door rather than ring the doorbell. He wasn't particularly surprised that Sylvia answered the door. When she saw who it was she pulled him inside and practically knocked him over with a big hug. "I'm so glad you're here. Tory's been waiting for you. It was hard to get her to rest, but I kept telling her that she had to give you a chance to take care of business. Boy, will it be great to have things back to normal."

Alvarez decided not to discourage her by telling her it would likely be some time before everything got back to normal. He had just disentangled himself from Sylvia's overly enthsiastic embrace when Tango rounded the corner. Spotting Alvarez much as one would spot a long-lost friend, Tango encircled him like a demented dervish, licking any exposed area he could reach and beating the detectives legs with his feverishly wagging tail. Alvarez thought he had felt nightsticks that were softer than this tail.

Sylvia grabbed the dog's collar and tried to restrain him. "See, he remembers you! And he's glad to see you, too! Tango doesn't like many people, you know."

Failing to think of an appropriate reply to this information, Alvarez decided to try another tack. "How is she doing?" he asked.

Tango sat panting at Sylvia's side. Sylvia was short of breath from the effort to restrain him, so they panted in unison, both looking adoringly at Alvarez, who tried to keep himself from being disconcerted by the spectacle. "Pretty good. They wanted to keep her at the hospital, but she wouldn't hear of it. But they wouldn't let her come home unless there was going to be someone here with her, so she called me. Cody and Lonnie will be home tonight—" she stopped and looked nonplussed at what she had said.

Alvarez ignored it. "Can I talk to her now, or is she asleep?"

"She woke up a couple of hours ago, and sent me over to the office to pick up some things for her. Typical Tory. She's back in her bedroom. You can go on back. I'll let her know you're here." She threw her head back and yelled, "Boss, Detective Alvarez is here!" Obviously satisfied that she had then discharged her duty as mistress of the sickroom, she winked at Alvarez and walked off toward the den where he had previously spent the night on the couch.

Tory was propped up in her bed, with papers in her lap. When she saw him she put the papers aside. Her left arm was encased in a cast that ran from her shoulder to her knuckles. Her face was drawn and pale, but her smile was one of welcome. "Have a seat," she invited him.

He sat in a straight-backed chair next to the bed. He couldn't resist the temptation to look around with a detective's eye for detail. So this is where she lives during the hours she's not being an engineer, he thought to himself. He was a little surprised, for although the room was Southwestern in motif, it was also unabashedly feminine, done in hues of sand and dusty rose.

"I got rid of all the furniture after Carl died and started over," she said, reading his mind. "I had enough of his ghosts to live with without keeping the bedroom the way it was when he was alive."

It sounded healthy enough to him, so he nodded his approval.

"So?" she asked after another moment.

He had to grin at that. "So? So I'm reporting in, as ordered."

She winced. "I'm sorry—I do get a little manic about things sometimes. I never meant to order you here. I just—"

"It's okay," he interrupted her. "You just wanted some answers to your questions. It's understandable; I'd feel the same way if I were you."

"I also never told you thank you for following me out to the site last night," she continued on doggedly, determined to make things right.

"You're welcome," he said easily, "although you handled things well enough without me. How are you, anyhow?"

"I'm okay. More than okay. Pretty lucky, I guess. I have a couple of cracked ribs, but they just taped those. My arm is broken in two places, but they say it broke clean and should mend okay. And I'm lucky it's my left arm."

"Yeah, otherwise you might have had to take a whole day off," Alvarez said drily, gesturing to the papers she had put aside.

Tory looked where he pointed. "I'm signing payroll," she explained. "I have a dedicated staff, but there's a limit to anyone's dedication. They probably want to get paid on Friday as usual."

"Sounds reasonable to me. You're being real restrained, Tory. I'm not used to you being so patient when you want to know something."

"Well, I'm used to you dangling me along whenever you're in control of the situation, so nothing has changed in that department."

"Okay," he said. "it looks like you kept your part of the bargain. Sylvia didn't even complain about you giving her a hard time, other than sending her off to the office to fetch some work for you."

"Payroll."

"Payroll, then. How about a story?" Without waiting for an answer, he launched straight into his tale. "Well, you already know that things weren't going too well between Colliney and his wife. According to Lester, she had spent years putting up with Colliney's bad habits, which included spending money he didn't have, in addition to running around on Lester's daughter. But Lester's daughter loved her husband. So Lester had to tolerate Colliney in his business and bail him out of bad debts when he couldn't make ends meet. I guess he'd pretty much had all he could take even before he found out about his daughter contracting syphilis, but maybe there was still a chance even then that he could have gotten rid of his son-in-law without bloodshed."

"So what happened?"

"Lester went out to the precast yard one night to go over his books to make sure everything was in order before he started legal proceedings to get Colliney out of the business. According to him, he didn't even realize that Colliney was scheduled to supervise a pour later that evening."

"Columbo told me that he had been assigned to supervise a pour of one of the stadium columns because they were starting to run behind schedule."

"Right. Well, when Lester got out there, his office was already occupied. By Colliney and some woman, he says."

Tory considered that. "I can see where something like that could drive Petey Lester over the edge."

"No kidding. It turned out the woman had driven Colliney out to the precast yard that night, which proved fortuitous for Lester later on. Lester threw her out of the office, and she took off, according to him. We're going to have to locate her to substantiate all this later, but there doesn't seem to be any reason at this point to question Lester's story." Alvarez heard a noise and looked up to see Tango coming in the room. He braced himself for another intimate encounter, but the dog walked over, sat down next to him, and adoringly placed his head in Alvarez's lap.

"That's strange," said Tory. "He doesn't really like that many people."

"So I've heard," said Alvarez drily. "Anyhow, according to Lester, he didn't really mean to kill Colliney, although he's very frank about the fact that he has no regrets about it. I guess he was roughing Colliney up a little when he bashed his head against the wall and stunned him. So, kind of on impulse, the way he tells it, Lester took him by the throat and strangled him with his bare hands."

Tory closed her eyes and turned even paler than she had been to begin with. "Are you okay?" Alvarez asked. "You're the one that wanted to hear this story, remember?"

"I was just thinking, that's the way that Bill Hartman was killed."

Alvarez looked at her quizzically. "You know, for a bright girl, you're not too smart, sometimes. I would have thought you'd have already figured out that Lester killed Hartman, too."

Tory stared at him for a moment. "Of course, that makes sense. I really hadn't thought about Hartman since I saw the hand fall out of the column."

"Well, do you want to hear the rest of this or not?"

"Yes, of course," she replied rather faintly.

"You can probably visualize the next part of the story better than I can. There Lester was with a dead body in his office, and a crew of workers outside in the precast yard."

"So he sent the workers home. Columbo said there would probably only have been two of them there."

"That made it even easier. According to Lester, he didn't send them home right away. He let them finish with setting up the form. Then he went out and told them that the plans had changed, the actual pour was to take place in the morning. This was where luck was with him again. The guys there that night weren't any of his regular laborers. They were both temporary workers, probably illegals, that had been assembled for the night shift. So he paid them off in cash and let them go." Alvarez watched Tango's eyes roll back as the dog's head slid off his lap and the dog slowly dropped to the floor, asleep before his head hit the carpet. It was like watching a drug overdose in slow motion.

"And then he completed the pour himself."

"Right. But not until after he'd cut out enough of the rebar to be able to fit Colliney's body into the form."

"You know, he was taking a terrible chance."

"Completing the pour himself?"

"No, putting Colliney in the middle of the column. I'm amazed that the column didn't break during transport. It would have been a lot safer to have put the body in one of the ends, because that wouldn't have affected the structural stability so much."

Alvarez noticed that Tory seemed to have gotten over her initial queasiness over talking about dead bodies. "Lester had probably determined that Colliney's skeleton would serve in place of the rebar that he had taken out," he said, curious to see how far she would go with this new technical question that had caught her attention.

"I hadn't thought about that," said Tory seriously. "I suppose you could get some reinforcing action from the skeleton. The spine would be running longitudinally and the ribs laterally ..."

"Lighten up, Tory. I was only kidding. Here was this guy with a body to get rid of, and he saw a chance to put it in the middle of a concrete column, so he did it. I'm sure Lester would have appreciated having you around to help him figure out the optimum place to put the body in the column, but it just didn't work out that way."

"And then I raised the questions about the other columns, and my company was authorized to study the structural integrity of all of them," Tory interjected.

"Right. Lester found out about that Saturday morning, before the party. Then he found out from talking to you that if the records regarding the procedures used to pour the columns checked out okay, there might not be any more investigation. So he checked out of the pool party early on Sunday afternoon and went down to the precast yard to make sure the records concerning the pour of that column would stand up to scrutiny and set everyone's mind at ease. But this was where his luck began to run out."

"Because Hartman was there, working on the records."

"Right. And Hartman had already realized that Colliney had never signed off on that pour. I doubt that Hartman ever realized what was at stake. He simply told Lester that he planned to document what he had found, and recommend that the column be investigated using physical tests, especially in light of Colliney's 'absence.' You have to realize that Hartman was being real cautious because of all the pressure you'd put on the precast yard. Well, Lester panicked. Throttling someone had worked reasonably well for him before, so he decided to try it again. After he killed Hartman, he figured he didn't have time to stick around and fabricate the pour records. He knew the night watchman routinely made his rounds about that time of evening, and he obviously didn't want anyone to know that he had been at the precast yard that night. So he took the records with him, hoping to solve that little problem later. He drove back to Las Cruces, where he had dinner with Harold Kemp and Director Henderson and your Lonnie Harper."

"He's not my Lonnie Harper."

"Whatever. Anyhow, on the drive back to Las Cruces, he had some time to figure out how to cover his tracks, and he came up with a pretty good plan, actually. He went up to see his daughter in her motel room. She routinely slept a lot and took tranquilizers to try to deal with her depression. He woke her up, pretending that he had just come up from the pool party. When she went into the bathroom for a few minutes, he set her clock and her watch back one hour. When she came out of the bathroom, he called her attention to the time, and she never questioned it.

"She told us he stayed there trying to convince her to go to dinner with him. Actually, he was solicitously having drinks with her and fetching her more happy pills, so that he could be sure that she'd refuse his invitation and fall back into bed the moment that he left. Which is what happened. So Lester went off to have dinner, after again calling his daughter's attention to the time, so she'd be able to substantiate both when he had entered and left her room. Then when he returned from dinner, he went back into his daughter's room and set the clock and her watch back to the correct time."

"I can't quite see it."

"Well, I know how much you like things in black and white, so I drew it up for you." He pulled a paper out of his pocket and handed it to her. She studied it:

Time (pm)	Alibi	Reality
2:00		
2:30		
3:00		Party
3:30	Party	
4:00		
4:30		Transportation/
5:00		Murder
5:30	with Tiffany	
6:00		with Tiffany
6:30		
7:00	Gets ready for dinner	Goes to dinner

"That's pretty cold-blooded, using his daughter as part of a cover-up for killing her husband."

"Yes, by this time Lester was rather fancying his life of crime. He figured he was actually going to get away with everything, except for one big stumbling block."

"What was that?"

"You. He was deathly afraid that you wouldn't accept whatever report he could fabricate as being consistent with the other pours, and he was afraid that you'd keep on investigating the columns and something unusual would come to light."

"So he was behind the letter, and the phone call, and the tire-slashing. It was Lester that knocked Jazz out and Lester that shot at me, wasn't it?"

"Yes, and it took me longer than it should have to put it

together. For someone who was a potential suspect, Petey Lester seemed to turn up missing just whenever something was happening to you up here. The night that his daughter tried to commit suicide, no one could reach him to let him know. I remember thinking that was damn strange, but then I got distracted with all the red herrings you kept throwing my way."

"I didn't throw them. You went looking for them."

"In any case, you were right. Petey Lester was behind everything that happened to you, and it all had to do with the stadium job. We started to get a lead on breaking his alibi when his daughter confirmed he was dressed for dinner when he first came to her room, not dressed like he had just come from the pool party. But I doubt we could have proven how he had enough time to kill Hartman without his confession."

"Was he serious about trying to kill me, or Jazz?"

"I don't think we'll ever know the answer to that. He says not. He says he just wanted to get you out of the way long enough to get this study of the columns laid to rest. But we have to remember that this is a man who discovered he rather liked killing after the first time he tried it. I'm sure that when he showed up on site last night and actually tried to physically remove that column, which was his very last resort, by the way, he was ready to kill anyone who got in his way."

Tory looked at him with big eyes, and they shared a moment of silence, remembering how close it had actually been. "So you were wrong," she said finally.

"Yes, I was wrong about your problems having to do

with your past. You may actually be able to keep that under wraps if everyone's attention is focused on Petey Lester and the body in the column. But I was right about the fact that you were headed on a collision course with trouble."

"Did you tell the police about the shooting?"

"Of course I did. I couldn't very well leave that out and have Petey Lester blabbing all about it in his confession, now could I?"

"I suppose not. Is it going to be okay?"

Alvarez stood up and stretched. He leaned against the wall and looked down at her. The dog on the floor beside Tory's bed was now snoring audibly and didn't move a muscle. "Good watchdog you have there. If you're asking if I'm currently unemployed, the answer is no," he smiled at her. "But I did decide to leave the little adventure at Webb Engineering just between you and me. But if I ever hear a report that something turned up missing from Emmett Delgado's office, I'll have to reconsider my decision."

"Thank you," she said simply.

"When does Lonnie get home?" he asked briskly, changing the subject.

"Why?"

"I want to ask him to keep an eye on you. There's going to be a lot of press when this thing breaks to the news services."

"I thought you didn't like Lonnie."

"Oh, I like him okay. I'm just not sure that I like him in close proximity to you." He continued to look at her consideringly. "I have the rest of the day off, believe it or not," he continued. "We could drive down to my place and spend a few hours together without any distractions."

She looked at him in shock. "Cast and all?"

"You're tough. Cast and all. I wouldn't have in mind anything too physically exerting. Not on your part, anyhow. And you can work around cracked ribs, you know. I'm speaking from experience."

"Are you asking what I think you're asking?"

"It depends on what you think I'm asking," he grinned, refusing to make it easy for her.

"What would people think?"

"I wouldn't have expected a cheap question like that from you. What do you think Sylvia already thinks?"

"I try not to think about that. I thought you only liked women of *La Raza*."

"I think you're avoiding the question."

"I think shared danger is a powerful aphrodisiac," she said carefully. "It wouldn't be appropriate to mistake your feelings for anything other than that."

"Don't hide behind some semantic philosophical answer. It was a simple question, and it deserves a simple answer. Is it going to be yes, or no?"

"Okay then." She looked really flustered, like some kid who had just been called on by the teacher and was trying to come up with the right answer. "The answer is no, for now."

"Well, if you never ask, you never find out," he said easily. "And here I thought you'd really like seeing the buildings in my neighborhood, since I live in a historic revitalization area. *Hasta la vista* and all of that, lady engineer. It's been real."

"So is this goodbye?"

"Do you have any idea how juvenile that question sounds?" he asked, feeding her words of a past occasion right back to her. "I'm not Lonnie, you know." He leaned over and kissed her a chaste kiss on her cheek. "Take care."

"What is that supposed to mean?"

"It means that patience isn't one of my stronger virtues." And he left her to finish signing payroll, wondering exactly when Lonnie and Cody would return, and if he had really meant to show her the buildings in his neighborhood.

She noticed that he was careful not to trip over Tango on his way out.

Sylvia jumped to her feet as Alvarez walked out of Tory's bedroom. One last loose end occurred to him. He joined her in the den and walked over to the breakfast bar. He shuffled through the assorted papers on top of the bar until he found what he was looking for. He handed Sylvia his card, the one that he had written his home phone number on just two nights ago.

"You give this to your boss, okay? Tell her to give me a call later this afternoon, because I just recalled that we need to discuss some of the finer details of this case."

Sylvia looked puzzled. "I don't understand. I thought Petey Lester was the one behind all of Tory's troubles, and he's in jail now."

"No, no. This has to do with clarifying the events of a couple of nights ago. It involves a certain Smith and Wesson thirty-eight, and the reputation of a detective who is near and dear to my heart." Sylvia looked at him in puzzlement. He decided that he better make things a little clearer.

"I have to make sure that Ms. Travers' recollection of that night's events correspond to mine in the utmost detail. Particularly the part where I walked into the trailer to come to her aid when she was trying to call the University Police to report a shooting. You know, it really rattles a person to be shot at. Her hands were shaking so hard she wasn't able to dial the number, so that's why the University Police weren't called in right away. At least, that's what I've told everybody. We need to go over that part of the story before she gives her complete statement to the police. *Comprende, señorita?*"

"No, I'm not sure I do," said Sylvia frankly.

"Well, if your boss seems to have any hesitation about contacting me to get our stories straight, just mention Emmett Delgado's broken file cabinet to her."

And, with a grin for Sylvia's puzzled look, he left.

EPILOGUE

The journalism student and his girlfriend came to the Mesilla graveyard in the late afternoon, partially to avoid the relentless daytime heat, and partially because he wanted to photograph the way the late afternoon sunlight illuminated the dilapidated gravestones. His girlfriend thought his summer term project of photographing old gravestones was creepy, but this was a new romance, and she was still in the mode of trying to appear enthusiastic about each and every one of his pursuits. She was frankly more interested in his broad shoulders and the way his sandy hair kept falling into his eyes, but not even the combined efforts of all her sorority sisters would have drawn that admission from her.

Privately cursing the decision to wear shorts and sandals (although they did show off her legs to a deliberate advantage) she followed her boyfriend into the heart of the graveyard, simultaneously trying to avoid the tumbleweeds and the *Iridomrymex pruinosa*, those tiny red desert ants who appeared to have the biological capability to outlast mankind and take over the world.

Her boyfriend plunged on ahead of her, looking for just the right gravestone for his subject, and exclaiming with glee over the epitaphs that were still legible. Thus occupied with looking at the ground, they almost walked into the *bruja's* final resting place before they realized it.

"What's this?" the coed asked edgily. She felt that graveyards were bad enough without encountering unforeseen physical structures. "It looks like a big cement casket."

"Maybe that is what it is," he answered her in excitement, already beginning to explore the object with his fingers in addition to his artist's eye. "There's no epitaph, but there's a date, and look, some kind of little gargoyle sculpture on the top. This is really weird, especially in a Catholic graveyard."

"Do you suppose the body is actually inside the cement?" she asked in horrified fascination.

"I don't know," her boyfriend answered, already selecting the spot he wanted to shoot from. "Sit on top of it for me, would you? That would be a great contrast. Youth and decay."

"Listen, this wasn't part of the deal. I don't want to sit on top of some dead body. It would be ... disrespectful, or something."

"Oh, come on, Clare. No one would actually put a body inside there. It's probably just some type of weird monument or something. And it's no more disrespectful than walking on all the graves that you tramped on to get over here."

And because innocence is not, after all, related to sexual experience, she complied, because in her innocence she still thought that willingness to please and a beautiful face were the main requirements for a happy life. And no one watching would have ever guessed her hesitation, because she tossed her head and mussed her hair and smiled her sexiest smile for the camera.

After he was satisfied he had gotten the exposures he wanted, he told her what a good girl she had been and laughed at her notion that someone would encase a body in concrete. "They only do that in Chicago," he teased her, and took her off to Padrino's for a beer to reward her modeling skills.

The dust was so fine and so dry that it took a while to settle after they had driven off. And in the late afternoon sun, secure in her final resting place, the *bruja* slept on.